Circle of Five

Jan Raymond

LOS ALAMOS COUNTY LIBRARY
MESA PUBLIC LIBRARY
2400 CENTRAL AVENUE
LOS ALAMOS, NM 87544

This edition published for Amazon Kindle

Copyright Jan Raymond 2013

ASIN: B00H6LS59E

This book is a work of fiction. Any references to historical events, real people, or real places are used fictitiously. Other names, characters, places, and events are products of the author's imagination, and any resemblance to actual events or places or person, living or dead, is entirely coincidental.

All rights reserved. In accordance with U.S. Copyright Act of 1976, the scanning, uploading, and electronic sharing of any part of this book without the permission of the publisher constitute unlawful piracy and theft of the author's intellectual property. If you would like to use material from this book (other than for review purposes), prior written permission must be obtained by contacting the publisher/author. Thank you for your support of the author's rights.

To Aish and Nayan

PROLOGUE

It was nearly midnight, and the tall trees obscured the meagre moonlight as the woman strode through the forest, her long cape flapping around her. She held up her lantern to see better, as she wove through the trees, in the still of the night. She was small and lithe with a delicate, waif-like face. She looked more like a young girl than the powerful Head of a community, which she was. Only her flashing green eyes which held a wealth of wisdom and experience gave her away. People tended to underestimate her because of her appearance, and she had long ago learnt to use it to her advantage. She peered into the darkness. She could barely see the path. She wondered how long it had been since anybody had walked along it.

As she paused, searching for the path in the dark, she heard the sharp sound of a twig, snapping. She froze, her hand curling around the hilt of the sword that hung from the belt around her waist. There was a low snarl, and she looked around warily. Probably a panther! She wasn't scared, she knew she could kill it with ease if it charged, but she didn't like to kill. She closed her eyes and concentrated on the animal.

'I will not harm you. You have nothing to fear from me,' she whispered softly.

She sensed the panther moving away. She opened her eyes, relaxing her grip on her sword. As she continued down the path, she wondered why the old man had called her. She had heard his summons while she and her guests were at dinner. She'd looked around the table, and realised the summons were only for her. She would have left sooner, but today's dinner was important, and it would have seemed rude and disrespectful if she had excused herself. She frowned as she considered the summons. No one sent for the Head of a community unless it was very important.

She hardly remembered the man she was going to meet. She had been a young girl, barely twelve, when she'd last seen him. She quickened her step, and turned off her lantern when she saw the outline of a cottage through the trees. It took her eyes a couple of seconds to adjust to the dark. She went around the cottage noiselessly, making sure she stayed out of sight of anyone who was in the cottage. There was always the possibility that this was a trap. Once she had made sure it was safe, she walked up to the front door and knocked. There was no answer. She knocked again, and when there was still no response, she twisted the doorknob and pushed. The door swung open.

The inside of the cottage was as dark as the outside. She went in, turned on her lantern and held it high, surveying the untidy room. There were books and papers on every piece of furniture in the room, and covering most of the floor. There were piles of books stacked against the walls.

'Hello!' she called out. There was silence.

There were two doors to her left. She gingerly stepped over the papers littering the floor, as she made her way to the first door and opened it. The smell hit her first, a putrid stench. She lifted her lantern and peered into the room. It was the kitchen. There was a sink filled with dirty crockery and the long table in the centre of the room, held rotting, half eaten plates of food. She stepped back hurriedly, shutting the door and the smell out.

She opened the second door and peeped in. Here, the smell was of sickness and decay. She walked into what seemed to be a bedroom. There was a single bed, and she could make out the outline of a figure lying on it, covered with layers of blankets. She walked with swift steps to the bedside table, cleared the papers and candle stubs which covered it and set the lantern down on the table. The figure on the bed, who she assumed was the man she had come to see, hadn't stirred. She looked down at the immobile figure wondering if she was too late. She placed her hand on the figure and shook him gently. He moaned softly but did not turn. She pulled away the blankets covering him.

Her memory of him was of a tall, well built man. The shrunken, emaciated figure on the bed bore no resemblance to the memory. She wondered how long it was since he'd eaten or even gotten out of bed. She gently turned him over and as she did, his eyelids flickered open. Faded, blue eyes looked at her, and she thought she saw relief in them.

'You came,' he whispered. 'I wasn't sure if you would. I wasn't sure if you could hear. I didn't have the strength to...,' he broke off into a bout of coughing, a harsh, guttural noise.

'Sssshh! Don't talk now,' she hushed him. 'You should have summoned someone earlier. You would have been looked after,' she said, pity welling up in her for this sad and lonely man, who had lived, and was now dying, alone. 'Let me get you something to eat or drink.'

'No! No! Here, take this,' he said urgently, trying to get up, holding out a crumpled piece of paper he had clutched in his hand. 'I had to give this to you. That was why I summoned you.'

She took the proffered paper, and he collapsed with a relieved sigh and closed his eyes. She could sense the life ebbing out of him. She flattened the piece of paper. He must have written it very recently as the writing was shaky and barely legible. Her eyes widened, and she gasped aloud when she read what was written on the paper. She turned and looked at the prone figure. He must have heard her gasp for he was looking at her now... with sympathy.

'Why didn't you summon me earlier?' she demanded.

'It happened today. I summoned you immediately. My time is almost over. I wrote it down in case you didn't make it in time.' His voice sounded stronger now.

'What should I do?' she asked, a feeling of helplessness sweeping over her.

He gave a ghost of a smile. 'I am merely the messenger. What you do with the message is up to you,' he replied.

She looked thoughtful for a few seconds, and then folded the paper and put it into the pouch which hung from her belt. It could wait for now. She fetched some water and gave him tiny sips with a spoon. She made him comfortable and covered him with the blankets again. She sat down beside him on the bed and held one bony hand between both of hers as he went back to sleep. She sat in silence, waiting.

It was almost dawn when she felt him slipping away. She put his lifeless hand down, picked up her lantern and went out of the cottage to look for a shovel. She found one at the back of the cottage. She picked a willow tree close to his house and started digging.

She buried him under the shade of the tree and placed a pile of stones, to mark the spot. She went back into the cottage and looked around. She would have to send someone to go through all the books and papers and catalogue them for the library.

She hadn't told anyone she was going away, and she wanted to get back before anyone noticed she was missing. Things were fragile as it was. And now this! She took out the letter from her pouch and reread it.

What should she do with it? What would be the consequences of sharing this information? Maybe... she should just destroy the letter and tell no one about her midnight visit. But, was that fair, was it right? Her thoughts whirled as she considered options. She folded the paper and put it back in her pouch. She would think about it some more and then make her decision. She stepped out of the cottage, pulled the door shut and latched it. She walked over to the grave.

'I'm glad you didn't die alone. But I don't know whether to thank you, or curse you, for the responsibility you've placed on me. My decision will affect not only us, but our future generations too. You did the right thing in summoning me. I hope I make the right decision too. Goodbye, my friend! I hope you've found peace at last!'

CHAPTER 1

SAMUEL

'Sammy! Sammy! Samuel! Hurry up!' Sam shot a disgusted look at his older sister, as he turned away from the beehive which was occupying his attention.

'Sam! It's Sam, not Sammy, not Samuel! It's Sam,' he growled, looking annoyed.

He'd always hated being called Samuel. Samuel! His parents had named him straight out of the Bible, and they called themselves atheists. Not only did they foist the name Samuel on him, but then they went and shortened it to Sammy which had stuck, when there'd been a perfectly acceptable Sam right there. Cassie insisted on calling him Samuel or Sammy, simply to irritate him.

'Blah! Blah! Whatever! Just hurry up, will you? Or, we'll be late for school,' said Cassie.

Sam watched his sister toss her red curls and flounce away. He shook his head and followed her down the empty street, littered with falling autumn leaves. It was a windy day and the leaves were being tossed around. They swirled in little circles as they fell down, only to be picked up and tossed again. It was like watching a dance. He loved watching the season's change, each one producing something new and unique when their turn came.

Anything new caught his attention, like the beehive today. He hadn't noticed it before. Maybe it was because the bees hadn't been this loud before. The beehive was a whirlwind of movement, as the bees went about their work busily, hoarding for the winter. He would have loved to spend the rest of the day watching the bees and their frenzied activity. It never crossed his mind that he might get stung. He had a way with nature. He knew the bees wouldn't hurt him, and it appeared that they didn't feel threatened by him either.

'Cassie's so paranoid. What was her problem?' he wondered. 'They had more than enough time to get to school. But no, Cassie had to be extra early.' He taunted her, 'Cas! Are you in a hurry to get to school early, to wipe the blackboard and write, "I love you, Ms. Cabot" on it, before she comes in?'

'Why do you always have to be such a jerk, Sammy? Is it part of being a special child?' she retorted.

'Well, you'll never know, will you? Cos, you're not! Special, that is,' he replied softly, 'in any way… however hard you try, four eyes.'

The shot hit home. If there was one thing Cassie hated, it was to be reminded of the thick glasses she wore. She was furious. For a moment, she forgot her need to get to school early as rage filled her. She swung her heavy school bag in a vicious arc at Sam, and though he tried to step aside, it glanced off his shoulder and he fell back. He felt his head hit something hard and everything went black.

CASSANDRA

Cassie looked in shock at what she had done. Sam had hit the back of his head on the edge of a mailbox which stood in the corner of the street. She could see the blood pooling around his head from the wound.

'No! Oh no! What have I done?' She panicked and looked around wildly.

The street was empty. The houses on the street were detached bungalows with huge gates. She briefly considered running into one of them and asking for help, but she didn't want to leave Sam lying alone either. She knelt down, lifted Sam's head gingerly, and rested it on her thigh. She pressed her hand against the wound and was relieved to see that the flow of blood stopped immediately. She applied pressure like she'd been taught in first aid class, and when she removed her hand after a minute, it looked like she had succeeded in staunching the flow.

'Sammy! Sammy!' She felt another jolt of panic course through her when she saw that he hadn't opened his eyes. 'Sam! C'mon… open your eyes. Sam!' She patted his cheek gently.

Sam's eyes flickered open. Cassie breathed a sigh of relief. She felt like a heel, as she gazed down at the delicate face which was looking up at her, dazed. She could feel his thin frame trembling.

Her mother's oft-repeated words echoed in her head. 'Cassandra, you cannot hit your brother or push him. He is very delicate and so we must treat him with extra care.' How she had hated those words and how often she had flaunted that cardinal rule in their house. She was only a year and a half older than Sam, and hadn't understood why he got to be special. She'd been jealous of Sam from the moment he was born. He had taken up all her mom's time.

She had understood as she grew older that her mom had spent more time with him because he was a sickly child. But it hadn't lessened her jealousy as she felt that he got more attention than her even now. She took out her hurt and frustration on him whenever she thought she could get away with it. But now, she seemed to have gone too far. Her mom would skin her alive if she found out what she had done.

'Sammy, you okay? I'm… I'm… er… I'm…,' she couldn't get the apology past her lips.

'Yeah! Yeah! I got it! Got stuck in your throat again, didn't it?' Sam shrugged off her hand from his shoulder and touched the back of his head gingerly. His hand came away covered in blood. He grimaced and reached for his bag which had fallen down. Cassie was quicker, and she handed it to him, solicitously. Sam grinned despite his pain. He was used to this routine. This wasn't the first time Cassie had hurt him. She would get angry, hurt him and then be very nice to him, hoping he wouldn't tell their mom. He never did, he wasn't the complaining sort. But even after 15 years, Cassie seemed to think he would sneak. And he let her think that. Now she would be nice to him, at least for a while.

He unzipped his bag and took out his bottle of water. He rummaged some more and pulled out a dirty napkin.

'Wait! Don't use that dirty rag. Here, take mine,' offered Cassie, pulling out a clean napkin from her bag.

'No! I'm fine. I'll use mine. You carry on to school if you want to. I'll clean this and catch up with you,' he said, not looking at her.

It was not like he was a small kid anymore and needed an escort to school. He could easily get to school by himself, and so could Cassie. But his mom insisted on dropping them both close to their school on her way to work, and now it had become a habit to walk up to school together. Usually when he dawdled, Cassie would leave him and take off. She probably would have done that today if she hadn't hurt him.

'No... I'll wait,' she said, looking nervous.

Sam shrugged, wet the napkin and started cleaning his wound as best as he could. Luckily, though there was a lot of blood, there were only a couple of drops which had splattered on his shirt. His school uniform was a white shirt with dark blue pants and a blue and yellow striped tie. Cassie had been afraid the blood may have stained his white shirt, but she didn't think the tiny droplets were noticeable.

She watched anxiously, torn between the need to get to school soon and knowing she should wait till he was done. She gritted her teeth as she watched him clean his wound, slowly, grimacing the whole time. Like he was in agony! She could see it was only a scrape and he was getting his kicks out of making her wait.

He was finally done. He got up, picked up his bag and took a few unsteady steps. Cassie turned around and started walking briskly towards school. If they hurried, they could still be on time. After a minute, she looked back and saw him lagging behind quite a bit.

'Can't you hurry up, for God's sake?' she shouted, exasperated. 'It was your head which got hurt, not your feet.'

'Maybe, but I feel dizzy if I walk fast. Maybe I have a concussion or something,' he said, looking at her innocently.

Cassie rolled her eyes. What an act! But she started walking slower, so he could keep up with her

SEBASTIAN

'What a drag! How'd I end up here?' wondered Sebastian, for the thousandth time, banking his bike alarmingly low while taking a corner, as he rode his yellow Ducati Monster to school. The heavy duty, two-cylinder, six-speed bike, thrummed under him, as he gracefully straightened out.

He knew he was going to get an earful when he went back home, as he was forbidden to ride his bike to school. But he loved the adrenaline rush and the sense of absolute freedom the bike gave him. When he was on the bike, it felt like all was right in his world. So once again, he'd left his Lexus at home and taken the bike instead.

It had meant leaving in the Lexus, and doubling back after his dad left to take the bike, but it was totally worth it. He didn't care if he got late to that dump which tried to pass itself off as a school.

'Holy Trinity? Who names a school Holy Trinity? It sounded more like a church, than a school,' he thought, scowling.

He hated the school he'd been forced to join. His dad had felt he was getting into bad company, running wild in his prep school and needed some grounding. Well, the bad company and the running wild were true, but his dad hadn't cared till now.

Sebastian knew it couldn't have been his dad's idea. Till recently, his dad had barely acknowledged his existence. But now, he had this new girlfriend, and Sebastian was sure this whole thing was her idea. Sebastian had rebelled against going to Holy Trinity. But his dad had threatened to cut off his allowance if he didn't, and Sebastian had to give in. He didn't know how to survive without the money. He was used to having money. So, he'd joined Holy Trinity. He hated the kids in his school… a bunch of losers! Well… if things progressed as they usually did, his dad would soon tire of his new girlfriend, and he'd get sent back to another prep.

He braked hard, as a bright pink Mini cut in front of him and raced ahead. He swore when he saw the pretty, Indian girl in the car which was racing away in front of him. He revved the bike and tore after it.

MAYA

Maya grinned, as she looked in the rear view mirror and saw the Ducati barrelling towards her.

'Ass!' she muttered to herself, as she pressed down harder on the accelerator. Not that she thought for a minute that she could beat the Ducati, but it gave her a kick to have riled Sebastian up.

'It's not my fault that your Dad's got the hots for my Mom,' she said aloud, as she twisted the tiny car into the path of the bike.

She too hated the fact that her mom was dating Sebastian's dad. She had no problem with the dad. Mr. Chastain, or Daniel, as he insisted she call him, was a cool guy. But she hated the sight of his handsome, lean, blonde, blue eyed son. Each adjective came out like an expletive in her mind. He looked down his nose at her school, her friends, and her. Not that she cared. She had more important things on her mind. Like how to catch the attention of a certain good looking, football player in school.

'Talk of the devil!' she muttered, as she caught sight of a familiar figure, pedalling swiftly on a bicycle towards school. She glanced at him, flipping her hair as she roared past, willing him to look up at her.

RYAN

Ryan looked up when he heard the roar and whoosh of the vehicles which raced by him. He recognized them. The pink car belonged to that Indian chick. He didn't know her name. She was junior to him. He frowned... she was driving too fast. So was that kid on his Ducati. He'd heard the kid on the Ducati was a big snob. Maybe it was time to take him down a notch.

Then he sighed. 'Let me first sort out my own problems... before taking on other people's,' he said to himself.

His girlfriend, Lisa, had kept him up on the phone till way past midnight. He'd woken up late, as a result, and he'd missed football practice. He wasn't sure how he had gotten himself into this situation where he danced to her every tune, but it wasn't pleasant. The fact that she was gorgeous might have something to do with it. He knew he was the envy of every guy in school. But she was always demanding more... more of his time, more of his money. The fact that she was born with a silver spoon didn't mean he was. She was thoroughly spoilt! He'd thought it was cute when they first started going out, but now, he really couldn't afford her. Plus, he was missing practice and his grades were falling.

'I need to have a talk with her,' he thought grimly, as he turned the corner. He kept putting it off because he didn't want to lose her.

He could see the school gates ahead. He freewheeled down the incline towards the gates, swung into school and stopped short.

The pink Mini and the yellow Ducati were parked on the left side of the long drive, which led from the school gates to the school building. He saw four kids standing glumly in front of Mr. Harris, the football coach, in the middle of the drive.

'Damn it!' he swore. 'Why did it have to be Mr. Harris on detention duty, today of all days?'

'Ah! Mr. Carter, do join us and complete the group. Late for school? And you didn't show up for practice last evening, or this morning either.'

Ryan looked down, shuffling his feet uncomfortably. 'Er... yes, Sir, I've had some... er... tests... and...,' he mumbled lamely, not looking up.

'Right,' said Mr. Harris. 'I'll see all of you in Room 103 after school, for an hour of detention,' he instructed and walked away.

CHAPTER 2

'What a bunch of losers,' thought Sebastian, looking around the room.

He and the other latecomers were in the detention room. It was on the ground floor of the school building, overlooking the quadrangle. He was sitting near the window, and he could see the last of the stragglers, making their way across the quad on their way home.

He was supposed to be solving a chapter of Math problems. But he'd been in detention many times and at many schools, and he didn't think Holy Trinity was any different when it came to detention. He knew most of the time, the teacher who had detention duty, never checked the work given in by the kids. As long as he pretended to write something occasionally, Mr. Harris wouldn't notice. He leaned back in his chair and tapped his pen thoughtfully on his long nose, trying to look like he was mulling over a sum. He looked around at the other kids.

He knew that the big, rugged, black guy sitting across the room played football and, more importantly, was dating that absolute stunner, Lisa. He couldn't understand what she saw in him. Sebastian had to admit, Bryan... Ryan... Bert..., he didn't remember the player's name, was in good shape. He guessed some girls liked the mocha skin and curly hair, but he must be as poor as a church mouse. He came to school on a bicycle, for God's sake! And Sebastian knew Lisa was loaded. He had seen her at the country club gala, looking gorgeous, in a blue gown with a plunging neckline. And this oaf had been there with her, looking super awkward in a tux. Sebastian wondered where he had gotten the tux from. Probably rented it, he thought derisively.

He looked at the scrawny, black haired kid sitting right in front of him, who seemed engrossed in his work. He'd never noticed him before this morning, but he knew the kid's name. Samuel! The kid's sister, Cassandra, was in the same class as Maya and him, and he had heard her complain about the boy, all the way to class that morning. She'd said she was late because the kid had slipped and fallen on the way to school. He could well believe it. The boy looked like a puff of wind could blow him over. He could see the lump at the back of the boy's head where he must have hurt himself, and the hair around it was still slightly matted with clotted blood. Sebastian leaned forward, pretending to write something and peeked over the kid's shoulder, to see what he was doing so intently. He almost gasped. The kid had sketched the entire room in front of him, in detail.

'Well, Mr. Johnson, astounding as this is, I thought I told you to do Math.' Sebastian and Sam looked up, startled. They hadn't heard Mr. Harris approaching.

'For such a tall man, he does move very quietly,' thought Sebastian as he bent over pretending to work on his sum.

'I finished them, Sir,' said Sam, looking up.

'The whole chapter?' asked Mr. Harris doubtfully.

'Yes, Sir… do you want to check?' Sam started flipping pages in his book.

'No! No! It's fine,' said Mr. Harris hastily. 'I'm sure you must have finished it. Hand it in before you leave.'

Sebastian covered his mouth trying to hide his grin. He was sure Mr. Harris didn't have a clue about Math. His grin turned to a scowl when he saw Maya sitting two rows away, also trying not to grin. She flipped her hair over her shoulder, exposing her long, graceful neck.

'Hm!' mused Sebastian. 'She's quite good looking with her long, black hair and honey coloured eyes.' She looked good in her uniform, with its dark blue, pleated skirt, white shirt and a striped blue and yellow tie. If his dad wasn't dating her mom, and if he didn't absolutely detest her, he might have even asked her out. He knew she was one of the most popular girls in his year, but strangely, though she had no dearth of admirers, and she was quite the flirt, she didn't seem to have a steady boyfriend.

He looked at the other girl in the room and frowned. 'Don't tell me she's actually doing her sums. She's such a… what was the word? Hyper kiss ass!… Kiss ass! Ah!' That was the word he was looking for. 'Kiss ass!' He rolled the word in his mouth, as he watched Cassie scribbling away. He couldn't stand girls like Cassandra. They got on his nerves.

They heard a ping. Mr. Harris looked down at his phone. 'Kids! I'll have to step out for a minute,' he said. 'I'll be right back. I want to see all of you in your seats, doing your work quietly, when I get back. Any misbehaviour and it'll be detention for the whole week, for the lot of you.' He left with that threat.

Cassie threw her pen down in disgust, as soon as the door closed behind him. 'I can't believe I'm in detention,' she said, rounding on her brother. 'And it's your fault. I've never been in detention before.'

'Seriously?' Sebastian asked with interest. He was familiar with the detention room of every school he had attended. 'Wow! So today, you can thank your brother for rounding off your education,' he added, winking at Sam.

Cassie ignored him and continued ranting at Sam, who returned Sebastian's wink with a rueful look. 'Women,' he mouthed. Sebastian found himself warming towards the kid. It surprised him. He never warmed to anyone easily and he hardly knew this kid. But there was something about him… he shrugged. He'd probably never see the kid again and even if he did, he doubted that he'd remember him.

'Cut it out, Cassie!' said Maya, annoyed. She'd listened to Cassie whine all the way to class in the morning, and she didn't feel like putting up with another round of the same.

Cassie turned towards her, 'What's your problem? I'm talking to my brother. Mind your own business.'

'Sort out your problems at home,' retorted Maya. 'If Mr. Harris comes back while you're raving… you heard what he said. Detention for a week.'

This shut Cassie up, and after another murderous look at her brother, she attacked her work once more. Maya peeked at Ryan, sitting two seats away, chewing on the back of his pencil.

'Er… do you need some help with your work?' she asked Ryan.

He looked at her blankly for a second. 'What?' he asked.

Maya blushed. 'N… N… nothing,' she said, cursing herself for her stupidity. She bent over her work, letting her hair fall over to hide her red face. 'What was I thinking? Asking a senior if he wanted help with his work? How stupid could I be?'

Sebastian had watched this interchange with interest. 'Hm! Looks like someone has a major crush.' He gave a wicked grin. He was going to have some fun with that. He looked back at Ryan curiously. 'What is with this guy? Why are women falling for him when I'm around?'

Sebastian checked his watch and realised there was still another half hour to go. Damn! He was bored. He closed his eyes and started daydreaming about the drive home on his bike. He wondered whether to swing by the country club. Chicks dug a Ducati and he'd look cool, riding in on one. Maybe Lisa would be there. And maybe he'd… a crash jerked him out of his reverie.

'Now, what?' He looked up in irritation.

The siblings were at it again and Sam had jumped up from his chair, tipping it over with a crash. They were both standing nose to nose, arguing heatedly.

'Bloody hell!' Sebastian wished they'd shut up. He leaned over, picked up Sam's book from his desk and rifled through the pages idly. The book was full of sketches, all drawn vividly and with precise detailing.

'What are you doing with my book?' He looked up and found Sam glowering at him. 'Give it back!' Sam snatched at it.

Sebastian stood up. He was easily head and shoulders taller than Sam. He held the book over his head and out of reach of Sam's hands. 'Where are your manners, kid? Say please!'

'Where are yours?' snapped Sam. 'Going through someone else's stuff. Give it back.' Sebastian held it higher, teasing Sam.

'Give it back, shithead,' growled Ryan, standing up. Sebastian wasn't intimidated. He never backed down from a fight.

'And what if I don't, numbskull? Whatcha gonna do?' he asked.

'Stop it, you two,' shouted Maya. 'All of you, just sit down. Mr. Harris will be back at any moment. I...,' she stopped, and her eyes grew wide as she felt her chair vibrating under her.

'You'll what?' sneered Sebastian. 'Tell on me... to my...'

'Shut up! Shut up! Listen!' shouted Maya. She could now see her pencil moving as her table started shuddering too.

'Listen to wha...,' started Sebastian and stopped, as he felt the floor vibrating under him.

'What's going on?' said Ryan, looking around confused. 'Is it an earthquake?'

'It's an earthquake,' screamed Cassie. 'Let's get out of here!' She started throwing her things into her bag.

'It can't be an earthquake,' said Sam. 'We're not on any fault line. We don't get earthquakes here. Leave your books. Let's get out of here before the building collapses.' By then, the windows were rattling and the cupboards were shuddering.

Sam raced to the door and tugged on the door knob, but the door wouldn't open. Ryan, who was standing with a dazed expression, suddenly snapped into action.

'Move, kid. Let me do this.' He ran up to the door and tugged at the knob. It still wouldn't open. Ryan wondered if Mr. Harris had locked it from outside. He slammed his shoulder against the door, but it didn't budge. The vibration was growing and with it came a strange humming noise. They could feel it reverberating in their skulls.

'Hurry!' pleaded Cassie, very frightened now. 'Open the door! Help! Help! Help! Mr. Harris! Help!' She was screaming.

Sebastian joined Ryan at the door, and they both slammed against it with their shoulders. They threw themselves at the door, over and over again, in vain. Sebastian tugged at the knob with no result. He twisted the knob the wrong way and pulled, and the door swung open. As it opened, they heard Sam scream. They turned around, alarmed.

'Aaaah!' Sam had fallen to his knees, and was holding his head in his hands and screaming. 'Aaaah!' He screamed again. Cassie and Maya started towards him, when they felt an incredible jolt of pain shooting through their heads. Sebastian and Ryan felt the pain hit them, seconds later. It felt like their heads were going to explode. All of them collapsed holding their heads. A bright, white light enveloped the room. One by one, they toppled over onto the floor and passed out.

CHAPTER 3

Ryan opened his eyes and winced as bright sunlight hit him. He wondered what time it was and looked at the clock. He swore and tumbled out of bed. He was running late, and he couldn't afford to be late for school, two days in a row. He didn't want to miss another practice because of detention. 'Detention!' he paused, with his hand on the bathroom doorknob. 'Detention!' He felt there was something about detention that he should remember, but he couldn't. It was just a niggling thought, at the back of his head.

'Forget it! If I can't remember it, it probably wasn't worth remembering anyway,' he decided and went into the bathroom. He looked at himself in the mirror as he picked up his toothbrush. 'Hello handsome!' he told his reflection. He had seen Jim Carey talking to his reflection in "The Truman Show" when he was much younger, and had started doing it because he had thought it was hilarious. Now it had become a morning ritual.

He bent forward to look at his eyes and noticed they were bloodshot. He frowned, wondering why they were red. He also had a throbbing headache. He decided to take a couple of pills, and hoped it would subside before he headed to practice.

He started brushing his teeth.

Maya took her second pill during the third period. She couldn't concentrate, her eyes burned. Maybe she was coming down with something. She pressed her fingers to her temples and tried to listen to what the teacher was saying. It was History, and she liked History. She was a very bright girl, for whom studying came easy and her only real rival, was Cassie. She frowned as she thought of Cassie and her brother fighting during detention, the day before. The girl had a serious chip on her shoulder. She looked at where Cassie sat, front row as always, right under the teacher's nose. Her frown deepened. Cassie was sitting in the same position as Maya, holding her head in her hands and massaging her temples.

'What on earth?' thought Maya and turned towards Sebastian, who was as usual in the last row, as far away from the teacher as possible. He had his head down on his hands and was fast asleep. She shook her head. Sebastian sleeping in class was nothing new. For a minute, she had a weird feeling her headache and Cassie's had something to do with detention the day before, though she couldn't say why. That was the weird part; that she couldn't remember. The last thing she remembered about detention was Cassie and her brother fighting, and then everyone was yelling, and... and... that was it. For the life of her, she couldn't remember how she'd gotten home, or when. By car obviously, it was in its spot in the morning, but she didn't remember driving home.

Sam was sitting in his class, quietly panicking. He was sure he was dying. His head pounded, and he seemed to be suffering from some form of memory loss. He knew he was wired differently from other people. He'd been put through hundreds of tests and seen many specialists. Though the tests varied, as did the opinions of the specialists, the results had always been the same. His I.Q. was through the roof, and he had an eidetic memory. He was also autistic, though surprisingly, his E.Q was also quite high. He had heard all these terms often enough and had looked them up. He knew basically what it meant was, he was an anomaly. He was different. People said special to be polite, but he had always thought it was way cooler to say he was different.

He had often wondered if being different would have any effect on his health. It already did, in a way. He was very fragile and fell sick often, though as he grew up, he was getting stronger. But he had always felt that with the amount of knowledge his mind could absorb, it would explode one day. And it looked like today was the day.

'I'm gonna die today,' he thought, in a panic. He was surprised at the panic. He'd always thought he would meet death with equanimity. But he only felt cold terror. 'I don't want to die!' he thought. 'Oh God! Now I feel nauseous.'

Luckily, he sat near the door. He held his hand against his mouth and tore out, not even stopping to ask for permission. He barged into the toilet and just about made it to the first cubicle, when everything he had eaten in the morning, heaved out. He retched a few more times, but it was over and with it, his headache seemed to have lessened. He stood up and flushed. Maybe, he wasn't going to die today after all, he thought with relief. He walked out to the washbasin. As he opened the tap, he found his hands were shaking, and he was covered with sweat. His knees felt weak, like they were about to buckle. He leaned on the basin for support, splashed water on his face and peered into the mirror. His eyes had been bloodshot in the morning when he'd awoken, but now they seemed fine. 'Must have been the headache,' he thought.

He was reaching out to pull some tissues from the dispenser, when he heard someone else enter the bathroom and hurry past him. He was wiping the water off his face when he heard a familiar noise. Someone throwing up in one of the cubicles.

He turned towards the sound which was coming from the second last cubicle. He was still debating whether to stay or leave, when he heard the main door to the bathroom bang open. Before he could turn around, someone barrelled past him, pushing him out of the way. It was Ryan, who stumbled into another cubicle and also started vomiting. He was in such a hurry he hadn't even bothered to shut the door.

Sam frowned. This was getting weirder by the minute He wasn't sure why, but he was willing to bet that the boy throwing up in the second last cubicle was Sebastian. Instead of going back to class, he pulled himself up onto the washbasin countertop and waited. Ryan came out first. He looked ill, and his shirt was drenched with sweat.

He brushed back the hair clinging to his sweaty forehead and said, 'Sorry, kid! Emergency! Sorry, I shoved you.'

Sam was surprised. He was used to being shoved around by the older boys. He had expected rudeness, maybe a couple of threats, not an apology. Ryan must be feeling quite lousy. Ryan splashed water on his face and over his curly mop. He tried to flatten the curls and make them more orderly. Only then did he seem to notice that Sam was sitting on the counter.

'Aren't you supposed to be in class?' he asked.

Sam tensed. 'Yes!' he replied.

'I don't feel too good, so I'm letting you off with a warning. I suggest you get off the counter and leave, before someone else comes in,' said Ryan, turning away.

'I think you should stay,' said Sam, quietly.

'What?' Ryan looked taken aback.

'I said, I think you should stay,' repeated Sam.

Ryan couldn't believe the cheek of the kid. Did he have a death wish? He was just about to chew the kid's head off and send him packing to class with a flea in his ear, when the kid raised a finger and silently pointed to the end of the room, where the door of the second last cubicle was opening.

The snooty kid, who was in detention with him the day before, walked out. He looked a wreck, dishevelled and sweaty. He staggered to the wall, leaned back against it, and after a few seconds, sank down to the floor as if his legs couldn't hold him. Ryan looked back at the kid sitting on the counter and recognized him. He'd been in detention too, the previous day.

'What the hell is going on here?' he asked irritated.

Sebastian looked up from where he was sitting on the floor. He didn't feel too good. He had woken up with a bad headache and had considered skipping school. But his dad was already mad at him for having taken the bike the day before, and he hadn't wanted to anger him further. So he'd come to school, but had slept through his morning classes, till he had awoken feeling nauseous. He felt better now after he had thrown up. But he was in no mood to take bull from anyone. He was about to say something nasty, when Sam piped up. 'Do either one of you remember what happened after detention yesterday?'

Sebastian looked at him. 'Hey! You're the kid who was in detention yesterday, the artist... Cassie's brother, right?'

Sam ignored the question and repeated his own. 'Do either one of you remember what happened after detention yesterday?'

Sebastian was surprised by the kid's cheekiness and then he grinned. He liked the kid's attitude.

'Yeah! I went home, ate dinner and went to bed, not that it's any business of yours,' he replied. Ryan didn't reply. He just looked thoughtful.

'What did you have for dinner?' asked Sam.

'Er... I... um... pasta? I don't know. I don't keep track of my meals. Probably pasta,' said Sebastian. 'What's this about anyway? What's going on?'

'I don't remember anything after detention yesterday,' said Ryan. 'When I woke up this morning, I couldn't remember how I got home. My cycle was in the shed, so I assume I cycled home.'

CHAPTER 4

'Why are you asking me all these silly questions? I have to get back to class,' said Cassie and turned to leave the toilet.

'Cassie! One sec! Humour me. Do you remember how you got home yesterday?' asked Maya.

'Yes, Sam and I walked back,' replied Cassie.

'Are you sure?' asked Maya.

'Of course I'm sure,' said Cassie. 'Now, can I go back to class?'

'I've had a horrible headache since I woke up this morning, and I just threw up. So did you! Did you have a headache when you woke up this morning?' asked Maya.

Cassie nodded. 'Yes, but it's normal for me. I get headaches all the time.'

'With nausea?' persisted Maya.

'Yes... with nausea. They're called migraines. Maybe, you just had your first one,' said Cassie, looking irritated. They both jumped, as the bell rang for break. It sounded extremely loud in the quiet bathroom.

'Now see what you did?' moaned Cassie. 'You made me miss the rest of History.'

'Cassie, I didn't make you miss anything. You were throwing up. That's why you missed class,' said Maya.

'Now I won't know what work he's set for us. I'll...,' started Cassie when Maya cut her off saying, 'I'll get it from someone and give it to you. Stop whining. Come with me. We need to find the others.'

'Others?' asked Cassie sourly.

'The others, who were in detention with us, moron. There's something weird...,' She was talking more to herself now. 'Something, I'm not sure, just come with me.' She caught Cassie's arm and pulled her.

'The only thing weird is you,' thought Cassie as she tagged along, annoyed. They went back to class to find Sebastian, but he wasn't there. Then, they checked Sam's class, but he wasn't in either.

'There they are,' said Cassie in a bored voice. She had refused to come into Sam's class and was waiting outside, leaning over the balcony overlooking the quadrangle. She was watching the kids in the quad and had spotted the three boys, walking across.

'Where?' asked Maya eagerly, peering over the balcony. Cassie pointed them out. 'Come on, hurry, we have to catch them,' said Maya and raced towards the stairs. She looked over her shoulder to see if Cassie was following her. She wasn't. 'C'mon,' she called out.

'No! I'm going back to class,' said Cassie stubbornly.

'Cas! If you don't come, I won't get the History assignment for you,' threatened Maya.

'Fine, I'll come, but I think you're mad,' said Cassie. Maya raced down the stairs with Cassie reluctantly trailing behind. Maya reached the ground floor first, turned the corner and ran full tilt into Sam.

'Listen, about yesterday…,' Maya and Sam stopped and stared at each other, when they realized they were both saying the same thing.

'Guys!' said Ryan, shushing them, as the bell rang for class. 'Let's head back to class now. We'll meet after school at the football stands? I'll see you there, yeah?' They nodded and returned to their respective classrooms.

After school, Maya, Cassie and Sebastian made their way towards the football stadium. Cassie was complaining loudly. 'I don't understand. Why do we have to meet? I have so much work…'

'Gosh! Give it a rest, Cassie,' said Maya, fed up with the whining.

Cassie turned to Sebastian. 'Do you know why we have to meet them?' she asked. He shrugged. Cassie gestured at Maya. 'She made me miss half the History period in the morning, with all her weirdness and now this.'

Sebastian found Cassie's whining equally annoying, but he was willing to put up with it, to taunt Maya.

'She's weird, isn't she?' he told Cassie, in a loud whisper.

'Yes, I think she's quite mad,' Cassie whispered back. 'She practically broke my arm this morning, dragging me down the stairs.'

'Really?' Sebastian pretended to be shocked. 'You should complain. I'm sure they'll expel her. She can't treat you like that.' Cassie looked gratified.

Maya, who was walking ahead of them, rolled her eyes. 'You know I can hear you, right? You'd enjoy it if I get expelled, wouldn't you, Seb? But I'm sorry, that won't be happening. I didn't drag her anywhere, much less break her arm. And Cassie, I borrowed the History notes for you. If you don't shut it, you're not getting it.'

They walked in silence after that. They had to pass the new block to get to the stadium. The main school building was an old structure, like most of the buildings in Skallen, the town they lived in. Skallen had started off as a farming community, and had been divided into the gentry and farm labourers. In the beginning, the farm labourers were an itinerant crowd, but over time they'd gotten married and settled down, in and around Skallen, as tenants in small shacks at first and later in cottages, built on the land of the people they worked for.

The village used to consist of a main street which had a store for provisions, little shops for odds and ends, and a pub where the labourers could get drunk and let off steam during the weekends. The pub still remained, but was now an elegant and expensive restaurant, aptly named

"The Tavern". With the advance in farming techniques, many of these agricultural communities around the region had disappeared, but not Skallen.

The community had adapted and persevered. People moved from farming to other professions and it had soon become a bustling town. A school for the labourers' children had been built in the old days, right where Holy Trinity now stood. The children of the gentry used to be tutored at home, or had gone to expensive boarding schools. The local school was called Holy Trinity, by the missionaries who had helped build it, and had originally consisted of one long, low building. There were still pictures of the school from those days, in the administration area of the main school building.

As the community prospered and grew, the old building was demolished and the new structure which still stood today was built. It had been funded by Lord Robert Dawlins, one of the landed gentry, who had died childless. He had left instructions in his will, for his money to be used for the construction of a new school building.

As Skallen grew, so did its community, and with change and growth had come the malls and theatres, filling in the gaps in the town and spreading outwards making it almost a city. But it still retained its old world charm; many of the people living there were direct descendants of the gentry or labourers, from when it was a village. Everybody claimed to have descended from the landowners, and even now the word "labourer" was a derogatory term in the community.

Like the main school building of Holy Trinity, many other old buildings too remained unchanged over the years, like the town library, the council buildings, the court, etc., and the people of Skallen were proud of their heritage. Any new additions to the old buildings had to pass through strict council laws and be approved before construction work could begin. In accordance with this, the new additions to the school building were built with care, so as not to compromise the look of the original building. It was quite a large campus and the main building stood near the front gates, closer to the main road. It was a square structure, with the quadrangle in the middle. All the classrooms were in the main building.

The new block stood behind the old one and contained the auditorium, indoor swimming pool, O.T. rooms, etc. Scattered over the rest of the campus, were the fields and courts for various sports. Holy Trinity had one of the best football stadiums in the region and many clubs and schools used their field for matches.

When the trio entered the stadium, there was a match in progress. Holy Trinity wasn't participating and the stands were mostly empty, and the few spectators sat near the locker rooms. Cassie pointed to an empty corner, high up on the stands. They climbed up and sat down to wait for the other two. They sat in silence, watching the match.

'There's Ryan,' said Maya, perking up, 'and Sam,' she added. Both the boys had entered at the same time but through different entrances. 'Guys!' Maya shouted.

Both looked up and saw the three of them. They made their way up the stands and sat down beside the others. All five watched the match in silence, for a couple of minutes. Nobody seemed to want to start the conversation.

Finally, it was Sam who spoke. 'None of us cares about this match... in fact, I know Cassie does not care for football or for any sport, for that matter.' He earned a scathing look from Cassie for the aside, but she didn't rise to it. 'So, that's not why we're here,' he continued, as he got up and climbed over the seats in the row below. He turned around so he could see all of them. 'Yesterday's detention... that's why we're here.'

Sebastian raised an eyebrow. 'You keep saying that, but I've no idea what you are going on about. I don't understand what the big deal is if I can't remember what I ate last night?'

To Sam's surprise, it was Cassie, who spoke, looking thoughtful. 'You know what? I can't remember what I ate either. And also… this is pretty weird, but I don't remember doing my assignment last night. This morning when Mrs. Lewis asked for our assignments, I thought I hadn't done it. I opened my book, trying to come up with some excuse to give her for why I hadn't finished it, but… it was done. I don't remember doing it.'

'Well, I don't remember doing my assignment either… because I didn't,' said Sebastian grinning. 'Homework is a bore.'

'So what did you do instead?' asked Sam.

'I… hm… what did I do? I… yeah… I watched a movie,' said Sebastian.

'Which movie?' persisted Sam.

Sebastian looked uncertain. 'Hm… let's see… er… you know what, I don't remember, and, what's more, I don't care,' he said, looking irritated.

'Did any of you wake up with a headache this morning?' asked Maya.

'Oh my goodness!', 'Yes!', 'Head was pounding!' All of them replied at the same time, their words overlapping each others. They looked at one another in surprise.

'Did you have a headache too, Maya?' asked Ryan. Maya nodded.

'I get migraines all the time… I'm used to it,' said Cassie dismissively.

'What's the last thing you remember about last evening?' asked Maya.

'Cassie and her brother were arguing,' said Sebastian.

'And then, you took Sam's book,' chimed in Cassie.

'Right, and he wouldn't give it back,' said Sam, his forehead scrunched up in thought.

Maya took over. 'Then, Ryan got up and asked Seb to…'

'… return the book to Sam,' finished Ryan, as he too remembered the sequence of events.

'Then something happened,' said Sam, his face still screwed up. 'Everything started shaking… I vaguely remember a light, dazzling light and noise?' He looked up. 'Do you remember that?' They shook their heads, looking at him strangely.

'You're off your rocker, you know that?' said Sebastian. 'And I've had enough of this nonsense. I'm leaving!' He got up and walked away.

'Pompous ass!' muttered Maya, as she watched him swagger away. She turned to the others.

'It's not nonsense. That's what happened,' insisted Sam.

'Sam! Now you are simply imagining stuff,' said Maya, gently patting his shoulder.

Sam pushed her hand off and said, 'I'm telling you something happened. In fact, Maya, you were the first to notice it. I don't remember what happened very clearly, but it appears to have caused memory loss, headache and nausea. All of us had the same symptoms… Sebastian too, he's just not admitting it. It can't be a coincidence, can it?' he asked, frowning.

Ryan considered what Sam had said. 'Well! Whatever it was, it's over. We're all feeling fine now, aren't we?' He looked around. 'Aren't we?' he asked again. They all nodded, Sam reluctantly. The truth was, he *was* feeling fine now. 'So I guess that's it then. I don't see how it matters anymore.' He picked up his bag. 'I'll see you guys around.' With that, he walked away.

'Yeah! I suppose he's right. We seem to be fine… so…,' Maya stood up and picked up her bag. 'Come on guys! Let's go home,' she said and followed Ryan down the stands.

'Cas!' Sam gave his sister a pleading look. She looked back at him, exasperated. She'd had enough of this.

'Sam! Let it go! Come on, we'll be late.' She picked up her bags and hurried down the steps.

'Something happened!' whispered Sam to himself, as he followed his sister. 'I'm not crazy. Something did happen.'

CHAPTER 5

SAM

Sam lay on the grass, looking up at the clouds. It was Sunday, and he was indulging in one of his favourite pastimes. When he was younger, he and his mom would lie down and watch the clouds roll by. They would weave stories around them. One cloud would be a castle and another, a giant, and... he sighed, as he remembered. It seemed like years ago. All that was before she started working. Nowadays, he rarely got to see her. She even worked weekends, like today. She was a paralegal and worked for a well known law firm.

His dad tried to compensate, but Sam still missed his mom. His dad was an investment banker and even when he was at home, he was either on conference calls or his laptop. He often said, "Money never sleeps". Sam didn't know about the money, but he knew his dad hardly slept.

His parents were childhood sweethearts and had married right after school. His mom had dropped out of school to support his dad while he finished college. By then, Cassie and he were born, and his mom had gotten busy raising them. His parents had decided the bustle of the big city was no place to raise children, and they had moved to Skallen, when Sam was a year old.

As the children grew older and more independent, his mom had started feeling she hadn't done anything for herself. She had blamed his dad for it, and they had often fought. It was only when they were seriously considering separating that they had decided to give it one more try, and had gone to a marriage counsellor. That had helped. His mom had realised she was young enough to still pursue her dreams, and his dad had been very supportive. His mom had gone back to college, got her degree and found a job. He was proud of his mom for having achieved what she had set out to do. But a selfish part of him wanted her to be just "his Mom" again.

He shook his head, pushing those thoughts away and relaxed his body and mind. He found it restful. His hyperactive brain needed to calm down, now and then. Over the years, with the help of therapists and later on his own, he had learned to push out all thoughts from his mind.

This was one of his favourite places to relax. He was lying on a little hillock which rose up behind his house. If he stood up and looked around, he would be able to see his house, with its white walls and dark green shutters. His street was called Landau Lane. It used to be a lane earlier, but now, it was a wide, tree-lined street with detached houses. The houses on his street were very similar, well maintained homes with gardens in front that ended at the pavement. Theirs used to be a well maintained home till his mom started working. Now their garden, or what was left of it, was a mess. There were more weeds than shrubs and the grass needed mowing.

They had a very active neighbourhood association, and he had heard from his friend, Colin, who lived down the road, that the association had decided to bring up the matter of the upkeep of the Johnson garden. Colin had overheard his mom, who was on the committee, telling someone that the Johnson's badly maintained garden was a disgrace to the neighbourhood and a letter was to be sent to his parents on the matter. Sam was grateful for that bit of information, as he fully intended to intercept the letter and make sure his parents never saw it. He knew that if they read it, his mom, who used to be on the committee, would want the garden cleaned up. It would fall to him and Cassie to do the dirty work, as his parents would be too busy. He had no intention of spending any time working in the garden. It could rot for all he cared.

His house was towards the upper end of an incline, and the slope continued on behind his house, ending at the hillock, on which he now lay. His house had a backyard, with a high hedge running around and a small wrought iron gate at the back. The gate led to a well trodden path, up the hillock. There were no houses behind the hillock and if he sat up, he would be able to see Lake Skallen to his left. To the right, the hillock sloped down gently to a small copse of firs. Lying here, he felt all alone in the world, just him, the sky, the earth and the plant and animal life around him. He felt at one with nature.

He sighed with pleasure, looking at the sky. The cloud he was looking at resembled a wolf. It only needed a bigger body and a longer tail. He moved his gaze to the next cloud… maybe a house or even a cottage… that could be Red Riding Hood's grandmother's cottage, with the wolf waiting near it. He smiled at his own stupid story. There were no more clouds, and the sky was clear after that. He looked back at the previous cloud.

'No way!' he spluttered aloud, sitting up. The cloud now looked exactly like a huge wolf, baring its teeth and waiting to pounce, with a massive body and a thick, long tail. 'That's weird,' he thought, looking at it with awe as the cloud broke up into smaller parts and dissipated. It had looked almost exactly like the wolf he had imagined. He smiled… that had been creepy, but also rather brilliant. He laughed aloud. It had put him in a good mood.

He felt… alive… like he could run for miles. He was also extremely hungry. He looked at his watch and realised it was almost lunchtime. He sat up and flipped his hair away from his forehead. He was a thin boy, with a pinched look on his face. He was the shortest boy in his year; even most of the girls were taller than him. The only two things which defined his face were his wide blue eyes and his shock of silky, black hair.

He pushed his hair back as he ran down the path, back to the wrought iron gate which opened into his backyard. As he ran, he felt exhilarated and had a crazy thought; he wanted to jump over the gate which led to his backyard. The gate was broad and short. A boy of Sam's height could clear it easily, but Sam wasn't very athletic. He'd been told all his life that he was very fragile and should be careful. 'No running... no jumping!!!' He had heard it so often, that it had become a way of life. He was, in fact, surprised at himself for running down the hill. He usually walked down the hill carefully. He was now almost at the gate. He braced himself and put out one hand. He caught the top of the gate and swung his body up. He felt the heel of his right foot hit the gate as he went over, and in that instant, he knew he hadn't made it. He came crashing down in a heap on the other side, winded.

His first instinct was to look around wildly. If anyone had seen that antic, he'd had it. He breathed a sigh of relief when he saw that no one was around. Then he moved his hands and legs. No broken bones! He stood up gingerly. He was wearing shorts, so he had skinned his knees, and he had a bruise on his arm, but otherwise he seemed okay. He gave another sigh of relief. He looked back at the gate. That was the most exciting thing he had ever done in his life. As the thought passed his mind, he realised how pathetic it sounded. He was fifteen, and that was the wildest thing he had ever done? What a sad life he led. But it was an incredible feeling. He could still feel the surge of adrenaline in his body. He knew he was going to try it again, although maybe not today.

He entered the house through the back door. The detached had two floors. The ground floor had a living room, drawing room, dining room, kitchen and a small guest bedroom which his dad, and now his mom too used as their study. The upper floor had three bedrooms and a den. A narrow passage led from the back door he had come through, with the utility room on his left. The passage opened out onto the open planned dining and kitchen area which was divided by a half wall. The kitchen was large and had a centre island, around which they usually ate. They only used the dining room when they were all eating together or had company.

'Hello! I'm home,' he called out, as he entered the kitchen.

His dad's head popped out from the study, a minute later. He gestured to his earpiece with one hand and mouthed, 'Conference call!'

Sam nodded, and his dad disappeared back into the study. Conference calls! On a Sunday! Sam shook his head and went into the kitchen. He opened the fridge and started pulling out stuff. There was some leftover pizza, frozen T.V. dinners, leftover roast chicken and a wilted salad. There was also some sushi, but he wasn't particularly fond of raw fish. He put on the T.V., turned down the volume so his dad wouldn't be disturbed and microwaved the pizza.

He pulled himself up on the kitchen counter and sat there, eating his pizza and surfing channels. There was nothing interesting on any of the other channels, so he turned to the local news and left it on. The anchor was talking about an electrical storm. He turned the volume a little louder. By then, the clip was over, and the next segment came on. It was about some corrupt, local politician. The microwave pinged.

Sam jumped off the counter and opened the door under the sink, to chuck the empty pizza box. It wouldn't fit so he stuffed it in as best as he could, but then the door wouldn't close as the edge of the box was sticking out. He made a mental note to throw it out before his mom came home. He took out the T.V. dinner that he had heated up, and got up on the counter again. He knew that the news was on a loop and the segment on the electrical storm would be shown again. It had caught his interest because it had looked like the anchorwoman was standing outside Holy Trinity.

He started on the T.V. dinner while he waited for the segment. He wondered where Cassie was. Probably studying. Sometimes, he felt bad for her as she was older by a year, but he was way ahead of her in most subjects. He did different subjects at different levels. He was doing Math and Physics, one level higher than her. He was doing quite a few subjects at Cassie's level. She had pleaded with their mom not to put him in her class. So, his mom had made sure that none of the higher levels he took were in Cassie's class. He only did English, Language and Social Science with kids his age. Even though he was doing subjects at a much higher level, he still found studying very easy. Cassie struggled... she did well because she worked that hard.

The downside of taking classes at different levels was that he didn't have many friends. He had no trouble with social skills, but the other kids found him odd because they couldn't relate to him. He honestly didn't mind that much. He found most of them boring.

His only friend was Colin, who lived down the road and was in his class. But they had an unspoken agreement. At school, Colin totally ignored him. But back home, they hung out. Well, they used to hang out a lot when they were younger but not anymore. These days, Colin spent his time with the cool crowd at the mall and went to movies and parties. He still chilled with Sam sometimes, but only when he had absolutely nothing else to do.

Sam looked down at his tray. He'd polished off the T.V. dinner. He eyed the roast chicken and salad and was wondering whether to make himself a giant burger, when the segment came on again. Margaret, the anchorwoman was saying that on Wednesday, there had been an electrical storm in the vicinity of the school. Apparently, there was no warning. The weather forecast had been clear. It had occurred about 4.15.p.m. The electrical storm had hit a tree, right outside their school and cleaved it in half. It had lasted for about five minutes and had disappeared as quickly as it had appeared.

'It was an unusual phenomenon,' said Margaret, 'and meteorologists are still trying to figure out what caused it.'

'Ah! Ha! That was what I saw. I knew I wasn't imagining things. The electrical storm occurred around the time we were in detention. That must have been the light I saw and the sounds I heard.' He jumped down from the counter, pleased with himself and started making his giant burger with the chicken and salad. He paused, as a thought struck him. 'I wonder why the others don't remember seeing it.'

'Are you going to eat all of that?' Startled, Sam almost dropped the burger he was lifting to his mouth.

'Cas? For God's sake! You scared the hell out of me,' he said, 'and yes… I am eating this whole burger. Do you have a problem?' he asked belligerently.

Cassie gave him a disbelieving look and walked to the fridge. She knew he'd never finish the burger. He was a poor eater, another reason for their mom to fuss over him… coaxing him to eat, "just a little more". Of course, all the fussing had stopped after she got her job. They used to feel fatherless, now they were motherless too. Not that it had made much of a difference in her life. Her mom's life had revolved around Sam anyway. Cassie had always felt like an outsider. She was actually happy in a perverse way that her mom was hardly home anymore. At least now, Sam and she were in the same boat. Now, their parents didn't have time for either of them.

'Where's the pizza?' she asked. She was sure there'd been more than half a pizza in the fridge. She had eaten a big breakfast, before going up to study. She had a test on Monday. But she had felt hungry again, and the thought of the pepperoni pizza she knew was in the fridge had kept distracting her from studying. She wanted to heat it and take it up with her.

'I ate it,' said Sam as he took another big bite of his burger.

'No, you didn't,' said Cassie, with a disbelieving look. 'The whole thing?' She looked at where he was pointing and saw the edge of the pizza box, jutting out from under the sink.

'You better chuck it out before Mom comes home,' she said huffily.

She was annoyed! She'd been fantasizing about the pizza, and she was miffed that it was over. She bent down and rummaged through the fridge, to see what else was there. She was sure there were a couple of frozen T.V. dinners. That wasn't what she wanted, but she was hungry, and it would have to do.

'There it is.' There were two. She pulled one out and shut the fridge door. She walked over to heat up her food, when she saw the remains of another T.V. dinner beside the microwave oven. She paused and turned towards Sam.

'Has Dad eaten?' she asked.

'Don't know. Don't think so,' replied Sam, with his mouth full. He was almost through with his burger.

'He must have eaten,' said Cassie, putting her food in and setting the timer. 'There's another T.V. dinner here,' she said, pointing to the one beside the oven.

'Me!' said Sam, stuffing the last bit of burger into his mouth.

'You, what?' asked Cassie, filling a glass with water.

'Me ate it!' said Sam.

Cassie stared at him. 'You ate pizza, a T.V. dinner and you're eating that burger?' she asked incredulously.

'Yup,' said Sam, looking pleased with himself. 'I was very hungry.'

Cassie took her food and pulled herself up on one of the tall stools which stood around the island. She decided to take a break and continue studying after lunch. She attacked her food hungrily.

'Look! Look! They're showing it again,' said Sam excitedly.

She looked up and saw him pointing to the T.V. The anchorwoman was talking about an electrical storm which had occurred outside Holy Trinity. She removed her glasses and wiped them. She couldn't see the screen clearly. Her vision was blurred. It had been getting blurred for the last couple of days, but it was getting worse today, and she was finding it difficult to study. Cassie hated her glasses. She had worn glasses from when she could remember. Big, thick ones! She did have contacts, but they were not the soft ones, like her friend Len wore. They felt alien in her eyes, so she hardly wore them. She hoped her power hadn't gone up. She put her glasses back on and looked at the T.V. The anchor who was standing outside their school, was pointing to a tree the electrical storm had apparently broken in half.

She looked at Sam. 'And how is this relevant to my life?' she asked sarcastically.

'Didn't you listen?' asked Sam. 'It happened when we were in detention. Right outside school. That was the noise I heard and the light I saw. Now, do you believe me? I wasn't imagining things.'

'Oh!' said Cassie and continued eating.

'Wait! It'll come again.' Sam was bouncing on the balls of his feet, in excitement. In a few minutes, the segment came on again. 'Watch! Cas! Watch!' Sam poked her.

'Ouch! Okay! Take a chill pill, will you?' She watched the whole segment.

'Well?' asked Sam. 'Now, do you believe me? Don't you think it's weird?'

'No, I don't. I mean… yes, I do believe you, but now you know what it was that you saw. It was an electrical storm. There's your answer,' said Cassie.

'Cas, the electrical storm isn't the weird part,' said Sam softly. 'The weird part is that it happened just outside school, when we were all there, and I remember seeing it and none of you do.'

Cassie paused with her fork halfway to her mouth, as she considered what he had said. She put her fork back down and swivelled around to look at Sam, her green eyes, troubled.

'You know what? You're right, Sam,' she said. 'It happened so close to us that even if we didn't see it, we should have heard it, right?' Sam nodded vigorously. 'It's funny none of us, except you, remember it. Maybe, the electrical storm struck the school too, and we all got electrocuted and our minds went blank. That's why we don't remember anything. Maybe, overnight the effects wore off, and the headache and nausea were remnants of the shock.' She felt like she was letting her imagination run wild, but it did seem like a good theory.

Sam seemed to agree. He nodded. 'Cas, that actually sounds plausible. It would explain a lot.'

Cassie picked up her fork again, when another thought struck her. She put her fork back down and turned towards him again. 'But then, how come we don't remember the electrical storm, and you do?'

Sam looked uncomfortable. 'I know you hate it whenever anyone says it, but the fact is I'm different. My brain absorbs more… my senses work overtime… so maybe, that's why I remember more,' he offered, waiting for the angry outburst from her about how he thought no end of himself.

Surprisingly, Cassie seemed to be contemplating what he had said. 'You're probably right,' she said.

She removed her glasses and wiped them. 'Damn! These glasses suck.'

'Language!' their father reprimanded Cassie, as he walked into the kitchen. 'I had to take that call. Sorry, kids! Ok, now, who wants what for lunch?' he asked, rubbing his hands together.

'Dad, we're done!' said Cassie, picking up her tray and moving over to the sink. She opened the door under it to chuck her tray. 'Sam, it's your turn to empty the garbage bag. Once you've put in a new bag, please put my tray into it… along with yours,' she said with a sweet, false smile which grated on Sam. Cassie always acted sweet and perfect, when their dad was around. He didn't reply.

His father hadn't even noticed the exchange. 'Have you both finished eating?' he asked, as he opened the fridge door.

'Yes, Dad, we were hungry,' said Sam.

His father peeked over the fridge door, his usual genial face looking troubled. 'I'm sorry, kids! I had to take that call,' he apologised again.

The kids were used to this. Their dad forgot the world when he was working, and when he finally came back to reality, he felt bad and tried to make up.

'Dad! It's all right! Honestly! Why don't you grab something to eat and I'll sit with you,' offered Sam.

'Er… if you guys have finished, then, I'll make a sandwich for myself and take it to the study. I can finish some work while I eat,' he said.

Cassie looked at her dad. She'd inherited her curly red hair and green eyes from him. Her dad was Scottish. Most of her dad's relatives were red haired and green eyed. She was glad she hadn't inherited the freckles too. Some of her cousins weren't as lucky as her. They had blotchy freckles all over their face. Now, looking at her dad, she noticed he seemed to have lost weight, and had bags under his eyes. Running the house and working was taking a toll on him. She felt bad for him, and she blamed her mom.

'Why don't you get back to work, Dad? I'll get you something to eat,' she offered.

'No! No, sweetheart. You go on. I'll find something to eat,' he replied, pulling out stuff from the fridge.

'Dad! I need to see the ophthalmologist,' Cassie said apologetically. 'My vision is blurred and it's getting worse. I think my power has changed.'

'Sure, hon! Will you book it? You know how forgetful I am,' said her dad, putting some bread, cheese and ham slices on the table. He started making a sandwich for himself.

'For when?' she asked.

'As soon as possible? We don't want you to get migraines again,' her dad replied. Cassie nodded and turned to leave the kitchen.

'Just let me know when you book it, so I can clear my schedule,' he called out after her.

'Okay, Dad,' she replied.

Sam took out the garbage bag from under the sink. He leant it against the wall and was lining the bin with a new bag, when they heard the front door open. Sam's eyes lit up.

'Honey! I'm home.' Cassie stopped halfway up the stairs, when she heard the voice.

'Babe! We're in the kitchen,' called out their dad, his face lighting up with pleasure too. Their mom walked into the kitchen, with a giant bag of Indian take away.

'I managed to get away. Calling me on a Sunday was bad enough, but asking me to work the whole day was a bit much. So I told them to take a hike. I come bearing gifts,' she said, raising the bag of Indian food, 'and hoping to be forgiven.'

'Honey! You are a life saver. You saved me from having a crappy sandwich for lunch,' said their dad, giving his wife a quick peck before taking the bags from her.

'Cas! Sweetie! Where are you going?' her mom called out, as she started climbing the stairs again.

'I've finished eating,' said Cassie. 'I have…'

Her mom cut her off. 'Nonsense! Come on… it's been so long since we've had a meal together.'

'And whose fault is that?' thought Cassie, sourly.

She was about to say she wasn't hungry, when her mom said, 'I've got curry.'

Damn! That was inconvenient. Chicken curry was her favourite. Maybe she'd have a small bite and get away. She came back downstairs.

'C'mon kids! Set the table,' called out their dad. The two kids scurried around getting plates and cutlery while their parents emptied the food into dishes and heated it up. Sam thought he wouldn't be able to eat much after his huge lunch, but surprised himself by polishing off quite a bit of the Indian food. Cassie watched in amazement. She too was stuffing her face, but she had always been a good eater. Even her parents seemed surprised at Sam's appetite.

For the first time in weeks, Sam felt truly happy. It was so long since they had sat down together and had a meal like a regular family that he had forgotten what fun it was. All thoughts of the electrical storm were erased from his head as he enjoyed the moment.

CHAPTER 6

MAYA

Maya and her mom were having Sunday brunch, when Maya saw the segment on the electrical storm. Sundays were a big deal for her mom and her, because it was the only day they got to spend time together, and catch up on what was happening in each other's life. They usually woke up late on Sunday and Maya would crawl into her mom's bed, to snuggle for a while. Her mom would get coffee and the papers, and they'd relax in bed, sipping their coffee, reading the papers and gossiping. Today, it was almost eleven, when they had finally gotten out of bed. Her mom had made brunch with sausages, bacon, eggs, and some of last night's tandoori chicken, and she had made fresh rotis to go with it.

They usually watched T.V. while they ate, and today was no different. The segment on the electrical storm had come on and the newscaster had said it had occurred just outside Holy Trinity. It had happened right around the time she and the others were in detention. Maybe, that was the light and noise Sam was talking about.

After breakfast, she spent the morning tidying her room. She was house proud like her mom. While she was studying or doing a project, she would let things pile up for a couple of days, but as soon as she finished, the first thing she did was tidy up her room. She liked a neat room.

She and her mom lived in a large apartment which had three bedrooms, study, drawing room, dining room and a den. It was well laid out, spacious and tastefully decorated. It had an Indian theme, with a lot of Indian artefacts and paintings and was a very cosy home.

Her mom and dad were both doctors, successful in their own fields. They'd gotten divorced when Maya was ten. Her mom had found a job in a well known hospital in Skallen and they had moved here, for a fresh start. After a while, her dad had also moved to Skallen, to be closer to Maya. He had lived only a couple of streets away and she'd seen him often. Her parents had an amicable relationship even after the divorce, so Maya had grown up secure and happy.

Her dad had remarried a couple of years ago, got a better offer in a hospital in another city and had moved away. Now, he had three year old twin boys. Maya had visited them once but hadn't felt comfortable. Her stepmom was nice and the twins were adorable, but she'd felt like an outsider. They were a unit now. It wasn't her home or her family. She'd not gone again.

Her dad visited her when he could, and she enjoyed the time she spent with him. But she didn't miss him when he wasn't around either and led a happy and contented life with her mother. She liked her school, her friends and her life. She didn't even mind her mother's boyfriend. Daniel and her mom had been dating for almost a year now, and she was now used to him. In fact, she was happy for her mom. The only thorn in her flesh was Sebastian. The mere thought of him was enough to bring a frown to her face. Thinking of him reminded her about detention and the electrical storm. She wanted to look it up on the internet. She googled electrical storm and browsed through some articles.

According to Wiki, electrical storms were also called thunderstorms or lightning storms. They were usually accompanied by heavy rain, thunder and lightning. She found that there were instances of sudden electrical storms, but they were very rare. Usually, there would be enough warning and the electrical storm would often be preceded by a thundershower. The articles said that an electrical storm could be very dangerous, and there were many government websites, which gave advice on what to do if caught in an electrical storm. The pictures of electrical storms were rather spectacular. There were even a few clips on YouTube. After going through some of them, Maya had only one question on her mind. If it was this loud, and this impressive, why did only Sam remember it, and not the rest of them?

'Maya! Honey! I'm going to the store. Do you want to come for a drive?' her mom called out, interrupting her thoughts.

Maya looked down at the assignment she should have been doing. She should stay and get started on it, but she didn't feel like it.

'Forget it,' she thought. 'I'll come back and do it.' She called out, 'Coming, Mom!' and pulled on her jacket, grabbed her bag and went down.

It started drizzling as they drove to the store. The nearest supermarket was not very far, but they had to get on to the main road, find the right exit and double back. It took a good half hour, so they only went once a week, unless it was an emergency.

'I didn't check whether we have milk for the next week,' her mother said, 'and what shall I make for dinner tonight? Indian, Continental or Chinese?'

'Indian,' said Maya automatically.

Indian food was her favourite anytime, any day. She felt lucky that she could have it whenever she wanted. Her friends loved coming over to her place because of the wonderful Indian food her mom made.

'What?' Her mom gave her a puzzled look.

Maya turned towards her. 'I said Indian,' she repeated.

'Indian what?' asked her mom.

It was Maya's turn to look puzzled. 'You asked me if I wanted Indian, Chinese or Continental… for dinner? I want Indian,' said Maya.

'Did I say that aloud?' Her mom laughed. 'I'm losing it. Soon I'll need to be institutionalized. I thought I was just thinking it.'

'You must have thought aloud,' said Maya, also laughing. 'Mom, you're so absent minded. What would you do without me to keep an eye on you?'

'It doesn't bear thinking,' said her mom, switching on the indicator and turning into the exit.

Maya chuckled. Her mom was so forgetful. She'd make a list so she would remember all that she had to buy when she went shopping, and then she'd forget to take the list. She forgot appointments, she forgot birthdays. Over the years, Maya had taken over the role of her mom's assistant, and she kept track of important dates and appointments and reminded her mom. She always teased her mom about how she was going to operate on the wrong patient one day. But apparently, her mom was extremely professional at the hospital. Maya visited the hospital frequently and knew almost everyone there. She saw the respect and esteem with which her mom was held. So, however scatterbrained she was at home, obviously, she was very good at her job.

They parked at the store and went in. Her mother tore her shopping list in half and gave one half to Maya. 'I'll meet you at Counter 3?' she asked. Maya nodded and set off.

She went to the home section and started picking out the things her mom had written down. There was another woman in the aisle. She was near the detergents.

'I wonder which is better... Comfort? Or Lenor?' she asked.

Maya glanced up at her. The lady was holding two bottles in her hand, one bottle of Comfort and one bottle of Lenor.

'Comfort,' said Maya, smiling at her. 'My Mom always buys Comfort,' she added.

The lady looked up at Maya, her eyes growing wide. She put both the bottles back, abruptly pulled her cart and hurried out of the aisle, giving a frightened glance over her shoulder at Maya. Maya watched her racing away, puzzled.

'Well, you're welcome, you crazy twit,' she told the now empty aisle, and continued with her shopping.

'I wonder if anyone will notice if I walk out with this flashlight in my pocket. I wonder where the cameras are.' Maya looked around to see who'd said that. She was still alone in the aisle.

Curious, she left her cart, walked around the shelves and peered into the next aisle. A young boy in cargoes and a T-shirt which said, "I'm cool", was looking at the hardware section in that aisle. He had on a Chelsea cap and his hair was long enough to peep out from under it. He looked like he was around twelve or maybe even younger. He was trying very hard to look nonchalant as he looked around for the cameras, his hand reaching out towards the shelf.

'I wouldn't do that if I were you,' said Maya gently. She pointed to the wall. 'You were wondering where the cameras are… there's one right there,' she said, pointing to the wall.

The kid's mouth fell open and his eyes widened. 'How'd you do that?' he asked, looking fascinated.

'Do what?' asked Maya. 'Know where the camera is? I shop here often, so I know where some of the cameras are. Like this one,' she said, smiling and pointing at the camera again.

The boy looked totally unfazed, that he was caught trying to steal. 'No, how did you know what I was thinking?' he asked. 'Do it again. I'll think of a number.' He screwed his eyes shut for a second and then opened them. 'Ok, tell me what number am I thinking of?' he asked.

'What are you talking about? I heard you saying you were going to take a flashlight. I don't think that's cool,' replied Maya sternly.

The boy's eyes grew wider. 'You heard that too. Wow! How did you hear what I was thinking? Are you psychic?' he asked.

Maya looked around uncomfortably, in case anyone was watching. No one was around. 'Listen, if this is your idea of a joke, it's not funny,' she said and started walking away.

The boy followed her. 'Go on, do it again. I'm thinking of a number. Guess the number.'

'Shoo! Go away, kid!' said Maya, looking around nervously.

People would think she was crazy. What was wrong with the kid? She went back to the aisle where her cart was, grabbed it and hurried away. Luckily, the kid's mom called to him, and after trying to get Maya to guess the number once more, he ran off looking disappointed.

Maya got all the things on her list and went to the counter to wait for her mom. She hoped the annoying kid had left. She looked around aimlessly as she waited. She was so hungry. She usually didn't eat till tea time, after her usual Sunday brunch. She looked at her watch. It was only two and she was ravenous.

CHAPTER 7

RYAN

Ryan had a hectic Sunday morning. His dad had come home drunk, again, the previous night. When Ryan had come down in the morning, he had found his dad on the sofa, fast asleep. The T.V. was still on, and there were beer cans, leftover food and cigarette stubs and ash on the sofa, the table and all over the carpet. He and his two siblings were used to this sight by now. His older sister, Tammy, simply ignored it. She was in college, and she worked as a waitress in the evenings, in a pub, to pay for college. She stayed out nights whenever she could. He didn't know if she had come in last night. She was never around.

Once, when he had accused her of not being there for her family, she had said, 'What family? That drunk? Kiddo, take some advice from me. Get into college and get out of here as fast as you can.'

But Ryan wasn't like Tammy. He felt responsible for his younger brother Joel, who was only twelve, and for his father, even if he was a drunk. It hadn't always been like this. They'd been a normal, fully functional family till his mother's death eight years ago from cancer. She had only been forty-two.

His parents had met when his dad had come to Skallen for a summer job. His mom's parents were rich and well known in the community. She had married his dad against her family's wishes. His dad had promised his mom when he married her that he would make enough money to keep her in the comfort she was used to. He had worked hard and become rich and successful.

His dad's whole life had revolved around his mom. He had gone to pieces after her death. He hadn't even tried to cope. He had simply given up. Except for a few old faithfuls, he had lost most of his clients. And whatever money he made went towards his drinking and smoking. Ryan worked as a valet in a hotel in the evenings and tried to manage as best as he could.

Their house was huge, a mansion by any standard. Their dad had built it in his heyday, as a final instalment of the promise he had made to his wife, soon after they were married. He had promised her that he would build her a mansion, right at the top of the most expensive road in Skallen. Ryan remembered how well kept and charming their house had been, when his mom was alive. Now it was an old and decaying building, with paint peeling off the walls and shutters hanging off the hinges, in the middle of a garden which was overgrown with weeds.

He cleaned up the mess his dad had made as best as he could, when Tristan ambled inside. He was a doleful looking basset hound, almost nine years old. His dad had bought the dog for his mom, the year before she died. He followed Ryan into their huge kitchen. Ryan squatted and rubbed his ears.

'Hungry, old man?' he asked.

He washed Tristan's dish and poured out some milk for him. He made sandwiches for his brother, to take along when he went to football practice. He had woken up Joey on his way down. Joey walked in as he was putting the sandwiches in a box.

'Ryan, I'm at Tim's place for lunch,' he said.

Ryan nodded. He knew Tim, and Tim's brother Randy was one of his best friends, so he was okay with that.

After Joey left for football practice, Ryan ate breakfast and had just started washing the dishes, when Lisa called. He left the dishes in the sink and went up to his room to talk to her. They got into a fight because she wanted to go out in the evening, and he couldn't since he had to work. She hung up on him. He debated whether to call back, but he didn't feel up to grovelling. Feeling annoyed, he sat down at his computer, idly going through his Facebook page and didn't notice the time pass. He looked at his watch when he started feeling hungry. It was past two.

He went back to the kitchen, feeling irritated and miserable. He hated fighting, but Lisa was spoilt and she didn't understand.

'When you have money, you don't understand how people without money live,' he thought bitterly.

When he entered the kitchen, he saw that he hadn't finished washing the dishes earlier. Nor had he given Tristan his lunch. He opened out a can of dog food and poured it into Tristan's bowl. The dog appeared like magic from wherever he'd been sleeping and wolfed down the food, after giving Ryan a reproachful look. He decided to finish doing the dishes, before eating. He was just filling the sink with soapy water, when his dad staggered into the kitchen.

'Where's my wallet?' he asked angrily.

Ryan ignored him and continued washing the dishes. His dad misplaced things when he was drunk, and Ryan was used to his offensive behaviour the next day. He had learnt to ignore it and today after the fight with Lisa, he was in no mood to put up with any nonsense from his father. But his dad seemed to be in a more belligerent mood than usual.

'Boy! I'm talking to you. Answer me!' he lurched forward, grabbed Ryan's shoulder and shoved him around.

A blind rage filled Ryan, and before he knew what he was doing, he flung his arm out and pushed his father away. His dad flew clean across the room, hit the far wall and collapsed in a heap. Ryan didn't care if his father was hurt. All the years of hurt and neglect filled him. He wanted to get out of there. He flung open the back door and took off, running. He didn't know where he was going and neither did he care.

After a while, he realised that he was running towards the cemetery where his mom was buried. He reached the cemetery and slowed down to a walk. The cemetery was behind an old church. The church was built when Skallen was still an agricultural community, and was almost as old as the town itself. He walked down the road which ran along the wall of the church. There was a little gate at the back that led to the cemetery. His mother was one of the last people buried here. There was a new one now, on the other side of town, on the banks of Lake Skallen. That was where Skallen buried its dead these days.

He opened the little gate and entered the cemetery. It was very quiet and peaceful inside. He wove his way through the old tombstones till he reached his mother's grave. It was covered with a pink marble slab and had a marble headstone with the words, "Here lies Grace Carter, wife of Harold Carter and mother of Tamara, Ryan, and Joel", and below that, "God took her home, it was his will, but in our hearts she liveth still."

He brushed away the leaves which had fallen on the grave and sat on the edge of the marble slab. He felt tears running down his face and touched his cheek in surprise. His rage was finally spent, and grief had taken over. He sat there, weeping unashamedly. Even after his tears finally dried up, he continued sitting there staring into the distance. He wanted to stay there forever.

He finally stood up and walked around the cemetery, picking some of the wildflowers which grew there. Once he had a little posy, he placed it carefully on his mother's grave. He felt his eyes blur with tears again.

'Mom! I wish you were here. I miss you. I don't know how long I can keep going. Please, give me strength,' he whispered brokenly. He looked wearily at his watch and was surprised to see that it was almost four.

'How long did I run, and how long have I been sitting here?' he wondered.

Joey must be worried. He thought of his dad. He hoped his dad wasn't hurt. His dad was a big man, and heavy. With all the drinking and no work, he had gradually packed the pounds. Ryan was young, and he was a strong boy. You couldn't play football if you weren't fit, and he was easily the best player in his school team. He thought of how he had flung his dad right across the room. He was strong, but he didn't think he was strong enough to lift his father and throw him across a room. He still wasn't sure how he had done that. He must have been that angry. Well, he had to go back and face the music. He turned away from his mother's grave and walked back through the gate. It took him a good hour to reach home.

When he entered the house, he heard the sound of the T.V. from the den. He walked softly past the door of the den, his head down, hands tucked deep in his pockets, hoping he could get upstairs without being seen. He started up the stairs, when his father called out to him. He went back to the living room, reluctantly. Joey and his dad were sitting on the sofa. His dad had his right arm in a sling. He got up and walked towards Ryan. Ryan waited for the tirade he was sure would follow.

His dad raised his left hand and slapped Ryan, hard across his face. Ryan raised his hand to his stinging cheek, in shock. His dad had never hit him before. Ryan didn't remember him ever hitting any of his children. He could see Joey's scared face peering over the sofa. His dad raised his hand again. As it descended, Ryan caught it.

'Stop!' he yelled. 'Don't you dare lay a finger on me, ever again.' He pushed his father away. 'I've put up with this rubbish for way too long, without complaining. We've carried on the best we could. If you lay a finger on me... or on Joey, I swear I'll call the cops. I... have... had... enough!' He brought his fist down on the console next to which he was standing, as he said that.

With a loud crack, the console broke in half. He jumped back, surprised. He saw his dad's and Joey's shocked faces. He stumbled back a few steps, bewildered, and then turned around and bolted upstairs.

He ran into his room and locked his door. He leaned against the door, panting. What was happening to him? First, he had thrown his dad across the room and now he had broken the console with one swing of his fist. The console was an antique, mahogany piece, heavy and thick and he had broken it in two, with ease. He hadn't even hit it that hard. It was like he was on steroids or something. He looked down at his hands. They were shaking. He suddenly felt ravenous and realised he hadn't eaten anything since breakfast. But he didn't want to go down and face his father again.

The den upstairs had a balcony with an ivy covered trellis running down its side. He and his sister had used it many a time to go out, without their dad's permission. He stepped out of the room and silently made his way to the den. He could still hear the T.V. He hoped Joey was okay. He didn't think his dad would hit Joey, but after today he wasn't sure. For a minute, he debated whether to go down and take Joey with him. But he knew that if he went down now, it would mean another showdown. He decided it would be better to keep out of his dad's way for a while.

He opened the door to the den quietly and made his way across the balcony. He shimmied down the trellis and went to the garage. His bicycle was there. He had a pickup, but most of the time he didn't have the money for gas, so he used his bicycle to get from one place to another. He used the pickup only when he was taking Lisa out on a date, or when he was going out with the boys. He wheeled his bike to the gate. When the house was new, the garage and the gate were remotely operated, but now neither worked. The garage door and the gates were always open. As he went out of the gate and freewheeled down the road, lined by swank mansions, he wondered what his rich neighbours thought of the eyesore at the top of the hill. His dad kept getting offers for the property, but he always refused them.

'Forget it!' He pushed the angry thoughts which kept boiling to the surface away, firmly. His stomach rumbled. He decided to pick up a pizza on his way to work.

CHAPTER 8

SEBASTIAN

It was well past noon when Sebastian crawled out of bed. He had been on the internet the whole night. Usually, he would have been partying till the cows came home, but after his little escapade with the Ducati, he was grounded. He had called the kitchen for coffee and the papers, when he awoke.

His home was enormous. It had two drawing rooms, two living rooms and a den. It also had a study, library and eight bedrooms. There was a recreational area in the basement, and indoor and outdoor swimming pools. The grounds, in the middle of which the house stood, were about half the size of the Holy Trinity campus. It was a long drive from the large, black, wrought iron gates to the main house.

His dad and he had their own suites. When his dad wasn't travelling, he was usually holed up in his study, a large, oak panelled affair. His mom was his dad's second wife and she was an actress. She was stunning to look at, and Sebastian had gotten his good looks from her. Their marriage had lasted six months, and it had produced Sebastian. He was born in France, which was where his mom had moved to after leaving his dad.

After three unlucky tries, his dad had given up on marriage, deciding that it was too much work. That was, till he met Maya's mom. He had sprained his ankle while jogging one morning. He had gone to the hospital to get it looked at and the rest, as they say, was history. Sebastian sincerely hoped his dad didn't end up marrying Maya's mom. He didn't mind Neha, Maya's mom; it was the daughter that he intensely disliked.

He usually didn't care who his parents dated. He wasn't close to either of them. Neither of his parents had wanted children. He was a mistake, one he knew they both regretted making. Neither had any other children, and they didn't bother much about the one they had either. He was brought up by a series of nannies, and when he was old enough, was sent away to boarding school. He had managed to get into trouble at every school he had attended, and been chucked out of every one. His holidays were spent with whichever parent was willing to have him. It was only now, after his dad had started dating Neha, that he had taken a sudden parental interest in Sebastian.

His coffee and papers came up. He lolled on his couch with the T.V. on as he had his coffee and skimmed through the papers. He was idly channel surfing a little later, when he saw the segment on the electrical storm.

'Is this what the kid was going on about?' he wondered aloud.

He got up and went to his computer. He googled electrical storm on the internet and went through some of the articles. This sounded like what Sam had said he saw. It was strange that he and the others hadn't heard it. As he was browsing the articles for more information on electrical storms, one of his ex-girlfriends popped up online, and he spent a pleasant afternoon flirting with her.

It was amazing how all his ex-girlfriends still kept in touch with him. But he was so charming, it was difficult to remain angry with him. Sooner or later, they always forgave him for dumping them. It was late afternoon by the time he got offline, and he felt hungry. He went to the kitchen, still in his bathrobe. Naomi, their cook and housekeeper, was lording it in the kitchen as usual. She looked at him sternly.

'Master Sebastian, do you know what time it is?' she asked.

Sebastian grinned. Naomi was more of a mother to him, than his own. Nannies, governesses, wives and girlfriends had come and gone. But, Naomi had been in his life from when he could remember.

'I don't know, Naomi. I just woke up. Do you know what time it is?'

he teased.

'Don't you flirt with me now.' She rapped his knuckles.

'It's almost five… and look at you, unwashed, and still in your bathrobe. Have you even brushed your teeth?' she chided.

Sebastian pretended to be shocked. 'My dear, of course I did. Now be a darling and feed me, please,' he said. 'I'm starving.'

'Hmph!' she said, trying to look stern and failing, her plump face breaking into a smile.

She was a short, genial, black woman and if there was anyone in the world Sebastian felt affection for, it was her.

'What do you want?' she asked him.

'A club sandwich, actually make it two and a large milkshake, to go,' he said, with a wicked smile.

'In your dreams. You will sit here, eat it and then go,' she replied in a severe tone. 'I hardly get to see you these days.'

'Fine, I'll eat here… since you miss me so much,' he teased.

He sat at the small dining table which was in the kitchen and switched on the T.V., to watch the Sunday races. Naomi bustled around the kitchen, getting his meal ready. She turned around from the cupboard, with some bottles balanced on one hand and reached out for the bread with the other. As she turned, she slipped and grabbed the counter for support. Two of the bottles slipped from her grasp and fell. Sebastian, immersed in the race, saw the movement from the corner of his eye and as he turned his head, he saw the bottles fall. He bounded across the room, caught the two bottles with one hand, and put out his other hand to steady Naomi. As Naomi steadied herself, he placed the two bottles on the counter and walked back to his chair.

'How did you do that?' asked Naomi, staring at him.

'What?' asked Sebastian, nonchalantly.

'Catch those bottles and me? You were right across the room, on the other side of the table. How did you get here so fast?' She looked flabbergasted.

'I guess all the Tai Chi is helping,' joked Sebastian. 'My reflexes are getting better. I can't say the same for you though. You should be more careful, Naomi. You could have had a bad fall.' Naomi didn't look convinced by his explanation, but she didn't pursue it.

Sebastian was glad she wasn't questioning him further because he was freaking out himself. How on earth had he done that? It was at least ten feet from where he was sitting, to where Naomi had been standing. And he'd been on the other side of the table. And he had not only gotten there, but had caught both the bottles, and Naomi. How had he done that? He looked down. His hands were shaking.

When Naomi finished making his sandwiches, he picked it up, muttered something about an assignment and hurried back to his room. She didn't say anything, just looked at him with a peculiar expression. Once he got to his room, he put the food on the table and sat down. He felt weak in the knees. First things first... food. He felt like he was dying of hunger. He wolfed down his sandwiches and gulped down the milkshake in a matter of minutes.

Then, he went to his desk, picked up a book and looked around. There was a glass vase on the mantel, above the fireplace. It was across the room from him, at least ten feet away. He took aim and chucked the book at the vase... and missed. He took another book and tried again. On his fifth attempt, the book glanced off the vase and the vase tottered around slowly, before falling. Sebastian took off when it was tottering. But he had only taken a couple of steps before it hit the ground and shattered with a crash, the pieces flying all over the place.

Sebastian frowned. His reflexes weren't any different than they'd been the day before. Then, what the heck had happened in the kitchen? He wondered whether to chuck more books at the identical vase which stood on the other side of the mantel.

'Forget it!' he muttered to himself.

He must have reacted so fast in the kitchen because he had thought Naomi was going to fall. Just a freak adrenaline rush! He wondered whether to call Naomi and ask her to send somebody to clear up the shattered vase, but decided against it. She would give him a lecture about his carelessness, and he didn't feel up to a lecture. He sat down at his computer again.

CHAPTER 9

CASSIE

Cassie was trying to finish her assignment. Maya had borrowed the History notes for her like she had promised. She had finished copying those notes and had started on her Math assignment. After her mom had returned home, she'd been trying to make up for having left to work that morning and had insisted on family time. She'd gotten mad at Cassie, when Cassie had said she had work to finish. She had become mean, saying, 'Oh, you don't have time to spend with your family' and, 'So, now you think you're too grown up to hang out with us.'

'Seriously? Look, who was talking!' thought Cassie angrily. It was so immature that Cassie hadn't even bothered to argue.

If her mom felt guilty about not spending time with her family, it was her problem. Taunting Cassie to make up for her inadequacies was not cool. Both Sam and her dad had looked uncomfortable and then Sam, in that quiet way of his, had turned his mom's attention to something else. As she went upstairs, Cassie had looked back and caught her father's eye. He'd looked sheepish and given an apologetic smile. Cassie hadn't responded. She couldn't understand why her dad let her mom get away with being nasty.

Now, because of the time she had wasted, it was almost ten and she was still doing her school work. Luckily, her mom hadn't insisted on her coming down to dinner too. She hated her mom. She sighed, laid her pencil down, leaned back in the chair and stretched. She removed her glasses. Over the day, her vision had become steadily worse and now, she had to squint through her glasses to make things out. That hadn't helped her mood either. She felt irritated and angry.

She had to book her appointment with the ophthalmologist. She rubbed her eyes with her palm and opened them. She looked down at her Math assignment. Funny! She could see a bit clearer without her glasses. The numbers were less blurred. Maybe, her power was coming down. The ophthalmologist had told her when she was younger, that for some people, their eyesight became better as they grew older. As Cassie had grown older, she had kept hoping it was true. But, it had only become worse. Cassie had concluded the doctor must have felt sorry for her and told her that small white lie. But now she wondered if the doctor had actually meant it. Maybe, her eyesight *was* getting better.

Well, that would be one good thing out of a totally horrid day. Her eyes fell on the cup of cocoa on the table and she smiled. Sam! She knew she was hard on him, but that had more to do with her mom. She also knew Sam understood that and felt bad about it. Her mom being a jerk was not Sam's fault, but when Cassie needed to vent, she usually took it out on him. Which wasn't fair… but hey, who said it was a perfect world and life was fair. Sam tried to make up for their mom's nastiness. The cup of cocoa was his way of trying to cheer her up. He had brought it up in the "Monster Cup". He had known it would make her smile.

The "Monster Cup" was a return gift she'd received when she was much younger, for some kid's birthday. The kid was a spoilt brat, who had thrown tantrums right through the evening, and had hit and bitten the other children. The return gift was this mug, with the face of that horrible child and "Happy Birthday" emblazoned below it. It was many years since she'd received the cup. Nearly all the other mugs in their house had chipped or broken, and been thrown away over the years. New ones had taken their place and in their turn, had broken and been thrown away. But the "Monster Cup" had endured. It was probably because no one wanted to use it. But if someone was making a hot drink for anyone else in the house, they would make sure they gave the drink in the

"Monster Cup". It was an inside joke in their family. She had skipped dinner that evening. Sam had made cocoa for her and brought it up in the "Monster Cup".

She groaned. Sam was so darn nice when she was so mean to him that it made her angry. It would have been easier if he were as mean to her. When he was nice to her, like this, it just made her angrier with him. She glared at the offending cup and wished it would break.

Clink! A jagged line ran through the cup, and it fell apart in two. Cassie was so stunned she didn't even notice that the cocoa was staining her assignment. Luckily, she had drunk most of the cocoa. It was only the dregs which had spilt out of the cup, and was spreading over the table and the edge of her assignment.

'That didn't happen! That so did not happen!' she whispered in amazement.

She saw the spilt cocoa staining her assignment, and hurriedly pulled it out of the way. She went over to her dresser, pulled out some tissues and dabbed the assignment with it, to soak up the liquid. She pulled out more tissues and wiped the cocoa off the table. She picked up the broken pieces of the cup. It had neatly broken in two.

'It must have been on the point of breaking. It's rather old. Must have been cracking anyway, and we hadn't noticed,' she thought. Her hands were shaking as she put the pieces in the dustbin.

That was so freaky. She wondered whether to go tell Sam about it, but decided not to. He'd either laugh or come up again with some half-assed theory about it. She wished she hadn't skipped dinner because she was feeling hungry now. She decided to go down and make some sandwiches before she finished her Math assignment. She hoped her parents had retired to their bedroom. She didn't feel up to another enforced family time.

CHAPTER 10

Ryan got back late on Sunday night, after his shift. The weekends usually meant more customers. More work, but also more tips. He peeked into the living room. His dad was sprawled out on the sofa as usual, with the T.V. on and the usual debris around him. His right hand was encased in a plaster cast and was dangling off the sofa. Ryan realised he didn't even know which part of his arm his dad had broken. The stub of a cigarette dangled off the end of his fingers, the ash leaving a barely visible trail on the carpet.

Ryan could see the scorch mark left by the cigarette, at the end of the ash trail. One of these days, he was sure he would come back to a burnt shell of a house. He shuddered, and only hoped neither of his siblings was in the house if, and when, it happened.

The carpet was full of scorch marks, especially nearer the sofa, and Ryan was sure if he shook the carpet, years of accumulated ash would rise. They had a cleaning lady who came in once a week, but he wasn't sure how long they would be able to afford her.

His dad was fast asleep, his good hand resting on his stomach, loosely holding the remote control. The remote rose and fell rhythmically, in time with his breathing. He gave soft, gentle snores. He must have just fallen asleep, thought Ryan. Once he went into a deep slumber, he sounded like a train. Ryan tiptoed to the television and switched it off. His dad made a sound and Ryan froze, but his dad was only mumbling in his sleep. Relieved, Ryan turned around to slip back out. As he crept out, he saw the bashed up console in the exact position it had been in the afternoon. He felt a pang of regret. It was one of his mom's favourite pieces.

He had eaten at work, and he wasn't hungry. He went into the kitchen and switched off the lights. He went upstairs and checked on Joey, who was fast asleep. Tristan was curled up at Joey's feet, and he opened one sleepy eye and looked at Ryan. Ryan scratched him behind his ears and straightened Joey's comforter. He switched the night lamp on Joey's bedside table and switched off the main light, on his way out. He closed the door, leaving a little gap so that some of the light from the landing filtered into the room. Joey didn't like to sleep with his door shut.

He walked over to Tammy's room. For the first time in his life, he understood how Tammy felt and why she acted like she did. If you cared too deeply, it sapped your strength. Maybe this was the reason behind Tammy's indifference. Tonight, he felt the need to talk about the day to someone. He wasn't the confiding sort, and he usually carefully guarded his feelings.

No one at school guessed at his unhappy family life. In fact, he knew most of the boys his age envied him, his looks, his popularity, his prowess on the football field. They felt that he led a charmed life. And most of the younger kids idolized him, and wanted to be like him when they grew up.

'If only they knew,' he thought, bitterly.

He knocked on Tammy's door. There was no answer. He looked down at the latch and saw it was locked from the outside. She wasn't home. He went to his room, suddenly feeling wiped out. He changed his clothes, brushed his teeth and set his alarm, before collapsing on the bed. He was asleep in minutes.

It felt like he had just gone to sleep before the alarm rang. He showered, got ready and crept down. His dad was still sprawled on the sofa, snoring deeply. He went to the kitchen and opened the fridge. He was opening one of the cupboards looking for a glass, when Tristan trotted in, looking hopeful.

'You greedy glut!' he told the sad-eyed dog.

He washed Tristan's basin and poured some milk for him. He poured out a glass of milk for Joey and drank the rest of the milk straight out of the carton. He opened the cupboard under the sink to chuck the carton, and saw that the garbage bag hadn't been changed. It was overflowing, and beer cans and packets littered the floor. He picked up everything and crammed it into the garbage bag.

Emptying the garbage bin was Joey's work. He was supposed to take the garbage bag, put it in the trash can and put a new liner in every night, before he went up to bed. Usually, Joey never forgot. Ryan remembered the chaos of the previous day. He didn't blame Joey. The kid must have bolted upstairs to his room as soon as he could, and he wouldn't have come down after that. Ryan wondered if he had also skipped dinner.

He pulled out the garbage bag and walked to the back door. Their back door had a thick wooden door inside and a swing mesh door outside. Ryan opened the wooden door and stopped in shock.

The mesh door was smashed in half and the lower half was hanging off its hinges, while the upper half was lying a couple of feet away, on what used to be his mom's vegetable patch. Ryan realised he must have broken it when he had barged through the door, after shoving his dad.

'Does rage give you this kind of strength?' he wondered, staring bemused at the shattered door.

He threw the trash in and looked again at the broken door. He couldn't believe he'd done that. He felt confused and scared. He wished he could talk to someone about what had happened.

He ate a couple of sandwiches and went to the garage. When his mom was alive, she would usually be there to see him off, giving him a peck on his cheek before he left. He pushed his bike out of the garage and took a deep breath in the early morning air. He pushed out the sad thoughts which were crowding his mind.

'Enough!' He gave himself a mental shake.

There was no use dwelling on those happy days. Time to move on! He got on his bike at the gate and freewheeled down the lane. He felt an instant lift in his spirits. He always felt his spirits rise when he left home, and he would feel it ebbing, on his way back home. He had to get out of the pit of despair his home had become. That was the reason he was working so hard to keep his grades up. He needed to make the grade, to get a football scholarship. He didn't know what he would do about Joey, if that happened, but he'd cross the bridge when he came to it.

He reached school, locked up his cycle at the stand and jogged to the stadium. Some of the boys were already in the locker rooms, changing and joshing around. They laughed and ribbed each other as they changed, and then trooped out to the field and started jogging. Mr. Harris, was already there sitting in the stands, waiting for them to finish their rounds.

'I think the guy lives here, mate,' said Sheldon, a blond, burly giant, who was their goalkeeper.

For someone so big, Sheldon was pretty light on his feet. The players on other teams were very wary of him. If anyone got in his way, they would usually end up with broken bones. After they finished jogging, they did some stretches. As they were finishing, Mr. Harris joined them on the field.

Football was a sport the Skallen community loved and followed avidly, whether it was local, league or international football. The Holy Trinity football team was called the "Skallen Raiders", and they had the whole town rooting for them every year, during their matches. Now the players paired off into two teams, took their places and started the game. At first, they merely passed the ball to one another, warming up. Soon, the game began in earnest.

Ryan, who was the team's best striker, intercepted a pass and dashed off swiftly with the ball, towards the goalpost. Sheldon, who was playing on the opposing team, was waiting for Ryan. As Ryan came tearing down the field, Sheldon charged out towards Ryan. Ryan feinted and tried to slip past Sheldon, to push the ball into the goal. Sheldon anticipated the move and he crashed into Ryan, and both went down. Sheldon let out a loud howl. Ryan, who had rolled away, jumped up and rushed to Sheldon's side. Sheldon was writhing in agony. His arm was at an awkward angle.

'Sheldon! Shel!' He tried to help him up, but Sheldon only howled louder. The other boys crowded around.

'Boys! Move! Let me through!' Mr. Harris pushed his way past the players and knelt down beside Sheldon. One look at the arm and he whipped out his mobile. He called for an ambulance and tried to calm Sheldon. 'Hang on buddy! The ambulance is on its way! Just hang on! Kids, move away! Give him some air!'

Since it was early morning, the ambulance reached the school in no time. By then, Sheldon had stopped howling, but he was pale. The medics rushed out of the ambulance and one of them gave him a shot for the pain. They waited a couple of minutes for it to take effect and then carefully lifted him onto a stretcher. He was so big that Ryan and a couple of other boys had to lend a hand.

'Sorry mate!' Ryan kept saying, over and over.

'Ryan, if you don't shut up, I swear I'll come there and mess up your face with this broken arm,' swore Sheldon, through his pain. 'Guys! Get him to shut up,' he added, as they strapped the stretcher in the ambulance.

Mr. Harris had climbed into the ambulance with Sheldon. As he sat down, he turned and gave Ryan a curious look. He still had a contemplative expression as they shut the ambulance doors. As the ambulance sped away, Ryan slumped onto the grass with his head in his hands. He felt so guilty. His dad, the table and now this! What was happening to him? Ryan felt overwhelmed.

'Mate! It's not your fault', 'Come on Ryan', the other players patted his shoulder and ruffled his hair, trying to cheer him up, but all Ryan could hear were Sheldon's howls. No one felt like practicing anymore. Soon, in twos and threes, they straggled away.

'Come on, man! Get up, champ!' said Randy and pulled Ryan to his feet.

They both walked into the locker room. Devon, the captain of their team walked up to Ryan.

'Mate! It's a rough sport. These things happen. Don't beat yourself over it,' he said sympathetically, before walking off to shower.

It didn't make Ryan feel any better. He didn't want to look at any of the other players. He felt that they must all be looking at him accusingly. He showered, changed, and left before the other guys came out of the shower. He didn't feel like talking to anybody, especially about Sheldon, and he knew that was what they would want to talk about right now. The only place he knew would be empty at this time of the day was the library, so he headed there. It wasn't open, so he sat outside behind a pillar, so he wouldn't be seen by anyone passing by.

He looked at his hands. He clenched his hands into a fist and brought it down with a resounding thump against the floor. 'Ouch!' he cried, as he felt a jolt of pain race up his arm from the impact. His knuckles were bruised and hurt like hell, but there was no crack on the floor. He couldn't figure it out. Was it hormones? He decided to check the internet, to see if there was any kind of information on what he was going through. He waited outside the library till he knew the campus would be pretty full, before venturing out. The first person he ran into was the last person he wanted to see. Lisa!

'Ryan! You jerk! You were supposed to pick me up yesterday evening. I was all dressed and waiting and you never turned up.' Ryan gave an exasperated sigh and turned away. He had told her the day before over the phone that he couldn't make it. She was simply picking a fight. 'Excuse me! Where are you going? I'm talking to you,' she said.

'Lisa, I'm sorry... but not now. I can't deal with this right now.' Ryan turned around and walked away. He left her staring at his back, her mouth open in disbelief. No one had ever walked away from her, in her life. She did the walking away!

Ryan went up to class. Randy was already there and he gave Ryan a questioning look. 'Where were you, champ? I was looking for you,' he asked.

'Just wandering around. You know, this morning... it freaked me out. I wanted some space,' replied Ryan.

Randy nodded soberly. 'Yeah, man. It was totally freaky. I mean, someone breaking Shel's arm. I never thought I'd see that. He must have been standing at an awkward angle... I...,' he stopped, when Ryan raised his hand.

'Can we not talk about it? It makes me sick, just thinking of him howling in pain,' said Ryan. Randy nodded sympathetically and left it alone.

During break, Ryan went to the office to see if there was any news about Sheldon. Miss Violet, who more or less ran the office and had been at Holy Trinity forever, told him, 'Yes, dear! He's fine. He has broken his arm. They've fixed it and sent him home.'

Ryan sighed with relief. He'd been so worried the damage had been worse. Broken bones mended. Shel wasn't going to be too happy about missing the next few games and their team would miss him sorely, but, at least, it wasn't a major injury. He was walking back to class, when he saw Mr. Harris coming out of the Principal's office. He looked at Ryan as he walked past, with the same brooding expression he had in the morning. It was creepy. Ryan dug his hands deeper into his pockets, hunched low and hurried back to his class.

CHAPTER 11

Maya thought she was going insane. She kept hearing voices in her head. She tried to get rid of the voices, tried to make her mind blank, but they kept intruding. Some, she recognized and some, she didn't. It happened randomly. Except for the weird encounter with the boy in the mall, the previous afternoon, the rest of the day had passed uneventfully. This morning, she'd been getting her books out of her locker when she had distinctly heard Leah's voice say, 'Look at that Indian snob! Tossing her hair and thinking no end of herself.'

Maya had swung around, shocked at the venomous outburst and had seen Leah, way across the corridor, with her friends huddled around her. But, she was looking straight at Maya. When she had caught Maya looking at her, she had smiled sweetly and looked away. One of the other girls was obviously in the middle of some juicy bit of gossip she was sharing with her friends, and Leah seemed to be listening to it. Maya had been baffled. She didn't have any beef with Leah, and Leah had always been nice to her. She had wondered if she was hallucinating.

She had dismissed it at the time, but it had kept happening. She'd hear someone say something; she would look around, and no one would be there. Later, when she was on her way to P.E. class, she heard a voice repeating, 'I hate P.E.! I hate P.E.! I hate P.E.!', over and over again.

She looked at Mary Anne and Felicity, her two best friends, who were walking with her, and said, 'What?'

They both looked up at her, questioningly.

'What, what?' asked Felicity.

'Did one of you say something?' Maya asked. They looked at her strangely.

'N... o,' replied Mary Anne.

'Listen, guys, this isn't funny. Is this some big joke you're playing on me? Did you get Leah to say that in the morning? It's okay, I'm not mad, but just tell me... it's freaking me out,' she said.

Both the girls looked genuinely puzzled. 'What on earth are you talking about Maya?' asked Mary Anne.

'Was one of you just saying, "I hate P.E." over and over again, just now?' she asked.

Mary Anne's mouth fell open. 'Was I saying that aloud? I thought I was saying it to myself,' she said.

'I didn't hear anything,' said Felicity, 'and I'm walking between both of you.'

'I guess I simply hear better than you,' Maya joked, though the last thing she felt like doing, was laughing. What was going on? She couldn't understand it.

She was frightened now. The other two girls were looking at her curiously, but just then, some juniors rushed past them, shoving Mary Anne in their hurry and she dropped her gym bag. In the confusion of picking up the bag, swearing at the kids and rushing to P.E., they didn't question Maya further.

They reached the grounds, changed and jogged out onto the hockey field. Maya and her friends hated P.E. They had chosen hockey for their P.E. credit, as it was one of the few games where they could waffle around the field and do absolutely nothing. They goofed around as usual, pretending to play, with as minimum movement as possible. As she stood in a safe corner, where she was sure the ball wouldn't reach, Maya found herself wondering again about the voices in her head.

'All this rubbish started the day after the detention,' she mused. 'I wonder if the other four have had any strange experiences. Maybe I should talk to them. I could speak to Ryan. It would be a good excuse to strike up a conversation with him,' she smiled involuntarily with pleasure, at the thought of talking to him. Then, her smile turned to a frown. 'Darn! He'll think I'm off my rocker.'

'What other four?'

The loud voice startled her. She looked around to see who had spoken. Had she been talking aloud? There was no one near her. As she scanned the grounds, she caught sight of Mr. Harris. He was standing on the other side of the field, and he was staring intently at her with a strange expression. It disconcerted her. She looked away and ran to join the scuffle happening near one of the goalposts.

Things got stranger that afternoon, during Physics class. When Maya opened her Physics book, a note fell out. It was folded in half, and then a quarter, and her name was written in capitals on top. The letters were in calligraphy and so beautifully formed, it looked like it was printed. She looked around to see who it could be from. But no one was looking at her. Everyone was busy taking out their books and opening them. She opened the note.

It said, 'Meet me at Room 103 after class.'

This was also written in long, graceful cursive. There was no signature and she didn't recognize the handwriting. Room 103! That was where they had gone for detention. Immediately, she looked up at Cassie. Cassie was frantically waving a note at her. Maya lifted hers up. They both turned to look at Sebastian. He was leaning back in his chair with his permanently bored expression. He hadn't even opened his books. Cassie looked around and checked to see what their Physics teacher, Ms. Cabot, was doing. Her back was to the class, as she wrote something on the board. Cassie turned around and waved her note wildly at Sebastian. He raised one bored eyebrow. Cassie mouthed something. Maya couldn't make out what she was trying to say, and she doubted Sebastian could.

'Cassandra! Is there something you'd like to share with the class?' asked Ms. Cabot.

'No, Ms. Cabot! Sorry!' Cassie subsided in her seat, looking mortified.

She had never been pulled up in class before. Ms. Cabot was her favourite teacher, and Cassie was extra attentive in her class, to the point of being cloying. Maya was equally curious to know if Sebastian had received a note. She sat somewhere in the middle of the classroom, and there was less chance of Ms. Cabot seeing her. Sebastian, of course, was as usual in the last row. She turned to ask him if he had received a note too. He had leaned back in his chair again and had now shut his eyes.

'God! He's such an ass,' she thought, irked.

She waved at Brett, who sat right in front of Sebastian. Brett looked eagerly at her. Maya knew Brett had a crush on her, and that was the reason for the eagerness. She felt bad when she saw his face fall, as she gestured to him to call Sebastian.

Brett turned around and gave Sebastian's desk a shake. Sebastian's eyes flew open, and he looked at Brett, annoyed. Brett motioned towards Maya. Sebastian looked at Maya and raised one eyebrow again. She pointed to his book, asking him to open it. He frowned, clearly displeased at being disturbed from his reverie. But he leaned forward and picked up his Physics book. He flipped through the pages and a note fell out. Both his eyebrows went up. He picked it up and opened it. He read the message and looked at Maya

'What is this?' he whispered.

Maya shrugged and waved her note. 'I got one too,' she whispered back. 'Maybe Ryan or Sam sent it.'

'Maya! Sebastian! Do you want to be sent out of class? I'm not amused by this behaviour,' said Ms. Cabot.

Maya turned around hastily. 'Sorry,' she muttered and bent over her book.

After class, the three of them hung back till the room emptied. Ms. Cabot was still at her desk, going through some work. Cassie and Maya walked over to Sebastian's desk. Since it was at the back of the class, there was no chance of Ms. Cabot overhearing them. They compared notes. Except for the names in capitals on the folded paper, all their notes were exactly the same.

Maya tucked her note into her jacket pocket. 'Come! Let's go!' she said.

'Why?' asked Sebastian, tucking his note into the pocket of his jeans. 'To listen to her brother's wild theories again?' he asked, nodding at Cassie.

Cassie hesitated. 'I… er… there's something I need to…'

'Children, what are you still doing here?' The three of them almost jumped out of their skins. Ms. Cabot was standing right behind them. She was a tall woman, taller than Sebastian, who was quite tall for his age. She had straight, thick, jet-black hair which hung straight down, almost to her waist and ended in a sharp widow's peak on her forehead. She had strong features, a fit body and she wore clothes which flattered her. She was strikingly attractive and most of the boys in school were in love with her.

'Why didn't you become a model, Ms. Cabot?' Cassie had asked her shyly one day, when she had hung back after class, pretending to have a problem with an algorithm.

Ms. Cabot had smiled sweetly and said simply, 'Because I love teaching.'

That answer had made her more of a benevolent and lovely goddess in Cassie's eyes, and she worshipped the ground Ms. Cabot walked on. Ms. Cabot was looking curiously at the three of them. Cassie hurriedly shoved her note into her bag. Ms. Cabot noticed the movement and turned towards her.

'What is that, Cassandra?' she asked.

Maya and Sebastian glared at Cassie, hoping she wouldn't take out the note. Cassie, whose hand was still inside her bag, pulled out a folded note. Ms. Cabot held out her hand.

'It's after class. We weren't doing anything,' protested Sebastian.

For some reason, Sebastian had taken an instant dislike to Ms. Cabot, from the moment he'd seen her. She'd been very nice to him, especially since he was new, and he had to admit she was totally hot. But there was something about her which put him off. He felt like she was a little too good to be true. He got the feeling she didn't like him much either. He was always getting into trouble in her class. She gave him an icy look as Cassie placed the note in her hand.

Cassie was blushing, looking embarrassed. Maya and Sebastian watched helplessly as Ms. Cabot opened the folded paper. She looked at it for a few seconds, looked up at Cassie and smiled gently. She folded the paper and gave it back to Cassie without a word.

Then, she said, 'Ok, kids! Don't hang around! Run along now!'

She turned around and went back to her desk. The three kids hurried out before she changed her mind and decided to question them further. Cassie still had the paper clutched in her hand as they walked towards the detention room.

'I wonder why she didn't say anything,' said Maya puzzled.

'Because this isn't the note we got,' said Sebastian. He dove forward and snatched the piece of paper from Cassie's hand. 'This is a page from one of our notebooks. The note we got was on some kind of stiff and expensive paper.' He was holding Cassie's note over his head, out of her reach

'Give it back! It's mine! Give it back, you jerk! Don't you dare open it,' screeched Cassie, as she jumped, trying to snatch the paper back from him. Sebastian opened it, still holding it over his head.

'Oh! My! What have we here?' he asked.

Maya could also see the paper. It was a beautiful but biased sketch of Ms. Cabot's face and all around it were tiny, red hearts. Cassie's face was red again and she looked close to tears.

'Seb! Don't be an ass! Give it back to her! If she hadn't had that, we would still be standing in class answering Ms. Cabot's questions, about the note and room 103.' She could see how upset Cassie was. 'The sketch is exquisite, Cassie,' she added, as Sebastian returned the note to Cassie.

'It is,' agreed Sebastian. 'You and your brother draw very well.' Maya looked at him in surprise. Sebastian giving a compliment? That was a first. Then he spoiled it by adding, 'Maybe, you should draw me sometime.' Cassie gave him a scathing look, tucked her note back in her bag and marched ahead of them.

When they reached Room 103, Maya opened the door and they went in. Both Ryan and Sam were already there, standing near the teacher's desk, their satchels on the table. They were both holding notes, identical to the ones the others had received.

'Hey guys!' called out Maya, as she and the other two walked in. 'What's up? Which one of you sent the note?' she asked.

'Neither of us sent it. We were wondering which one of you sent it,' replied Sam, waving his note.

'Listen! This is so not funny. I'm sick and tired of this. Who sent this? Seb, if it was you, just say so. You've had your fun… we'll all have a good laugh and get home.' Maya was mad now.

Sebastian frowned. 'Whoa! Why are you blaming me? Why would you think that I sent the note?' he asked.

Maya pulled out the note from her jacket and held it out, in front of his face. 'Because this paper looks bloody expensive and of the five of us, you are the one most likely to pull a stunt like this and think it's funny.'

'Hey! Hang on! I got one too,' he said, pulling out his note.

'Well, we would have known it was you if you hadn't received one, wouldn't we?' retorted Maya. She shook her head. 'It's just like you to think this was funny, with no thought for anyone else. You're such an ass. Well, you've had your fun. I'm leaving.' She picked up her bag and turned to leave.

'I didn't send it… but feel free to leave. You're only taking up space here. In fact, just die. You're taking up space on Earth,' Sebastian replied heatedly.

'Stop it, you two,' said Cassie irritated. These two were worse than Sam and her when they got going. 'If none of us sent it, then who did?' she asked with a frown.

'I did,' said a familiar voice at the door. They all turned towards the door. Mr. Harris was standing there, looking as unkempt as ever.

'I didn't do anything. Why do I have detention?' protested Cassie.

'Sir, is this about what happened this morning?' asked Ryan.

'What happened this morning? I don't know what happened this morning. I didn't have anything to do with whatever happened this morning.' Cassie's voice was getting shriller by the second.

'Cas! Please shut up!' said Maya. She turned to Ryan. 'What happened this morning?' she asked him.

'Kids!' Mr. Harris raised his voice and put up his hand. They fell silent immediately and looked at him. 'First, Cassie this isn't detention and Ryan, this is not about this morning… well, not entirely. Why don't you sit down?'

He waved them to the chairs. The children sat down uneasily, looking at each other, wondering what was going on. Mr. Harris pulled himself up into his favourite position, on top of the desk, and looked at them.

There was silence in the room. Mr. Harris seemed quite comfortable in the silence. He was dressed as usual, in sweatpants and T. shirt with a Holy Trinity jacket over it. His clothes looked like they'd been picked out at a jumble sale. But more than his clothes, it was his hair which made him look so untidy. It was a bit too long and he never seemed to comb it. It was usually all over the place, making him look like a mad scientist. He always had the beginnings of a stubble. People were put off by his appearance, but he was proving to be an amazing football coach and that was enough for Holy Trinity.

As usual, it was Sam who piped up first. A thought had just struck him. 'Mr. Harris?' he asked. 'Do you remember the electrical storm?' Sam had just realised that apart from them, the only other person he knew for sure was at the school during the electrical storm, was Mr. Harris.

Mr. Harris looked at him. 'Yes, Sam! During your detention last week, right?' he asked. Sam nodded.

'I had stepped out to make a call if you remember. When the electrical storm struck, I wasn't in the room. I hurried back though, as soon as I heard it, to see if you kids were okay?'

'And?' asked Sam.

'And what, Sam?' questioned Mr. Harris.

Sam asked, 'Were we okay?'

Mr. Harris frowned. 'Er… I guess you were. You were doing your work. I thought you seemed okay. Were you not okay?' he asked.

The kids looked at each other again, not sure what to say. Again, it was Sam who raised the question on all their minds. 'And, did we all just go home after that?'

Mr. Harris gave a quizzical look. He seemed to be wondering if they were messing with him. 'Ye... es. Why are you asking me these questions?'

'Because we don't remember anything from when we were here for detention, till the next day morning. Total blank... all of us.' Sam blurted out. 'And we all woke up with awful headaches and we were nauseous. Same symptoms... all five of us... five of us!' He jabbed at the air with his palm, his fingers spread out, to emphasize his point.

To their surprise, Mr. Harris didn't look very perturbed. 'Really?' he asked.

Sam nodded vigorously. 'Is that normal?' asked Sam, feeling better when he saw that Mr. Harris didn't look surprised. 'You know, I thought it was because of the electrical storm. Does that happen? Is it normal?'

Mr. Harris seemed to be considering his question. 'Well, that depends... it's not normal for most people... but I guess you kids are not most people, are you?' he asked, with a smile.

The kids looked at each other uncomfortably. 'What do you mean?' asked Sam

'Ryan, do you want to start with what happened this morning. By the way, it wasn't your fault,' he added.

Ryan didn't want to talk about it, but the other kids were looking at him. He told them what had happened on the football field in a few brusque sentences. He finished his story and then looked up at Mr. Harris, who simply stared back at him.

'Is that all, Ryan?' asked Mr. Harris softly. Suddenly, involuntarily, everything came tumbling out. Ryan told them about what had happened the day before, shoving his dad, breaking the back door, the console... everything. He felt so much lighter after it all came out. The other kids looked at him stunned, but he couldn't care less. He looked at Mr. Harris to see his reaction. He looked sympathetic. Ryan took a deep breath and let it out in a long sigh.

'Do you feel better after talking about it, Ryan?' asked Mr. Harris gently.

Ryan nodded. He made a fist with his right hand and brought it down hard on his desk. It made a loud thump which made them all jump.

'What was that for?' asked Cassie irritably.

'Don't you see? Nothing happened to the table. It didn't break. It happens randomly,' said Ryan. He spread his hands out and looked at Mr. Harris, who nodded back at him.

'Oh my God, Ryan… that's freaky,' said Maya.

'I know,' shrugged Ryan. 'You don't have to tell me. I feel like one,' he said, looking pained.

'No! No! I don't mean you are a freak. I mean, it's as freaky as the voices I've been hearing.'

'Hm? Voices?' prompted Mr. Harris, looking interested.

'Yeah! I can hear what people are saying,' she whispered, and looked around to see their reaction.

'Even I can hear what people are saying,' said Sebastian, whispering back, imitating her. 'In fact,' he hissed. 'I heard what you said just now.'

Maya glanced at him annoyed, but decided to let it go. 'No! Let me rephrase… I can hear what people are thinking,' she said.

'Seriously?' Now, Sebastian looked interested. 'Tell me, what am I thinking of right now?'

Maya shook her head in irritation. 'I'm sure I can guess what you're thinking, Seb… you're not much of an enigma. But it's like how Ryan said. It's random. I hear it sometimes, but most of the time I don't.'

'Anything else?' asked Mr. Harris, looking around at the others.

'Well, something did happen yesterday,' said Cassie. 'I was doing my assignment and there is this cup we have at home... you know the monster cup you brought me cocoa in last night?' She looked at Sam. He nodded. She looked back at Mr. Harris. 'Well, we all hate that cup and keep hoping it would break. We feel bad to throw it away... but anyway, yesterday, Sam brought me cocoa in that cup, as a joke. I was looking at the stupid cup and I wished it would break... and...,' she paused dramatically, '... it broke.'

'Okay, try this for freaky,' said Sebastian, getting involved, and he told them about how he had caught Naomi and the bottles in the kitchen. 'I tried to repeat it again, but ended up breaking things. It was just the one time.'

'Mine too,' said Cassie. 'I tried to break other things, but I couldn't, so I assumed the cup must have been on the verge of breaking anyway.'

They sat in silence for a few minutes, digesting each other's stories and then, one by one, they turned and looked expectantly at Sam.

'Well, Sam?' asked Mr. Harris. Sam looked cut up.

'Well, what?' he asked, roughly.

'Have you had anything weird happen to you?' asked Mr. Harris.

'No,' said Sam, looking disgruntled. He looked around at the others. 'Do you mean to tell me that all of you have some kind of... some kind of...?' He couldn't seem to find the word.

'Power?' suggested Mr. Harris.

Sam ignored that and continued, '... some kind of freaky thing going on. I'm the only one who actually remembers the electrical storm and I don't get anything?' he asked, in an aggrieved tone.

For the first time, Mr. Harris looked surprised. 'What do you mean, Sam? You don't feel different in any way?'

'No, okay? Stop rubbing it in,' he growled. 'Apparently, I'm not good enough. I mean, Cassie gets her freak on, and... I... Come on!' he said, looking disgusted.

'Er… one sec… Mr. Harris, how do you know all this? And, why isn't this freaking you out? It sure as hell is freaking me out,' said Ryan. The others nodded in agreement and looked at Mr. Harris.

'Do you know something we don't?' asked Ryan

'Did you do this to us?' asked Maya, looking scared.

'Kids! Kids! Hang on! All in good time!' He jumped off the table and went around to the other side of it. He bent down and picked up the bag he had brought into the room with him. He unzipped it, pulled out some belts and handed them around.

'Here, take one each,' he said, 'and strap it on.' Maya and Cassie hung back, but the boys took it readily enough and examined it.

'This is fancy,' said Sam, turning it over in his hands. 'It looks totally high tech.'

'What does it do?' asked Sebastian, looking at the belt he was holding, in fascination.

'You'll find out soon enough. Sam, don't fiddle with the settings. Come on girls, take one,' Mr. Harris urged.

The girls took theirs reluctantly. Mr. Harris buckled his belt on and gestured to them to do the same. The boys buckled theirs on at once. The girls looked at each other with misgiving.

'What, Maya? Are you chicken?' taunted Sebastian. That did the trick. With a determined look, Maya strapped hers on.

Cassie looked at them. 'Oh, fine, if we're all being crazy… here goes nothing,' she said and buckled hers.

'Can you see that green button? Press it,' instructed Mr. Harris. They all did as he told them. For an instant, there was a bright green light followed by the sensation of falling.

CHAPTER 12

The kids landed in a heap, crashing one on top of the other. They picked themselves off the floor and looked around, dazed. Mr. Harris seemed to have landed on his feet. Evidently, he was used to this mode of transport. They were in a large circular, white room with perfectly smooth walls. It had a patterned floor. There were strange symbols etched on the floor with coloured stones embossed in it. The ceiling was dome-shaped, with the top quarter made entirely of glass, like a skylight. They could see clear, blue sky through it. The room was empty of furniture or people. There was a door on one side, set so perfectly into the wall that if it hadn't been for the dark green doorknob, they wouldn't have known it was there. Ryan stepped forward towards Mr. Harris. Looking around at the weird room, he now had misgivings about having blithely put on the belt, and followed Mr. Harris's instructions. As the oldest, he felt he had to take charge of things.

'Listen! I don't know who you are and what you did to us. I don't know what this place is,' he waved around at the room, 'or where you've brought us, but you better let us go, or I'll smash your head in,' he threatened.

'Whoa! Stand down, soldier! I'm trying to help you… I promise,' said Mr. Harris, smiling as he put up his hands. Ryan walked straight into them shoving Mr. Harris back.

'Why should we believe you?' he growled. 'You just…,' he stopped, as he felt a tug at his arm. He looked around. It was Sam, looking up at him, his face pale.

'Don't worry, Sam. I won't let him hurt us,' he said, trying to reassure the kid.

Though it was obvious Sam was scared, he said, 'Ryan, let's see what he has to say. Come on!' He tugged at Ryan's arm again.

Ryan looked indecisively between Sam and Mr. Harris, and then he nodded. He took a couple of steps back. 'Explain! And make it quick!' he said, gruffly.

Mr. Harris gestured towards the door. 'If you will, take off your belts and come through here?' He started taking off his belt.

The children looked nervously at each other as they started removing their belts. Mr. Harris opened the door and walked through it. The kids hesitated for a couple of seconds, still unsure. Then, Sam took a deep breath and walked towards the door, and the rest followed him out.

They had entered an enormous room. It was the size of almost three football fields. The ceiling stretched away, high above them. They had entered through a side door and the room was laid perpendicular to it. From the far left, where the room ended, to the far right, which looked like the entrance, were hundreds of fluted pillars which ran the length of the room. They walked forward, passing between two of them, looking around as they went.

The entrance to the room was through two enormous wooden doors which were shut. A stunningly patterned carpet ran in the centre, all the way from the entrance through the entire length of the hall, to finish at a low dais that stood on the other end of the room. Three elaborately carved chairs, one large and two smaller ones were on the dais. On either side of the carpet, up to halfway up the room, were less ornate chairs. These were positioned just in front of the pillars. The wall at the end of the room behind the dais was made entirely of glass. In the centre, was a large, white lotus, made of panes of frosted glass. The lotus was surrounded by vividly coloured panes of stained glass. The side walls of the room were hung with richly woven tapestry.

Mr. Harris walked briskly down the carpet, towards the dais. The children scuttled after him. There were three people, two women and a man, sitting on the chairs on the dais. The other chairs on either side of the carpet were unoccupied. The children looked around in wonder as they walked behind Mr. Harris. The room was fascinating, yet terrifying in its strangeness. They reached the dais.

Mr. Harris stepped aside, and with a dramatic flourish, he said, 'This is them!' gesturing at the children.

'Them?' Maya involuntarily looked behind, to see if there was someone else there that Mr. Harris was pointing at. 'Why is Mr. Harris talking like those people would know us?' she wondered.

She'd never seen them before in her life, and looking at the faces of the other kids, she didn't think any of them had either. There was silence, as the three people on the dais observed them. The children shuffled their feet, feeling uncomfortable. They felt like lab rats, being examined.

The woman, who sat cross legged on the large chair in the centre, was serene and beautiful. She was completely bald, which added to her ascetic appearance. She didn't look very old, her face was smooth with no wrinkles, but her eyes held the wisdom which came with age and experience. She was dressed in simple, but elegant robes.

The woman on her left, could have been, maybe was, her sister. They looked identical, except that the second woman had long silvery hair which hung loose. It gleamed, red and blue in the light that filtered through the stained glass. Her robes were also elegant, but more colourful and embellished.

The hawk-nosed man on the right seemed to have trouble sitting still. He looked old… much older than the two women. He had a lean face, long wavy hair which fell to his shoulders and a short French beard. In contrast to the two women, he was dressed casually in jeans, a black pullover and black boots.

'Is this it?' he burst out, like he couldn't bear to keep it to himself any longer.

'Marcus! You of all people should know how deceiving looks can be,' said the woman in the centre, softly. Her voice was melodious and soothing. 'Come here, child!' she gestured to Sam. He hesitated and then shuffled forward, closer to the dais. She held out a slender hand to him. He climbed up the dais and placed his trembling fingers in her hand. She clasped his fingers gently and closed her eyes for a few seconds.

When she opened them, she said, 'Don't be frightened. There is nothing to be afraid of. You are in a safe place.' She smiled sweetly. Sam felt oddly reassured by the gentle touch and her words. 'You must be Sam,' she added. Sam was surprised. How did she know who he was?

He felt like he had stepped into a dream. He glanced around to make sure that the others were still there. Ryan took two steps forward, but Sam shook his head imperceptibly, and Ryan paused. Cassie was pale and looked like she might pass out.

He turned back and pulled his hand away. 'Would somebody like to tell us what is going on?' he said rudely.

Marcus looked at Sam in anger, but the two women turned towards Mr. Harris. 'I didn't tell them anything,' explained Mr. Harris.

'You didn't tell them anything?' asked the silver-haired woman, raising an eyebrow. 'And they just came with you?'

'That was foolish!' said Marcus.

'Or, very brave!' she retorted.

'I told you… they are different,' said Mr. Harris.

'Why? What can they do?' asked Marcus.

Mr. Harris shrugged. 'I don't know yet. They… don't know yet… but if…,' He paused as the woman in the centre interrupted sharply.

'All will be revealed in good time, Marcus.' She turned to the children. 'I understand how frightened you must be. Blane should have been more forthcoming before bringing you here. But,' she said, turning to Mr. Harris, 'I understand why you didn't. I apologize, children. Let me introduce myself and welcome you. My name is Iola. This is my sister, Sybil. And this is Marcus,' she said, gesturing to the other two. 'I've been waiting to meet you for a long time. I wish you could stay longer, but Blane tells me that you have to get back.' She looked at Mr. Harris, who nodded. 'Blane will take you back now. I look forward to seeing you again… soon, I hope. You must be confused and frightened. You don't have to be. Blane will try and answer the many questions I'm sure you have. Goodbye, till we meet again. Go, with peace in your hearts,' she said, smiling serenely. She got up from her chair gracefully and walked away, followed by the other two. They went out through a door in the far left corner of the huge room.

Sam was still standing on the dais. Sebastian called out. 'Sam! Yo, Sam! You okay, bud?' Sam turned around and walked back towards them, looking dazed. That striking face… that melodious voice… his hand still tingled from where Iola had touched it. He looked up at Sebastian, who was grinning now. 'Looks like someone got bit bad,' Sebastian said, laughing, and slapped Sam on the back. 'Snap out of it, kid. She's old enough to be your… your… how old is she?' He turned to Mr. Harris, who smiled.

'Iola tends to have this effect on people. It'll pass. Come along, kids,' he turned and started walking away. As the others made to follow him, Ryan stretched out his hands, holding them back.

'Stop!' he said firmly. 'Let's get some answers first and then we'll come.' Mr. Harris turned around and saw Ryan's protective stance.

He smiled. 'Ryan, I promise I'll explain after I take you back. We don't have much time. It's almost four. You need to get back home before your folks start worrying. So, shall we go?' he asked.

Ryan looked at Sam… who nodded. Ryan lowered his hands and said, 'Okay… let's go.' Mr. Harris, who'd been watching the two boys with interest, turned and led them out.

They walked back through the doorway by which they had entered. The belts were still on the ground where they had left them. They each picked up one and strapped it on. Sam put his hand on Mr. Harris's arm. 'Before we go, where are we?' he asked.

'Tibet,' replied Mr. Harris. He looked at the children's disbelieving looks. 'I'll explain once we get back. Now, press the orange button,' he said, 'at the count of three… one… two… three.' They pressed the orange button, there was the sudden flash of light and they were falling again.

With a crash, they landed on chairs and tables, knocking them over. They were back in the detention room. They untangled themselves and got up shakily. Mr. Harris held out his hand for the belts. The girls handed it back eagerly, the boys with a bit more reluctance.

Mr. Harris put them back in the bag and zipped it up. He looked at his watch. 'Ok, who wants to go first? Raise your hand.' He smiled, as all five hands went up. 'Let's take it from the oldest… Ryan?' He nodded towards Ryan.

'Where did you take us, truthfully? Who were those people? Who are…?' The questions tumbled out of Ryan.

Mr. Harris interrupted him. 'One question at a time. As I said, we went to Tibet,' he said.

'No way,' said Sebastian. 'How do we know it was Tibet?'

'Do you know it wasn't?' asked Mr. Harris.

Maya waved her raised hand to catch Mr. Harris's attention. 'Ok, forget that, we'll take your word for it… not that it matters… but who were those people and why did you take us there?' asked Maya.

'Iola, Sybil and Marcus, head the council of Pha-yul, an ancient community which has existed for centuries. It consists of people who have special powers. When we find people in whom the powers manifest, we help them understand these powers, control them and enhance them.'

'Who are you? Why don't you live there?' asked Sam.

'And what are your powers?' added Sebastian.

'I too belong to that community, but I live outside it. There are many others like me, who live in the outside world. We act as teachers and guides for... freshers... if you will... like you. When we find people with special abilities, we train them and help them understand their powers.' He looked at Sebastian. 'You don't need to know what my powers are. You need to figure out what yours are.'

'Is the community like a school? Do we have to live there and learn to use our powers?' asked Sebastian, looking hopeful.

'I'm afraid not. Usually, you would not be taken to Pha-yul till you were ready. You will be trained here,' replied Mr. Harris. Sebastian looked disappointed. For a wild moment, he had thought he was rid of Holy Trinity.

'When would we be ready?' he asked.

Mr. Harris shrugged. 'When you are!' he replied.

'This is so freaking cool... I can't wait to start,' said Sebastian, sounding excited.

Mr. Harris frowned at him. 'Sebastian, there is nothing freaking cool about this. It's a big responsibility you've been given. I would advise you not to use your powers in front of others, if you can help it. I also hope you won't abuse it, till you learn to control it or you could end up hurting someone. Of course, it's only advice... but I sincerely hope you take it.'

'I have a question,' said Cassie, who'd been quiet till then. 'What did she mean, when she said she had been waiting for us?'

'They have powers too,' said Mr. Harris. 'They may have known you were coming.'

'And what was the whole thing with Sam?' asked Ryan. 'How did she know who he was?'

'She can read people's minds, like Maya. If you remember, she said I had told her you need to get home. I didn't say it aloud. She read my mind. She would have known who each of you were, as soon as you entered the room,' said Mr. Harris.

The kids looked at one another. They didn't know what to think. It was all a bit too much to digest.

'What do you want from us?' asked Ryan, after a couple of minutes of silence.

'Nothing,' replied Mr. Harris. 'It's more of, what I can do to help you.'

'Do we have to join this... this community?' Ryan asked.

'Children! There is nothing you have to do. Nobody is forcing anything on you. All I'm offering is help... to help yourself. Ryan, you of all people should know by now, what happens when you have a power that you can't control. So, I suggest you go home and think about it. I'll let you know where we'll meet again. You can decide whether to come or not. Does that sound fair?' he asked.

'Totally,' said Sebastian. 'Count me in. Tell me when and where.'

He picked up his bags, waggled his fingers at the other kids and turned to leave. The others didn't look as excited and straggled out slowly. Sebastian had already disappeared by the time they walked out.

'Guys,' Ryan sounded anxious. 'I'm the oldest. I feel I should know what we should do... but I don't. What do you think?'

'I'm not sure this is a good idea either,' said Cassie.

'I think we should talk about this some more before deciding, right?' said Ryan.

'Yeah!' said Maya pensively. 'I have piano class now. Why don't we meet up later?' The others nodded.

'Where?' asked Cassie.

Maya thought for a minute. 'How about Silver Creek Park? Cassie and Sam have to walk and it's close enough to them. I have a car and Ryan, you can cycle down. He's an ass, but I think we should call Seb too. Sam, will you call him? He won't come if I call,' she added, making a face. Sam nodded and they split up and went home.

CHAPTER 13

Ryan was the first to arrive at Silver Creek Park. There had been a little brook called Silver Creek which had run through the area, when the park was designed almost sixty years ago, but it was now just a dry ditch filled with rotting leaves. It had been fed by the Skallen River, but after the Sentinel Dam had come up a couple of decades back, the level of the Skallen river had dropped and Silver Creek Brook had dried up, though the name still remained. The pathway, with wrought iron railings and wooden benches set at intervals, still ran the entire length of the dried up brook and ended in what used to be a little pond, but was now a dry hollow.

A decade back, the town council had raised enough money to build an artificial lake on the other side of the park, and visitors to the park now went there, since it also had a playground and food stalls around it. Ryan sat on one of the wooden benches near the new lake, and waited for the others. A little plaque on one side proclaimed, "Silver Creek Lake" proudly. Ryan was worried. He stared at the people walking around the lake without seeing them, his mind on the strange events which had happened that day. From the moment he had heard this new found strength he had was permanent, all he could think of was how it would affect his football and consequently his scholarship. He had wanted to bash Sebastian's face in, jumping around like a jackass, thinking he was so cool. What an oaf! Unlike Sebastian, who found his power cool, Ryan felt it was a curse.

He'd been so scared to move during practice in the evening, in case he hurt someone again that he hadn't scored even once. He'd jumped aside if anyone came too close. But he hadn't cared. He'd felt he'd rather lose than break someone else's bones. Though, he thought, he wouldn't mind making an exception in Sebastian's case. He would gladly bend that nose out of shape. Mr. Harris had watched Ryan play badly, but he hadn't commented. Right now, Ryan was irritated with Mr. Harris too. He had enough problems in his life; he didn't need any more. He didn't want anymore.

His phone rang and he took it out of his jacket pocket. It was Lisa. Shoot! He couldn't catch a break. She was going to be mad. He had told her he'd meet her at the mall, before work. He had completely forgotten. He flipped open the phone.

'Hey Lis!' he said, trying to sound casual.

'Ryan! Where are you?' she sounded cross.

'Sorry Lis! Mr. Harris has me doing extra workout. I don't think I'll be able to make it to the mall,' he said.

'Ryan! All the boys are here. Randy is here!' she said irately. 'So don't give me this bull.'

Ryan swore to himself. He'd forgotten Randy and the boys were heading there after practice. But he knew the boys would cover for him. 'Babe, you're welcome to come on over to the gym and check out what I'm doing. I'd enjoy the company. Mr. Harris asked me to stay back, not the other guys,' he said. He hated lying, but he found he was doing quite a bit of it with Lisa these days.

'Whatever!' She hung up on him. Ryan flipped the phone shut and looked up as a shadow fell across him. It was Maya.

'Hey!' she said shyly.

'Hey!' said Ryan, moving over to make room for her on the bench. She sat down. They sat in awkward silence for a couple of minutes.

'So, where do you stay?' asked Ryan, trying to make small talk.

'On Trudeau Road… near the Skallen Museum?' Maya answered, relieved to break the awkward silence.

Ryan said, 'Yeah… I know the place. Darren lives there.' Maya nodded. She had no idea who Darren was.

'Where do you stay?' she asked him.

'Parley Place,' he replied, and waited for the look of surprise. Ah! There it was. He was used to it. It was the most expensive neighbourhood in town, and he always got the "You… live there?" look, whenever he told people where he lived.

There was a long pause again. Maya couldn't stand it any longer. 'Ryan', she started tentatively. 'What do you think of,' she waved her arm about vaguely, '… about all this? Honestly?'

'Honestly? I wish, whatever picked me… chance or fate…whatever… hadn't picked me. I have enough on my plate as it is. I feel like this heavy, new responsibility has been thrust on me,' he said. 'I honestly wish, someone else had been picked.' Maya looked at him sympathetically. 'What about you?' he asked.

She considered his question for a couple of seconds. 'I won't lie. I'm curious. I found the whole experience fascinating. I feel like we've been given this opportunity to do more… I guess… I guess, what I'm saying is that I feel chosen… like… special… which is very immodest, I know,' she was rambling now. 'I'm not sure how to explain it,' she ended lamely, thinking to herself, 'God, why do I keep acting so stupid around him?'

'No, I understand. I guess if I didn't have all these problems to deal with, I'd probably be excited too. It's normal,' he said, shrugging. Maya wanted to ask him what his problems were. She wished she could help. He looked utterly unhappy.

'Hey, you love birds! Getting it on, are we?' Sebastian's cheerful voice rang out. Maya glared at him, as he sauntered up. He was annoying and inappropriate. 'Scoot up!' he told Maya and perched himself next to her. 'So, what's this all about? Sam wouldn't tell me anything. Simply told me to come here. Wait! Don't tell me! He has some other crazy theory that he wants to share with us?'

Maya was crushed between the two boys. She wriggled out and got up. As she stood up, she saw with relief that Cassie and Sam were walking up towards them. She sat down cross-legged on the grass, and Cassie and Sam threw themselves down beside her. They were all so used to Sam starting the conversation that they all turned towards him, expectantly.

'What are you looking at me for? You are the ones with the super powers. I'm a mere mortal. I don't even know why I'm here,' he said grouchily.

'Sam! Maybe, you haven't discovered your power yet,' said Cassie kindly. Sam looked at her in surprise. Cassie had been super nice to him the whole evening. He didn't know how to handle "Nice Cassie!"

'Fine, I'll start,' said Maya. 'So, what do you think of the whole thing? Huh? Ancient community? Tibet? If all of you hadn't also seen it, I'd have thought I'd dreamt it. I still wonder if he hypnotized us. I mean those people… who were they? Tibet? Seriously?'

'You know, I considered it while we were there, that we were in some kind of mass hypnotic state or mass hallucination. It's possible you know, to plant an idea like that in our heads… theoretically. It was all just too fantastic,' said Sam contemplatively.

'I know… wasn't it? Do you think we would be able to do mass hypnosis? Do you think they'll teach us?' asked Sebastian.

'Frankly, I don't know what to believe,' Ryan said. 'Mr. Harris said training… I don't even understand what he means by that? Training in what? If it has anything to do with studying, let me tell you, I'm won't fare very well. My grades are barely up as it is.'

For the first time, Sebastian looked put out. 'Study? You think he'll make us study?' he asked. 'I'm not very good at that,' he said glumly.

'Maybe not studying, but whatever training he's going to put us through, I'm sure it involves a lot of hard work,' said Sam.

'I'm not very good at that either,' said Sebastian gloomily. 'Stop breaking my bubble! At this rate, I'll get bored with the whole business in no time.'

'That's nothing new,' said Cassie, shaking her head. Sebastian was getting on her nerves, frayed as they were with the turmoil of the last few hours.

'Whoa!' said Sebastian, looking at her. 'I thought Maya's the one who takes pot shots at me. When did you join her?'

'Shut it, Seb. Guys! Did you believe all that Mr. Harris said? What if he had some kind of ulterior motive?' asked Maya.

'Like what, Maya? Did he try to torture you into a web of lies?' Sebastian laughed. He looked around when he realised no one was laughing with him. 'Come on, you're not taking her seriously, are you? I mean, if the guy had wanted to do something to us, he didn't have to take us to Tibet. He had all the time in the world to do whatever he wanted with us, right here.'

'We shouldn't have gone,' said Cassie. 'It was a bit foolish of us.'

'A little too late for that, don't you think?' asked Sebastian drily.

'I wouldn't have let anything happen to you,' said Ryan.

'Oh, my hero!' said Sebastian, throwing his arms around Ryan.

'Gerroff me!' Ryan struggled and shoved Sebastian away. Sebastian went flying into the air and fell in a heap, about ten feet away. They all froze for a moment, in shock. People were looking at them. They hurried over to Sebastian, who was staggering to his feet, a little shaken but unhurt.

'Man! That was a sucker punch!' He didn't seem upset. He looked wonder-struck. 'If your shove did that to me, I'd have given anything to see your charge this morning,' he said.

'No, you wouldn't,' said Ryan savagely. 'You didn't have to hear the howls Shel made, when I broke his arm. There was nothing funny or cool about it.' He looked down at the ground, looking upset as he relived that moment. 'That's why I've decided I'll start training with Mr. Harris,' he said, 'not to be cool, not to enhance my strength, but to learn to control it. And Maya,' he looked at her. 'Do you like hearing people talk and not being able to stop it?' Maya shook her head. It was driving her crazy. 'Maybe he can help you control it.' He got up and picked up his bag. 'What I'm trying to say is, there is no harm in doing what Mr. Harris says, for now. Let's see what happens. I have to go now. I'm late for work.' He hurried away, breaking into a jog.

Sebastian sat down on the bench again. 'Man that was something else. Did you guys see that?' He paused and then said, 'You know what? He's the one it happens to all the time… the powers, I mean.'

'That's not true,' said Maya quietly. 'I know that the woman in the red shirt is wondering whether she should make chicken for dinner, or fish. That woman in the pink skirt is hopping mad with her boyfriend. I don't want to go into all the bad words she's using about him.' She shook her head, trying to rid the voices and looked at them. 'As Ryan said, it's not pleasant, not being able to control it.'

'So, what's she saying about her boyfriend?' Sebastian asked, with interest.

Cassie shook her head. 'Did they drop you on your head when you were a baby?' she asked. 'Is that what's important?'

Sebastian looked at her, surprised. 'Again? You're being mean to me, again? You're spending too much time with her. You're going to turn into a jerk like her, if you're not careful,' he told Cassie and then turned back to Maya. 'So go on, what was she saying?' Cassie shook her head in disbelief and turned away.

'Not telling you, Seb,' said Maya, looking irritated

'Why not?' He looked disappointed. 'Fine, if I'm not going to be entertained, I might as well leave. Ciao, kids. See you when I see you!' He walked away, whirling his key ring on one finger.

'Why do you fight so much?' asked Cassie, curiously. 'You fight like us,' she pointed to Sam and herself, 'like siblings.'

Maya put one finger in her mouth and made a puking motion. 'Please, don't even say that.' She watched Sebastian, as he walked away jauntily. 'My Mom is dating his Dad and neither of us is happy about it,' she explained.

'Oh! ... Oh... you're jealous, because he gets to spend time with your Mom and you don't?' Cassie nodded sympathetically. She could understand how that felt.

Maya looked at Cassie in surprise. 'No! I'm not jealous of him. I just don't like him. He's such an ass!'

Sam gave a half shrug. 'He's ok,' he said.

Maya opened her eyes wide. 'Sam, have you even met him? Seriously? If you think Seb is ok... I'm sure you're still hallucinating. But, I better get used to him. I have no choice now. Till now, I could pretend he didn't exist, most of the time, but now if we're going to be spending time together, I guess that's no longer an option.' She sat down heavily on the bench, as the enormity of everything that had happened hit her.

'Why us?' She looked up at both of them unhappily. Unlike Sebastian, she didn't feel this was exciting or cool. She had told Ryan she felt special. But she didn't feel that way when she was hearing other people's thoughts. She didn't want to listen to other people's secrets, or hear what other people were thinking of her. If she resisted, she got a headache, like the one she was getting now because she'd been trying to keep the thoughts of the people around her out. She was constantly popping pills. If she didn't, the headache grew worse, till she threw up. If it went on like this, her mom would think she was bulimic.

'So, we'll do as Mr. Harris says?' asked Sam. 'Ryan, Maya and Seb are on board. I guess you are too, Cassie. I'm not sure why I should tag along, but why not? I might as well.'

'Well then… we're decided,' Maya said. She looked up at the sky. 'It's getting dark, guys. Shall I drop you home? It's on my way.' They nodded gratefully. As they walked toward her car, she asked, 'By the way Sam, do you know who Darren is?'

CHAPTER 14

The next day, they all found notes in their lockers during break. It was in the same expensive paper, with the same exquisite handwriting. Their messages were all identical, asking them to come to the football grounds after school.

Ryan was already on the field with his teammates when the other four trooped in, one by one. Mr. Harris was also on the field. The four of them sat in the stands and waited for Mr. Harris. Ryan noticed them as he jogged past and gave a half wave.

'I don't know how they practice like this, morning and evening. It looks tiring. I wish Mr. Harris would hurry up. I have a date this evening,' said Sebastian, tapping his foot impatiently.

Mr. Harris gave instructions to some of the players and then walked towards where they were sitting, Ryan in tow. The other football players looked at them curiously, but at a bark from Mr. Harris, they continued with their practice.

Mr. Harris called out to the kids, 'Leave your bags and come down here.' Sebastian felt a thrill of excitement, as he scampered down ahead of the others.

'Ryan,' said Mr. Harris. 'I want you to put them through their paces. Maybe, twenty laps, some stretches and two sets of exercises? We'll take it from there.'

'What?' spluttered Sebastian. 'I thought you were going to help us hone our powers. What is this?' he said, looking upset.

Mr. Harris turned to him. 'Your powers use your body and your mind. You cannot hope to understand or use your powers, till you can understand and control both.'

'I can control my body,' said Sebastian, roughly. He was getting annoyed. This wasn't turning out like he'd imagined.

Mr. Harris smiled. He stepped away from the group and told Sebastian, 'Punch me!'

Sebastian stared at him. 'What?' he asked.

'You heard me. I said, punch me!' repeated Mr. Harris.

'I won't punch you. I'll hurt you,' said Sebastian.

Mr. Harris was taller than Sebastian, but Sebastian was sure he was stronger than the older man. He had the advantage of age and strength. He knew he could easily knock Mr. Harris down. He didn't want to.

Mr. Harris said, 'Punch me!' again. Sebastian looked around at the others, who were looking uncomfortable.

He shrugged. 'Okay,' he said.

He had done a bit of boxing in one of his prep schools, and he had discovered to his surprise that he was quite good at it. It was a phase, and as usual, he had soon gotten bored with it. But for a year, he had trained. He had even ended up second in his weight category. He was sure it would come back to him. He took his stance.

Sebastian waited for Mr. Harris to also take his stance, but he just stood there, very still. 'Go on,' he said softly. 'Punch me!'

Sebastian took a swing. It wasn't a hard punch. He didn't want to hurt Mr. Harris. His fist struck air, as Mr. Harris rocked back on his feet. Sebastian lost his balance and almost fell. He steadied himself and followed through with an uppercut. He missed again, though Mr. Harris hadn't moved. Sebastian frowned. He started bouncing on the balls of his feet. He feinted to the left, but whipped back and hooked a right. He missed again.

For five minutes, he jabbed and punched, but didn't connect once. Mr. Harris just moved his body, rocking back and swinging his body to the left and right, out of the way of Sebastian's fists. He hadn't moved his feet at all. Sebastian stopped, drenched in sweat. He bent over, his hands on his knees, breathing hard.

'That was just brilliant,' said Sam. 'I don't care if I don't have powers. I'd like to learn how to do that.'

Mr. Harris didn't say anything. He gestured for Ryan to take over and walked back to the other football players. Some of them had stopped to watch the little exchange between Mr. Harris and Sebastian, and now there was a soft cheer, clapping and whistling for Mr. Harris as he walked back. He lifted his hand and waved in acknowledgment. Sebastian's face was red with anger and embarrassment, while the other four tried to stop laughing.

For the next two hours, Ryan made them run, stretch and exercise, and when they felt that they couldn't move anymore and their knees felt like they were about to buckle, he'd give them a five minute break and then start all over again. Except for Sebastian, who played tennis occasionally, the others had never played an outdoor sport in their lives. Sam had never been allowed to play and neither of the girls was into sports.

'Stop! Please! I can't!' Maya threw herself on the ground.

Ryan hadn't expected much from the four. None of them looked fit. But of the four, Maya was able to hold out the longest. The others had given up earlier and were lying sprawled on the field. Ryan had exercised with them and hadn't even broken a sweat. Mr. Harris must have been keeping an eye on them because he jogged up now. He looked a bit put out by their total lack of fitness.

'Ryan, go on and join the others,' he told the older boy. As Ryan walked back to join his teammates, Mr. Harris looked at the four who were sitting or lying on the grass, drenched with sweat and looking flushed.

'O… k then, we need to do more, don't we? You may leave now. I want to see you at five, tomorrow morning. The other players come in only at six, so that gives us an hour alone. We can work on other skills then. When the football team turns up, you can start the workout Ryan showed you today.' They all groaned in unison. More of this! Sebastian wasn't enjoying this at all.

'When will you teach us how to use our powers?' he pestered again.

'When you are ready, Sebastian!' replied Mr. Harris.

'You keep saying that… but when would it be?' persisted Sebastian. He was annoyed. He hadn't signed up for all this running and jumping. He only wanted to learn how to use his powers. 'I don't want to do all this,' he said.

'Seb, shut it, will you? Don't you get it? It's all part of the package. Were you sleeping when he explained, or are you actually that dumb?' Maya asked. She was equally worn out and the thought of having to get here by five the next morning was torturous. And Sebastian wasn't helping, with his complaining. Sebastian turned towards Maya to say something nasty, but Mr. Harris interrupted.

'Sebastian… enough! This will be your schedule. You have to be here at five in the morning and you will train till class starts, and then you get back here straight after class. You don't get weekends off. Every day of the week, one of you will stay back after school, to work alone with me for an hour. Any questions?'

'What about our school work, extracurricular activities?' asked Maya.

'Figure it out. Make time! As I told Sebastian earlier, you have a big responsibility. So, this has to be your priority now. At least, until you master your ability. Remember what Ryan did to Sheldon? If you don't learn to manipulate your power, you could end up hurting people or harming yourselves.'

They nodded soberly. 'Right, off you go then. I'll see you at five sharp, tomorrow,' he said and went back to his team.

The children dragged themselves off the ground and went to pick up their bags from the stands. As they turned to leave, they saw Ryan making a run with the ball, leaping over a player, and they couldn't help envying how fit he was, and the ease with which he played.

CHAPTER 15

By the time Sebastian reached home, he was running late. He took a quick shower and got ready.

'Ouch! Ouch! Ouch!' he went, as he put his shirt on.

His muscles were protesting and he hurt all over. He knew he would feel a whole lot worse the next morning. He would have preferred to spend the evening soaking in a hot bath, but he had a date… at the club… with the lovely Lisa!

Sebastian didn't have much of a conscience. His philosophy was simple. You want something, take it. He didn't dwell too much on right and wrong. As long as he could live with it, he was okay. He had bumped into Lisa the day before, at the club, where she was hanging out with her friends. He had flirted with her and she had seemed flattered. Taking that as a good sign, he'd asked her out and she'd accepted.

He had asked his dad's permission to take the Porsche and to his surprise, his dad had said yes. It was promising to be a pleasant evening. He had asked Lisa if she wanted to be picked up, but she had said she'd come on her own. Sebastian left to the club a bit early, so that he would be waiting when she arrived. He prided himself on being a ladies' man, and he knew these small things made a big impression.

Ryan had gone straight to work after practice and reached home quite late. As he walked into his room, his phone rang. It was Lisa. After standing her up the previous evening and then ignoring her in school most of today, he was sure she was hopping mad at him. Their fights, which seemed to be happening more often these days, followed the same pattern. She'd get mad at him, and he'd have to grovel and beg to get her to forgive him. Today, for the first time, he'd had too much on his mind to even think of her. It had been a long day, and he was still trying to process all that had happened. He'd decided to deal with Lisa and her moods later. He had known he'd have to eventually grovel, but he hadn't felt up to it in school.

And her being mad at him, had given him some much needed time alone. So he'd spent the entire day ignoring her, instead of trying to make up as he usually did. He had slipped into class, just as the teacher walked in. He'd made himself scarce at break and at lunchtime, and had gone to practice right after class. He'd left to work after that.

He answered the phone and waited for the petulant outburst. Instead, she was all sugar and honey. She told him she was sorry for putting so much pressure on him, and that she understood he was trying his best and was dealing with a lot of stuff. He was baffled. At first, he had thought she was being sarcastic, but then he realised she meant what she was saying. They had spoken for a while and made up. He couldn't believe it. He had no idea why she was being nice to him, but he wasn't about to look a gift horse in the mouth.

Maya was reading in bed, when she got the threatening phone call. It hadn't frightened her, but it had left a bad taste. She called up her friends, Mary Anne and Felicity, and put them on conference to tell them what had happened.

'Guys! I had the weirdest call,' she said, as she drew up her covers and got comfortable in her bed. 'The number was blocked and I didn't recognize the voice. But whoever it was, said, "Stay away from Ryan or I'll cut up your ugly face, you...", it was followed by a bad word,' she said.

'What? Why would they say that?' asked Felicity. 'Ryan Carter? Why would they think you were seeing Carter? Are you?' she demanded.

'No! Like I would hide it from you guys,' replied Maya indignantly.

She hadn't told them about any of the craziness that was going on in her life. The two of them were her best friends, and they told each other everything. But Maya knew that she couldn't tell them about Mr. Harris and her abilities. They wouldn't believe her or they'd think she was crazy.

'I'm not seeing Ryan, but Mr. Harris has selected me along with a few other kids, he wants to... um... train us,' she was thinking fast, making up the story as she went, '... er... for a marathon. And Ryan's in charge... it's not only me. There are other kids there as well,' she added defensively.

Her friends started laughing. 'You? He picked you to run a marathon? Seriously? This is too funny.' She joined in their laughter. It sounded preposterous, even to her. She wished she had come up with a better excuse.

'I know! I told him what a bad athlete I was. You should have seen me at practice today. It was hilarious, but he's promised me extra credit, anyway, that's not the point... focus... the call?' said Maya.

'Right,' said Mary Anne. 'The call... do you think it was Lisa? She's Carter's girlfriend and she's mean.'

'But why would Lisa...,' Maya paused, thinking.

She thought about the gruelling evening of practice Ryan had put them through. Lisa, and some of friends, had been hanging around the stands for a while. Maya had done much better than the others, and she remembered Ryan had patted her back and high-fived her, a couple of times. She'd been thrilled, of course. But, maybe Lisa had seen that.

'What?' asked Felicity, hearing the pause. 'What aren't you telling us?' Maya told them what she'd just thought of. 'What a nutjob... it must be her, or one of her cronies,' said Felicity. 'They're all mad, and they think no end of themselves.' They spent a happy half hour, tearing Lisa and her friends to bits before going to sleep.

CHAPTER 16

Five o'clock the next morning, found Ryan, Maya, Cassie and Sam on the football field. Maya, Cassie and Sam, had found it difficult to get out of bed that morning. Their muscles were groaning in pain. Mr. Harris was already on the field, waiting for them. Sebastian hadn't turned up, but Mr. Harris didn't comment on it, or ask them why Sebastian hadn't come.

'Before we start, there is something we need to discuss,' said Mr. Harris. 'I'm sure there will be some curiosity about what we're up to? I've already told the Principal that there is an inter-school competition and that I've chosen five children for it. I have your letters ready for your parents to sign. Take it from me before you leave this evening. Stick to the same story, all of you. We have this one hour in the mornings and most of the weekend, when we can train unobserved. I'd like to use this hour in the morning to strengthen your concentration and focus. We'll use the weekends to learn other skills.'

There were five mats spread out on the ground. It was like he knew Sebastian wouldn't turn up. They sat on the mats.

'To harness your power and learn to control it, you need to be able to control your body and mind, as I was explaining to Sebastian yesterday. You are now sitting in the lotus position. The lotus is the symbol of Pha-yul. It symbolizes all that is good and pure. It stands for peace and harmony. It sits calmly in a lake, undisturbed and motionless. We call that state of mind "nirvana". It is a Sanskrit term and means "calm". The closer you get to that state of mind and body, the more control you will have over your powers. Let us begin.'

They started with simple breathing exercises, and then he took them through a series of stretches. It was a bit like yoga. Maya had taken yoga for a year, and she found some of the stretches familiar, but not exactly yoga. It was more intense, and by the end of ten minutes, they were covered in sweat. Maya and Sam were able to do most of the stretches quite easily. Ryan had the hardest time. Even the simplest posture was difficult for him. The ones which required balance completely threw him off. He swore as he fell yet again.

Mr. Harris said, 'Ryan, these exercises are to be done calmly and economically. Getting angry won't help you. Do as much as you can. It will come more easily as you practice.' His words seem to calm Ryan down, and he went through the next few steps with more ease.

Mr. Harris kept them at it for a half hour, and then told Ryan to take over and get them started on their workout. The kids groaned when they heard that. But the stretching they had done seemed to have limbered their muscles, and lessened the ache with which they had awoken. They were jogging around the track when the other football players started showing up. Ryan gave the three of them instructions on what exercises to do, and went to join his teammates.

Around half past seven, Sebastian sauntered into the grounds. He doubled over with laughter, when he saw their red, sweaty faces. 'Oh my God! You look fit to bust. How long have you been at this?' he asked, grinning.

The three of them ignored him and continued with their workout. 'Hey, Mr. Harris is coming,' whispered Sam, and they stopped what they were doing, to watch what would happen.

'Why are you here, Sebastian?' asked Mr. Harris.

Sebastian turned around, his grin vanishing. 'I wasn't feeling too great. My body hurt this morning after all that…'

Mr. Harris interrupted his excuse. 'Sebastian, you may leave. When you are ready to follow instructions and train, you may join us,' he said in a firm voice.

Sebastian opened his mouth to protest again, but Mr. Harris was already walking away. Sebastian turned around and saw the others grinning at him.

'What were you saying, Seb?' teased Maya.

Sebastian turned and walked away, his face red with anger. He was pissed off. He'd been in a bad mood since the previous evening, when Lisa had stood him up. He had waited for her like a fool at the club. She hadn't answered his calls either. And to top it all, his dad and Maya's mom had turned up to have dinner at the club, and he had ended up spending the evening with them. He'd show them all. He was sure if he focused hard enough, he'd learn to use his powers. He didn't need Mr. Harris and all his bloody training. As he walked past the stands, he saw Lisa and a couple of her friends. They were looking at him and giggling, which didn't do anything to improve his mood.

Sebastian didn't turn up for training in the evening either. No one commented on his absence. Ryan put them through another rigorous workout. Before they left, Mr. Harris gave them the letters they had to get signed, and told them, 'Today, Ryan's staying back for an hour with me. Tomorrow will be Maya, Cassie on Friday, Sam on Monday and Sebastian on Tuesday.'

They looked at him in surprise, for having slotted Sebastian in. He saw the look. 'He'll be back,' he said confidently.

The next few weeks were simply a whirl for the kids. They woke up early in the morning, trained, went to class, trained again, went home, finished their schoolwork, and they were so tired they were asleep as soon as their heads touched their pillows. As Mr. Harris had predicted, Sebastian returned with a sad face and an apology the next day. He was on the field well before the rest of them turned up at five, and was talking to Mr. Harris. He quietly joined the others for training without any smart aleck comments.

Weekends were equally hectic. Mr. Harris had started them on taekwondo and fencing. He had them use sticks instead of swords for duelling. The one hour that each of them had to spend alone with Mr. Harris, after practice in the evening, was the strangest time. Each of them were given a task and asked to practice it.

Ryan was the first to be given his task. When the football team finished practice in the evening, Mr. Harris called out to Ryan and asked him to wait. The rest of the team looked at him curiously. Randy gestured, asking him what was going on. Ryan shook his head… he honestly didn't know why Mr. Harris was asking him to stay back. He hadn't been there when Mr. Harris had explained the training schedule to the other kids. After the players had gone in to shower and change, Mr. Harris took him under the stands. There was a pile of rocks there. Mr. Harris picked up one and tossed it to Ryan, and asked him to crush it. Ryan squeezed the rock… nothing happened. He squeezed harder and harder, his muscles straining, the veins on his right arm popping up, but it just wouldn't break.

After trying for five minutes, he looked up at Mr. Harris and said, 'I can't do it.'

'Yes, you can.' Mr. Harris picked a rock, bigger than the one Ryan held. He moved it around in his hand for a couple of seconds, and then he applied pressure using only his thumb and the rock shattered into pieces. Ryan jumped back with a yelp, as a flying piece barely missed his cheek.

'Oops! Sorry,' said Mr. Harris.

'How did you do that?' asked Ryan, amazed. 'Is strength your power?'

'I am afraid not, Ryan, though it is yours. There is a reason that you are training your mind and your body. With enough training, you will get strong enough eventually to shatter the stone with your body strength alone, like I just did. But the amount of energy you would have to use when using only your body, is much more than if you use your body and mind in tandem. Feel it! Feel the stone! And, break it!' he said. 'This is your first task. This is what you have to practice. Practice hard. The sooner you are able to control your ability, the less the chances there are of you harming someone by accident. Right?'

Ryan nodded and looked down at the rock. He moved his fingers over it, like Mr. Harris had done. Mr. Harris left him to it and went back to his office. Ryan had no idea what he was looking for. Feel it... Mr. Harris had said! Feel what? The rock felt smooth to his touch. He went back to squeezing it.

The next day was Maya's turn. She was nervous. She asked Ryan how his training had gone when she saw him in the morning. Ryan looked glum.

'Badly,' he replied, looking cheesed off. 'He gave me these stones... rocks actually, and asked me to crush them, one by one.'

'How many did you crush?' asked Sam. The others stopped their workout and listened too.

'None,' said Ryan. The other four looked at each other, trying not to smile. Ryan looked so sad for himself.

I'm sure you'll be able to crush them soon,' said Sam, trying to cheer him up. 'Very large, were they?'

'They're there, under the stands. Please... go on, have a look,' said

Ryan, continuing with his sit ups.

The others got up and checked to see if Mr. Harris was looking. He was busy with some of the football players. They hurried over to where Ryan had pointed, ducked under the stands and saw the small rocks. Sebastian burst into laughter and soon the others were giggling too.

'These stones? He's kidding, right?' said Sebastian.

'Don't say anything to him. He's already feeling bad,' said Sam.

'Well, he should. He breaks a guy's arm and he can't break these stones. That's… that's… so funny,' said Sebastian, and they started giggling again.

They walked back to where they'd been working out. Ryan, who had finished his sit ups, was walking off to join his teammates for practice.

He looked at their barely concealed grins, sourly. 'It's not funny. I spent a whole hour, trying to break one rock… just one!' he said.

'Yeah! Gosh! Those rocks! Man, they're huge… what was Mr. Harris thinking?' said Sebastian, with a straight face. The others couldn't help it. They burst out laughing and so did Sebastian.

Ryan put his hands on his hips. 'I'm waiting to see what he has lined up for you… let's see who's laughing then,' he said, turning around and walking away in a huff. This sobered Maya up, though the others were still giggling. Ryan had only made her more nervous about her session.

After practice in the evening, the others left while Maya hung back. She waited for Mr. Harris to finish with the football team. She heard voices and looked up at the stands. She saw Lisa and her friends sitting there. Lisa saw Maya looking up. She leaned over to her friends and whispered something. They all turned to look at her. Maya felt herself going red. She felt very open and vulnerable, standing in the middle of the field, so she went across to the other side of the stands, and sat there, waiting for Mr. Harris to finish with the football team.

He was done in a bit and loped over to her. 'Get a couple of mats, Maya... the ones we use in the morning,' he called out. Maya went to the room where all the sports paraphernalia were stored and hauled out a couple of mats. She spread them out in the shade.

Mr. Harris had disappeared again. She sat down on one of the mats and started doing breathing exercises.

'They're gone.' She opened her eyes when she heard Mr. Harris's voice. 'I was waiting for that lot to leave,' Mr. Harris said, and sat down on the mat opposite hers.

'Okay, close your eyes,' he instructed.

Maya closed her eyes and waited. She felt a sudden sharp pain shoot through her head.

'Ow!' she cried out, holding her head. She opened her eyes.

'Did you feel that?' he asked.

'Hell, yeah,' she answered, rubbing her head. It had felt like something sharp had been jabbed through the back of her head. She took her hand away from her head and looked at her fingers, fully expecting to see blood. There was no blood.

'What was that?' she asked.

'It was me,' said Mr. Harris. 'I jabbed you with my mind. The thoughts you hear... other people's thoughts, come from here.' He pointed to his head. 'So I can send out a nasty jab into your mind, like how I just did. You have to try and resist it.'

Maya nodded and closed her eyes. She felt the sharp jolt of pain again as Mr. Harris jabbed. She tried to resist it, but by the third jab she could feel her head start throbbing. She turned over on all fours and threw up beside her mat. Once she was done throwing up, she rose shakily to her feet and went over to where she had left her bag.

She took out her water bottle and washed her face and mouth. She looked back at Mr. Harris as she drank some water. He was waiting patiently for her. She reluctantly made her way back, pulled her mat away from her vomit and sat down again. She took a deep breath and closed her eyes. Jab! Jab! Jab! She groaned, holding her head.

Mr. Harris kept at it. He'd wait till she was ready and hit her again with his thoughts, each one piercing her harder than the last. Maya wasn't able to block any of his thoughts. There was no image or voice, only a sharp pain that seemed to pierce right through her head. After a half hour of this, and after Maya had thrown up thrice more, Mr. Harris relented, and said, 'That'll do for today.' By then, there was nothing in her stomach to throw up. She was simply retching, over and over, holding her pounding head in her hands.

Mr. Harris waited till she composed herself. 'This is what you have to do. I want you to learn to keep thoughts out. Not just here in the field but all the time. I want you to block every stray thought you hear. Understood?'

Maya nodded. Even that hurt her head. 'Now, you can put the mats back and clean up the mess, before you leave,' he said.

Maya could hardly stand, she was so weak and shaky, but she followed his instructions and cleaned up, trying not to groan as her head throbbed with pain. She was miserable that evening. The headache was overpowering by the time she reached home. She called up her mom when she couldn't bear it any longer, and her mom returned home immediately, with a heavy duty headache pill for her. It still took more than an hour for the headache to recede, though a dull throb remained. She left her school assignments undone and quietly went to sleep.

The next day at school, she found some strange looking pills in a bottle along with a note, in her locker. The note said, "Take a pill, if you feel a headache coming. Keep practicing." But Maya didn't want to practice because she didn't want to suffer through another headache like the previous day. So, she didn't try to block thoughts the whole day. She had the pills in her bag, but hadn't needed them.

That evening, as she walked onto the field, she heard Mr. Harris's voice in her head, clearly. 'You aren't resisting, Maya.' His voice was reproachful. Maya looked around sheepishly, thinking of an excuse. To her surprise, Mr. Harris was standing across the field, talking to one of the football players.

'How is he even doing this?' she wondered. 'He's carrying on a conversation with that guy, and talking to me too. I wonder if he could hear me if I replied.' She thought she'd give it a try. 'I'm sorry, Mr. Harris,' she thought in her mind and waited to see if there was any reply. There was silence. She felt stupid. He couldn't hear.

She felt bad for not having practiced, and she decided she would start practicing from the next day. She started blocking thoughts right from when she woke up in the morning, the following day, starting with her mom. She felt a headache start immediately, and she took one of the pills Mr. Harris had given her. It was effective! She didn't get a headache the rest of the day, though she blocked thoughts whenever she could.

Cassie's session with Mr. Harris didn't last long. She stayed back the next day and when the football players left, Mr. Harris came over to where she sat. She stood up and waited as he walked over. He had a pencil tucked over one ear. He sat down with his legs on either side of the seat. He gestured to Cassie to sit in front of him, facing him. She too swung one leg over and sat down.

He took out the pencil from his ear and placed it between them on the seat.

'Move it,' he said.

'Huh?' asked Cassie.

'Move it,' he repeated.

Cassie wondered if this was a trick. She put one finger out and pushed the pencil. It moved a few inches. She looked up at Mr. Harris, wondering what she was supposed to do next. He was smiling.

'I meant, move it without touching it,' he said. 'I should have been a bit more specific.'

'What?' asked Cassie. She was sure she hadn't heard right.

'Use your mind and move the pencil.'

'Er… I don't think I can,' said Cassie.

'Try,' he said. 'Focus and try, this is your task… simple, huh? When you move this pencil, you can move on to your next task,' he said. 'I'll be in my office finishing up some work. Call me, when it moves,' he said and walked away. Cassie sat there for the next hour, staring at the pencil, willing it to move. It stayed obstinately still.

When it was Sam's turn, for the first time, Mr. Harris seemed at a loss. He asked Sam to break things, to read his thoughts, to try and block thoughts, but Sam couldn't do any of them. He had then tried to make Sam move a pencil, run, jump, swim, dive, with no result.

After two sessions of this, he had said, 'Sam, I'll think about your task some more. I'll consult with Iola and decide on what to do.'

As Sam later joked with the others, he wasn't sure whether Mr. Harris called Iola or he went all the way there, but for Sam's third session, he seemed to have made a decision.

'Let's work with the talents you possess, Sam… your mind.' Since then, Sam's sessions had consisted of solving problems of increasing difficulty which Mr. Harris set out for him.

Sebastian spent his whole session with Mr. Harris, running. Mr. Harris was waiting for him with a football. He kicked it high and long and told Sebastian to run and catch it. Sebastian spent the entire hour chasing footballs, but didn't catch one. At the end of the hour, Mr. Harris seemed disappointed.

He said, 'I want you to practice. This one hour isn't enough. You need to work on this more. I suggest you go to the tennis court and use those ball machines. I want you to try and catch the balls as they come out.' Mr. Harris said.

Sebastian followed those instructions, he had a feeling that if he didn't, Mr. Harris would find out. He started going to the tennis court and practicing. He hardly ever caught anything, except by accident, but after the first two days of getting battered all over by the flying balls, he became quite adept at stepping out of the path of incoming balls.

CHAPTER 17

As the days passed, the kids got used to the change in their life. Getting up and going to practice was not a pain anymore. Sebastian had always wondered how sportspeople did it. That had been a major deterrent to him taking up a sport, but now he realised that once you started, you soon got used to it. Their bodies were now used to getting up early, used to the workout, their muscles didn't protest anymore after the intense training. They managed pretty well even when Ryan changed or increased their workout, or when Mr. Harris introduced them to new contortions.

Cassie had felt worried when they started training that her studies would suffer. But to her surprise, she found she wasn't struggling with her subjects anymore. In fact, her concentration had increased and studying had become easier. She was able to concentrate better in class, and when she went home and revised, she remembered most of what had been taught in class. For the first time in her life, she didn't feel overwhelmed with her school work.

Another pleasant side effect was that her eyesight had improved, remarkably. She could see perfectly well now without glasses, but her ophthalmologist had still insisted on giving her glasses with a very slight power. The doctor was amazed at the dramatic improvement in her eyesight, and so were her parents. She never used the glasses the ophthalmologist had prescribed for her, except if she was around her mom. Her mom insisted she wore them.

Ryan had also observed with pleasure that his grades were improving. He was also performing spectacularly on the football field. He was a blur on the field these days. He had learnt a simple trick to avoid hurting anyone. He tried to play football, without letting anyone get close to him. He wasn't a defender, so he didn't have to cover or block anyone. His main work on the field was getting the ball away and to the goal. He ran faster, and twisted and jumped out of everyone's way, and had so far managed not to injure anyone. Randy had joked, 'Mate! I think you can win the game on your own!'

Even Sebastian seemed to have perked up with all the exercises. He no longer slept through class. Maya noticed that he even seemed to be listening in class. He raised his hand during lessons and asked questions. They were usually silly questions which would send the whole class into giggling fits, but Maya suspected that it was more of an act, to protect his carefully built up unsavoury reputation.

Another person who seemed to have noticed the change, was Ms. Cabot. She observed during one of her classes, after clearing a doubt for him. 'Sebastian, I'm pleased to see you are taking an interest in your studies. I see a change in you... for the better. Keep it up!'

Sebastian had replied, 'Ms. Cabot, you're such an incredible teacher that it makes me want to be a better student,' with a straight face. That had set the class laughing, but though she hadn't said anything, Ms. Cabot looked displeased.

A couple of days later, Ms. Cabot asked Cassie, Maya and Sebastian to stay back after class.

'What's going on with the three of you?' she asked. 'Cassandra and Sebastian, your work has improved remarkably. You are also training together, all of you, with Mr. Harris... or that's what I heard?'

'Yes, Ms. Cabot,' said Cassie, smiling. 'We train in the mornings and in the evenings and in the... ow,' she trailed off, as Maya stamped her foot. She glared at Maya.

'I'm sorry, Cassie. Did I hurt you? I slipped,' said Maya, smiling apologetically, while glaring at Cassie at the same time.

Ms. Cabot ignored the interruption. 'Go on, Cassandra,' she urged softly.

'Ms. Cabot, I think, maybe you should ask Mr. Harris about it. He would know more,' said Sebastian, smiling sweetly at her. 'We just do what he tells us to.'

'And what is that exactly?' asked Ms. Cabot. She was still looking at Cassie, who was getting flustered.

'A bit of jogging and some exercises… the usual,' said Sebastian, answering again.

'Yeah!' added Maya, also covering up for Cassie. 'It's a bit of a bore really, but he's promised us extra credits and it doesn't hurt to get some extra credits, does it?' she added, with a lame laugh.

Ms. Cabot looked like she would like to question them further, but Sebastian smoothly interrupted, 'Is that all Ms. Cabot? Because, we better hurry. We're already running late for practice and Mr. Harris doesn't like us to be late. He'd want to know why we were late.' He was practically pushing Cassie out ahead of him as he spoke. Ms. Cabot merely nodded and dismissed them with a wave of her hand.

As soon as they were down the corridor and out of Ms. Cabot's hearing, Sebastian and Maya rounded on Cassie. 'Cas! You cannot tell her,' said Maya, in a shocked voice.

'Cassandra Johnson, I don't care how infatuated you are with that woman, but not another word about us and what we're up to.' Maya was a little taken aback by the vehemence in Sebastian's voice. But Sebastian detested Ms. Cabot, and was annoyed at the little interrogation. 'This is none of her business. Nosy, prying woman! You make sure you're never caught alone with her again,' he warned Cassie.

Suitably chastened, Cassie nodded and the three hurried down to the field. They didn't tell Mr. Harris what had happened, as they didn't want to get Cassie into trouble. But, they told Sam and Ryan, who were equally mad at Cassie for blurting out what she did.

Later, as they made their way home, Sam teased Cassie, 'Seriously, Cas! What's going on with Ms. Cabot and you? I mean, just give me a heads up, will you? I'm your brother. I'd like to know.'

Cassie, who was already angry and embarrassed by the whole business, lashed out at Sam. 'Samuel! I'd shut my mouth if I were you. I don't even know why you hang around with us, or what Mr. Harris sees in you. You have nothing... you're a joke,' she said cruelly. She saw the hurt in his eyes, and wished instantly that she hadn't said that. Darn! Not a good day at all. She turned around and walked away. Sam didn't say anything. They walked in silence, the rest of the way home.

After that day, Cassie found that Sebastian was never far from her side if Ms. Cabot was around. Maya hung out with her friends most of the time in school, and often forgot to keep an eye out for Ms. Cabot. But apparently, Sebastian took his role of guardian angel pretty seriously. He made sure that Cassie never got caught alone with Ms. Cabot.

By the end of three months, Ryan had yet to crush a rock, and Cassie's pencil stayed obstinately still. But Maya had gained more control over blocking other people's thoughts without getting a headache, or wanting to throw up. She didn't need the pills Mr. Harris had given her, though she kept them with her at all times, just in case. She was even able to resist Mr. Harris's mind jabs, most of the time. She wasn't always successful with him, though. She could see he was pleased with her progress.

Sebastian had also improved a lot. He was able to catch most of the balls that Mr. Harris kicked at him. He wasn't consistent, but he was definitely much better than when he had started. The only problem was that he wasn't sure whether his progress had anything to do with his powers, or whether he'd simply become a better runner and catcher, through sheer practice.

All five children were becoming lean, muscular and strong, thanks to their intense training. They had started training at the end of July, and now it was almost October. They could now jog for miles without breaking a sweat, and went through their workout without any trouble. While they had all become more fit, the person who had changed the most was Sam. He was no more a short, scrawny kid. Over the three months, he'd shot up quite a bit, and had filled out considerably. He was still not as big as Sebastian, and nowhere near Ryan's size, but the change was most obvious in him.

His mom had gotten worried about the sudden and dramatic change in Sam's physique, and ignoring his dad's, 'He's just growing up. It's natural that he fills out and grows taller,' she had fixed an appointment with their doctor. The doctor, who had seen Sam from when he was a toddler, was delighted with the change in Sam. He told Mrs. Johnson that Sam must be going through a growth spurt and it was perfectly normal.

CHAPTER 18

The first snowfall of the year was in mid-November. In Skallen, winter set in by the end of October, or early November. It had started getting cold at the beginning of October, and because the five of them had been practicing in the cold, they were used to it by the time the snow started. Mr. Harris hadn't cut them any slack when it started getting cold. They'd still had to report at five, and had run or worked out in the early morning cold, bundled up in sweaters, removing layers as they went through their exercise routine, and it became warmer. When the snow started, and they couldn't practice outside anymore, he made them start practicing indoors. In the gym, on the basketball court, around the indoor swimming pool, whichever area happened to be free that day. The kids preferred this. Most of the indoor courts were centrally heated, and it was an improvement to running in the cold.

Ryan missed training sessions often when he went for out of town matches. The Holy Trinity football team was on a roll. They had won every match they'd played that season, mostly thanks to Ryan. Sheldon was back too, fit, healed and raring to go, and with Ryan and Sheldon in their current form, the team knew they had a very good chance of winning the Raiken Trophy, this season. The entire region competed for the Raiken Trophy, annually. It was a major event.

Holy Trinity hadn't won the Raiken Trophy in years, but they'd already been tipped as the team to watch out for, this year. With football practice and training taking up all his time, Ryan hardly had any time for Lisa. But surprisingly, she was very supportive about his tight schedule. Very often, he'd find her sitting in the stands with her friends after her cheerleading practice, waiting for him to finish training. He'd load his bike in the back of her car, and then she'd drive him to work, just to snatch a little time with him.

He was pleased with her support and understanding. For his part, he too tried to make time for her whenever he could. He'd drop in to see her if he was able to get off work early. He was glad that instead of fighting, they were trying to find a way to make their relationship work.

Mr. Harris, being the coach of Holy Trinity's football team, had to accompany them for their away games. Cassie, Maya, Sam and Sebastian, were thrilled whenever they heard there was going to be a match out of town. With Mr. Harris not around to keep a hawk eye on them, they could ease up on their training. Sebastian usually didn't bother turning up at all. The other three would do an excuse of a workout and leave as fast as they could. They hoped Holy Trinity kept up this winning streak.

The change in all five kids hadn't escaped attention. They kept answering questions from friends and family on why they were training this hard. They had discussed the matter with Mr. Harris, and had told him that "competition", and "marathon", were not cutting it anymore. He asked them to stick with the story for as long as they could, while he thought of some other excuse.

Lisa was curious like everyone else, about why Ryan and the other kids were training. When she had questioned Ryan, he had replied as vaguely as possible, but she wasn't having any of that. She had given him the third degree and asked pointed questions, trying to get more information out of him. She'd been particularly interested as to why the five of them were picked.

'What do you mean?' Ryan had asked. 'Mr. Harris picked us. I don't know why.'

She'd raised her eyebrows. 'Don't give me that, Ryan. How can you not know? I mean, I know why you were picked. But why was, why was that… for example, that girl Maya picked?'

'I don't know why… seriously. You'll have to ask Mr. Harris. He sent us these notes which said we were selected and to report for practice,' he replied.

Another day, she had quizzed him about their weekend training. She had landed up with her entourage, one Saturday morning, while they were practicing taekwondo. Mr. Harris had given them an earful and thrown them out of there. Ryan had tried to explain, but he could hear how vague his answers were and knew she wasn't satisfied. But luckily, she'd left it at that.

Before they knew it, December was upon them and it was time for exams. Mr. Harris had reduced their training and had given them one day off on the weekend, from the first week of December, to prepare for their exams. Sebastian, of course, used the time to catch up on his social life. There was a small crowd of rich kids he had met at the club. He had started hanging out with them. It was at one of their houses that he had met Anna, the girl he was currently dating. Her father was a shipping magnate, whose parents lived in Skallen. Anna went to a prep school, and she was visiting her grandparents in Skallen, when Sebastian had met her. She was funny and gorgeous and rather taken up with Sebastian. She now came down to Skallen every weekend, and the weekend dating suited Sebastian perfectly.

Cassie was studying like her life depended on it. She was a hard worker by nature, and she made full use of the extra time, studying. She was having some trouble with Physics. On Thursday, a week before her exams, she approached Ms. Cabot after class and told her that she needed help with it. Ms. Cabot asked Cassie to meet her after class.

The whole week had been blustery and windy, with heavy snowfall predicted over the weekend. On Wednesday, after practice, to their delight, Mr. Harris had told them to take Thursday, Friday and the entire weekend off, to study. So, when Ms. Cabot told Cassie to see her after school, Cassie agreed readily. After the last bell rang for the day, she hurried to the class Ms. Cabot had asked her to come to. Ms. Cabot was busy at her desk, correcting books, when Cassie reached the classroom.

Cassie said, 'Excuse me, Ms. Cabot,' timidly.

Ms. Cabot looked up and waved Cassie to a chair. Cassie sat down and took out her Physics book. She turned to the chapter she was having problems with and waited.

Ten minutes later, Ms. Cabot finished correcting the last book in the pile and got up. She came around the desk and sat down beside Cassie.

'Now, what is it you're having trouble with?' she asked. Cassie showed her the chapter, and Ms. Cabot explained it to her. After that, she gave Cassie, sums based on the principle and asked her to solve it. She went back to her desk to correct another pile of books. Now that she understood the principle, Cassie was able to solve them pretty fast. When she was done, she went up to Ms. Cabot's table and waited.

'Done?' Ms. Cabot asked, surprised. 'That was quick.'

'Once you explained, it was easy,' said Cassie, pleased by Ms. Cabot's reaction. Ms. Cabot went through the sums. They were all correct.

'Well done, Cassandra,' she said. 'I'm impressed with the progress you've made.' Cassie flushed with pleasure.

'You know what, Cassandra,' said Ms. Cabot, leaning over her table and pointing her pen at Cassie. 'You remind me of myself, when I was younger.' Cassie went pink. 'When I was your age, I wanted to be a physicist. I was going to discover things, create things… I was going to make a difference in the world. I had such big hopes and dreams. You seem interested in Physics, and you are a hard worker. I see ambition in you. You should seriously consider a career based on the subject. There are many options these days,' she said. Cassie wasn't particularly fond of Physics. The only thing she liked about Physics was Ms. Cabot.

'Why didn't you become a physicist, Ms. Cabot?' asked Cassie.

She couldn't believe Ms. Cabot was confiding in her. It was like they were almost best friends. Ms. Cabot sighed and got up. She towered over Cassie, who had to look up to see her. She came around her table and perched on the edge of it, swinging one long leg. She looked sadly at Cassie with her big, blue eyes.

'My Dad, Cassandra. He wasn't well. I couldn't leave him. I couldn't pursue my dream. I hope you get to realise yours,' she said, reaching out and patting Cassie's shoulder.

'What about your mother, Ms. Cabot?' asked Cassie.

Ms. Cabot made a face. 'My mother didn't care. Nothing my Dad did was ever good enough for her. Sometimes, I feel she was the reason my Dad became sick. She hated me and doted on my younger sister. When my Dad became sick, my mother packed up, took my sister and left. I've never seen them since. I was in my last year of college. As soon as I finished, I came back to look after my Dad. He didn't want me to.' Her eyes filled with tears at the memory. 'But, I couldn't leave him alone. I was all he had.'

Cassie wanted to reach out and comfort her. She wanted to tell her that she understood, and that she hated her mom too. She wanted to confide in Ms. Cabot, and let her know she wasn't the only one with those problems. But she felt too shy and scared.

'You have a brother, right Cassandra?' asked Ms. Cabot. She had removed a tissue from her bag and was dabbing her eyes with it.

Cassie nodded, glad to change the topic. 'Yes, Ms. Cabot, he's a year younger,' she said.

'Sam, if I'm not mistaken?' asked Ms. Cabot. Cassie nodded again. 'I think he takes one of my classes? You said he's younger. But, I think I'm taking Physics for him at a higher level,' she added.

Cassie scowled and said, 'Sam is kind of a child genius. My Mom thinks he's descended from heaven.'

Ms. Cabot nodded sympathetically, her hair swaying like a curtain as she moved her head. Cassie stared at it, mesmerized. 'It can be difficult, being a sibling to a special child. You probably think nothing you do will ever be good enough,' said Ms. Cabot. Cassie looked at her with wonder. Ms. Cabot seemed to understand exactly how she felt.

'Yes, Ms. Cabot. He's so good at everything it's annoying,' she said, with a grimace.

'You know, sometimes people like him have other special abilities too,' Ms. Cabot said, looking thoughtful. 'Is he gifted in any other way?' she asked.

Cassie hesitated. She wanted to tell Ms. Cabot that for all his brilliance, Sam didn't have any special powers, though she herself did. She wanted to share her secret with Ms. Cabot. Sebastian's face flashed through her mind, and all she said was, 'He draws very well. He has adactic... didactic... memory? I think it means...'

'Eidetic?' suggested Ms. Cabot.

'Yes. That's it. I guess it's a special ability,' she said

Ms. Cabot looked weirdly disappointed. 'Are you sure that's all he can do? He seems very... different,' she said.

Cassie wasn't very pleased with the direction the conversation was taking. She didn't like Ms. Cabot's interest in Sam.

'It always somehow becomes all about him,' she thought, irritated. 'Believe me, if he had any special abilities, he'll throw it in my face,' she said aloud, grumpily.

Ms. Cabot laughed, a lovely tinkling sound. She reached over and patted Cassie's cheek. 'Now, now, Ms. Grumpy. You just wait and watch. One day, you will grow up and be a famous scientist. And when you look back, none of this would matter. You're clever, you're smart, and you're pretty. No one, not even your Mom, can take that from you,' she said.

Cassie glowed with pleasure. Ms. Cabot thought she was pretty… and clever.

'Thanks, Ms. Cabot,' she breathed tremulously.

'Ok, now run along. You have a lot of studying to do. And I expect great marks in Physics,' she added with a smile.

'Yes, Ms. Cabot,' said Cassie, smiling back.

She picked up her bag and walked out, feeling on top of the world. Ms. Cabot thought Cassie was like her. Cassie was walking on air. She went over the conversation with Ms. Cabot, all the way home and right through dinner. It was her last thought before she slept that night. She decided to work even harder and score well, especially in Physics. She wanted to make Ms. Cabot proud of her.

Since Mr. Harris had given the weekend off, Cassie had spent the whole of Saturday, studying. It was past ten, when she decided to take a break and watch television for a while. She walked over to the den. Sam was sprawled on the couch, watching television. There was a pile of junk food on the table, and on the ground next to him. He looked up when she came in.

'Hey, Cas! Done studying?' he asked, yawning. He had the glazed look of someone who'd spent the entire day watching television

'Nope! Just taking a break!' she answered, going through the junk food and taking the chicken nuggets. She took the soda too, and curled up in an armchair.

'Sam! Check out what else is going on,' she asked.

'No! I'm watching this,' said Sam, eyes glued to the television again.

'Come on, Sam! You've been watching the whole day,' she whined.

'Fine,' relented Sam. 'But after this episode. I'm halfway through it.'

'I've got to go back to study by then. Tivo this, and we'll watch something else,' she suggested.

'Nope,' said Sam.

Cassie looked around for the remote control. It was on the table next to Sam. She slowly put her chicken and soda on the ground, next to the armchair, and made a lunge for it. Sam seemed to have been anticipating this. He snatched up the remote before her fingers closed around it, and swiftly moved it to his other hand, away from her.

Cassie sat back and glared at him. 'Give it to me!' she hissed furiously.

He twirled the remote in his hand, as he continued watching television. 'Nope,' he said again.

Cassie looked at the remote, twirling in Sam's hand and wondered if she could snatch it if she lunged fast enough. He looked like he was immersed in the show, but she knew him better. He'd move the remote before she was out of the chair. He was such a pain. He had watched television the whole day. This episode would be telecast again tomorrow. Twice! He could watch it then. She looked at the remote, twirling in Sam's hands. If she could just… maybe… it may not work, but there was no harm in trying. She concentrated on the remote.

For the past month, when she practiced with her pencil, there were many times when she felt that she was almost there, almost going to move it. It was like how you felt when you wanted to say something, and couldn't find the right word. You felt like you knew the word, it was at the tip of your tongue, but it just wouldn't come out. She'd been feeling that way about the pencil, like she knew how to make the pencil move, but was not able to translate the thought into action.

She reached out with her mind to the remote, and held out her hand. As she focused harder, she felt something shift in her mind. For a minute, it looked like the remote slipped out of Sam's hand as he moved it around. He made a grab for it as it slipped, but instead of falling, it whizzed across the room and into Cassie's outstretched hand. Sam and Cassie stared at the remote in Cassie's hand with disbelief, and then looked at each other. The television and their fight over it were forgotten.

Sam gave a yelp and jumped up. 'Cas! You did it! Oh my God! You did it! Did you see that? That was so bloody cool, Cas.' He was jumping up and down with excitement. Cassie just sat there with a dumbstruck look, staring at the remote resting in her hand.

'What the hell is going on? Who's shouting? Keep it down, will you?' Their dad's sleepy voice interrupted them. He was standing at the door, yawning. He looked at Sam jumping. 'Sammy! What's wrong with you? Do you want to wake up the whole street?'

'Sorry, Dad.' He threw himself on the bean bag next to Cassie, and reached over and took the remote from her. He waited for their dad to leave and whispered, 'Do it again!'

'I don't know if I can!' Cassie whispered back.

'I'm sure you can. Just do exactly what you did before. Come on,' he urged.

Cassie concentrated again on the remote and this time it was easy. It was like she knew which button to press. She reached out, lifted the remote off Sam's hand and let it hover in the air, above his hand. She was able to hold it for five seconds before it fell back into his hand.

'Again!' said Sam. 'Wait! Try moving this.' He picked up the soda bottle, which was half full and placed it on the table.

Cassie focused again, but she found she wasn't able to move the bottle. She tried harder and harder. Finally, the bottle gave a wobble, tipped over and fell off the table. Cassie started getting a headache, though Sam didn't want to stop. He picked up a wafer, placed it on the table and looked at Cassie expectantly.

Cassie shook her head. 'No, Sammy! I'm not strong enough yet. I'm getting a headache and I still have to study.' Sam looked disappointed, but he nodded.

'Can I tell them... please, can I tell them?' he asked eagerly.

Cassie smiled and nodded. 'Sure,' she said, as she got up to go, massaging her temples.

'Now?' he called out after her.

'Sure, if they're still awake,' she replied as went to her room. She shut the room door behind her. Her heart was racing, and she felt flushed with excitement. She hadn't wanted to show how excited she was to Sam. He didn't have any powers and to show off her power had felt like she was rubbing his nose in it. She wanted to try using her power again, but the promise of a headache was still hovering over her, and she didn't want to push it. She felt too excited to study. She prowled around her room, calming herself down. When she felt more composed, she sat down and opened her Physics book.

Maya was reading in bed, when her phone rang. It was late and she was sure it was Mary Anne or Felicity, with something they simply had to share right away. She rolled over and picked up her phone from the bedside table. She was surprised when she saw it was Sam calling. He sounded excited, but she couldn't understand a word he was saying.

'Sammy! Slow down! I can't... I don't understand what you're saying,' said Maya.

Sam spoke more slowly, 'Cassie moved the remote. It flew right out of my hand and into hers. She did it twice. Maya, it was so cool. You should have seen it.'

'Sam, are you sure it wasn't a fluke?' she asked.

'No... this was the real deal. She's figured it out. She was able to do it again and again. She started getting a headache, so she stopped. I guess she has to practice,' said Sam.

'That's great, Sam,' said Maya quietly.

Sam was puzzled. 'I thought you'd be more excited,' he said. There was silence. 'Maya? You there? Maya?'

'Yeah! I'm here, Sammy. I'm excited for Cassie, of course, she's been working so hard... it's not that,' she hesitated, and then said in a rush, 'the fact is, I'm also scared, Sam.'

Maya had wanted to confide in someone for a while now, but the last person she had thought she'd end up confiding in was Sam. But she couldn't hold her doubts and fears back any longer.

'Scared about what?' asked Sam.

'About what we're doing. We've completely put our faith in someone whom we know nothing about and we're following what he tells us, without any questions. We're lying to our friends and our family. I've never lied to my Mom in my life. And, we don't even know if Mr. Harris is leading us in the right direction. We've only got his word for it.'

'He's helping us, Maya,' said Sam. 'In fact, he's helped you the most. Without him, you'd still be hearing other people's thoughts. You hated that.'

'That's true,' agreed Maya, 'but...,' she paused, 'but Sammy, have you realised he's training us to be soldiers... he's teaching us to fight, with our minds and bodies.'

'Maya, he's doing that to help you defend yourself. Helping you block out voices? How is that teaching you to fight?' asked Sam.

'We passed that stage long back, Sammy. For the past month, he's been teaching me to read minds, consciously. You know how random my power used to be. I'd pick up stray thoughts from anyone around me. Now, I can block that and if I direct my mind towards someone consciously, I can hear what they're thinking,' she said.

'Wow! I didn't know this. Why didn't you tell us?' he asked, accusingly.

'Mr. Harris told me not to, and this is another reason I feel uncomfortable. We're a team and we share everything. Now, he has me lying to you. Okay, maybe not lying, but holding back things from you. And you know what, I don't know if it's okay… I mean, he gives us instructions and we just follow it. We don't question him. I'm wondering whether that's a good thing.'

'I think we should talk to the others about this,' said Sam. A thought struck him. 'Can you hear our thoughts?' he asked suspiciously. There was no answer. 'Maya? Have you tried reading our thoughts?'

'Once.' He could hear the discomfort in her voice. 'Mr. Harris asked me to try. I didn't want to… but,' she paused.

'Listen, I'm not judging you. He orders… we obey,' he said quietly. 'But tell me the truth.'

'Sammy, it was only that once. I couldn't read Ryan or Cas at all. I could hear some of Sebastian's thoughts, but I had to try very hard. But I'm able to hear your thoughts without trying much at all. I felt so miserable after, and I told Mr. Harris that I didn't ever want to try to read your thoughts again. He told me that I was stupid. That it was a gift, I should work to strengthen. But I've refused to try again… so far. I'm sorry,' she added.

'Hey!' said Sam softly. 'It's not your fault. We're all floundering, trying to figure this out. I only hope I wasn't thinking of anything weird. Look, I'm not sure why Mr. Harris asked you to do that, but I'm sure it was for the right reasons. I trust him,' said Sam.

'Then, why is he now training me to attack with my mind, Sammy?' asked Maya. 'Why would I need to attack anyone? In any way?'

'Attack with your mind? What do you mean?' asked Sam.

'He would jab my mind with his. He's done it to you. You know how painful it is. I've learnt to block his jabs. Now, he's making me practice jabbing his mind, with mine. He's strong, but I think I punch through, now and then. He sometimes winces when I jab these days,' she said.

'Wow! You're up to some pretty weird stuff, huh?' said Sam chortling. 'Hey! Can you read his thoughts?'

'Once.' Maya laughed. 'I don't think he expected it. He was thinking of mountains, and a big lake and a field with people fighting. I don't know whether it was a real place, or some fantasy. It was just for a moment before he blocked it. I thought he'd be angry, but he merely smiled, and said, 'Clever girl! But don't do it again. You could get hurt.' I don't know what he meant by that, but I haven't tried it again. I can see glimpses though when I jab, different things, but it's hazy and I can't make much sense of it.' They were both quiet.

'Maya,' Sam started. There was something which was eating at him, and he'd wanted to get it off his chest. 'What am I even doing here? I do sums during every class with him. I see him looking at me sometimes, and he looks... disappointed. Darn it... I'm disappointed. It's almost six months. I got nothing.'

'Sammy, there was a reason you were there that day, when we had detention. It wasn't a coincidence. Hell, you were the one who figured out something was going on, before anyone else did. And when we went to that place, Tibet or wherever, and met those people, who was it that Iola asked for? You! She didn't even look at us. You will discover your power.

I fully believe that and the other thing I'm sure of is that you will be incredible,' she said, smiling. Sam smiled too. She'd made him feel better.

'You think?' he asked hopefully.

'I know,' she replied.

CHAPTER 19

They had training only for an hour on Monday, after the exams. By then, the others knew what Cassie could do, and there was much excitement. Mr. Harris seemed quite pleased too. They had another couple of weeks of school, before their Christmas break. Cassie and Sam were going to Trinidad and Tobago. Mr. Harris had told them he'd be away for a while too. He asked them to practice on their own whenever they could, till school started.

The five of them were excited about their upcoming vacation. Maya and Sam forgot all about wanting to talk to the others about why Mr. Harris was teaching them to fight. This was their first real break in six months, and they were looking forward to it. Except Cassie, who promised herself that she would practice every day for at least a couple of hours, none of the others had any intention of doing any training. They couldn't wait for school to get over and their vacation to begin.

Sebastian's girlfriend, Anna, was coming down to spend Christmas break with her grandparents in Skallen. There were quite a few parties during the Christmas and New Year season, and Sebastian had invites to most of them. Lisa was thrilled Ryan was all hers for the entire Christmas break. Felicity and Mary Anne were going away for the weekend, right after their exams, but would be back soon. They and Maya enthusiastically made plans on what to do, once the girls returned. Everyone knew that once school started, they would be back to their crazy schedule, and wanted to make the most of their Christmas break.

Sam and Cassie had left to Tobago, the day after school closed. They'd been at the resort for a couple of days now. This morning, Sam was sitting by the poolside, staring morosely at the swimming pool. It was a still day, with an occasional puff of wind. He was lying on a deck chair, under the shade of a large beach umbrella. His vacation sucked. Big time!

He couldn't believe it was only two days since they'd left Skallen. It seemed like years. The fighting had started at the airport, with his mom getting mad at his dad. His dad had gotten a business call just before they left for the airport, and had insisted on taking it. Consequently, they had gotten late and missed their flight. They'd had to book themselves on the next flight, which was almost six hours later. As the airport was quite a distance from their house, it had seemed pointless to go back home. They had waited for six long hours at the airport, for the next flight. His dad had spent most of the time on the phone, much to his mom's annoyance.

When they had finally reached the resort, things hadn't improved. The cottage they had booked had been cancelled since no one had called to confirm. That was their mom's fault. She was supposed to have called to confirm, and she had forgotten. His dad was upset, mostly because he'd had to sit sweating in the open lobby and do his work there. They visited the resort every year during Christmas, and the staff knew them well. It was thanks to sheer goodwill that they'd managed to get a suite by evening. The front desk had promised to try and get a cottage for them, as soon as possible. It had been rather late by the time they'd settled in their room. Since they were sharing, it was a tight squeeze, and everyone had gone to bed in a bad mood.

The resort had managed to get a cottage for them, by the next afternoon. By then, the suite they'd been occupying was a complete mess. Sam and his dad could make a mess of a room in minutes, and half a day had been more than enough time for utter chaos. His mom had gone to the spa in the morning, after breakfast, and when she came back, the room had looked like it had been ripped apart by a tornado. She'd been so mad because they'd had to repack their things before they could send their luggage to the cottage. They'd all stayed out of each other's way, once they'd reached the cottage.

Sam had hoped things would cool down after that, but it had only become worse. His parents hadn't stopped fighting. Her mom had started being nasty to Cassie, as a result. And as usual, Cassie had started in on Sam. Cassie had gotten so mad, she'd started using her powers unashamedly around Sam, causing things to drop on him, fall from his hands and being a total jerk. He seemed to be spending all his time cleaning up. It had happened so often that his mom had finally yelled at him, when the bowl he was eating breakfast from, tipped over, and his cereal had fallen on the carpet. She never yelled at him.

He'd quietly slipped away after breakfast and mucked about the resort for a while, finally ending up at the swimming pool. He'd been sitting here since. He had his iPod and was listening to music. Though it was a tranquil day with a clear blue sky, he could feel a storm brewing. He could sense the static in the air and his hair was standing on end. He looked around at the sky, but as far as he could see, it was cloudless. There were no rainclouds, or even white, puffy ones for that matter.

Sun and Surf, the resort they were staying in, was on the island of Tobago. It lay sprawled over miles of sun-kissed beach. There was a clubhouse, which had two restaurants and a coffee shop. It also had a movie room, entertainment area for kids, video arcade and a giant swimming pool with water slides, close to the clubhouse. Most of the families tended to congregate there, during the day. Each suite of cottages had its own smaller pool, around which the cottages stood. The swimming pool near the cottages was usually empty during the day. That was why Sam had decided to come here. He wanted to be left alone.

He groaned inwardly as he caught sight of Cassie walking up the path to the swimming pool, carrying a book and a beach towel. He lay back and closed his eyes, hoping she'd go away. She ignored him and chose a deck chair on the opposite end of the pool. She spread her towel on the chair and lay down. He peeked at her through half closed eyes, wondering what new hell she was planning. He fully expected the umbrella to fold in on him, or have some object flying at him. She didn't seem to be planning to swim, and she wasn't reading either.

The book was lying face down on her stomach, and she was staring fixedly at the pool. He glanced down at the pool. There was a beach ball floating in it and she was making it spin around the pool. He looked around to make sure they were alone. She was being stupid and careless, moving the ball in the open. She seemed to be doing things like this all the time now, making things move. Often, she didn't seem to be aware of it. He'd noticed she was doing it more often after they had left Skallen, especially since the fighting had started.

He remembered how excited he'd been when she'd first moved the remote. Now, he hated her ability to make things move as she seemed to be using it mostly to annoy him or get him into trouble. He looked away from the spinning ball. He wished there was something he could do, to get back at her. His skin prickled and he felt a light breeze ruffle his hair.

'Here comes the storm,' he thought, 'at least, Cassie will get wet.' He looked up, but the sky was still clear.

He felt another puff of wind. It moved the dust and dry leaves on the ground. He could feel the wind around him, surrounding him. He lifted his head up, to feel the breeze on his face and looked up at the trees. The leaves on the trees were perfectly still, though he could feel the breeze. He looked down at the dry leaves on the ground, and as he looked, they gradually moved again, flying up into the air, before settling gently back on the ground again.

He sat up. Was he doing this? There was so much static… and… and power in the air. His mind seemed to be filled with limitless energy. He felt like it was bursting out of him. He could still feel the storm, and it felt like it was in him. He blanked his mind and focused on the energy. It felt tangible; as if it had mass… he felt like he was holding it with his mind. It filled him, his mind and his body.

He sent the energy he could feel in his mind towards the leaves on the ground and gently nudged them. They flew up into the air, swirling crazily like a small twister. He found that with a nudge, he could move it about. Fascinated, he moved it over the water. The pressure from his little twister caused the water to spin too, and there was a slight depression over the spot that it was spinning over. He lifted the revolving mass high into the air, and then brought it down onto the surface of the water, on the side of the pool he was sitting on.

The level of the water in the pool went down on his side and rippled out. By the time it reached the other side of the pool, it was a fully formed wave which went roiling out over the other side, crashing over Cassie, who was sitting up now, watching in disbelief. Once he'd started, he didn't seem to be able to stop. All his anger and rage came pouring out. He hit the water over and over, causing wave after wave to crash over Cassie. She jumped up with a scream and ran, slipping and falling. She picked herself up swiftly, raced around the pool and onto the path that led back to their cottage.

Sam let his breath out in a whoosh, and looked around. He was standing at the edge of the pool, his hands clenched; his body tense and he still felt so angry. He could feel the storm so clearly in his head, the thunder and lightning and the pure energy which made up the storm. He reached out into the storm… he could feel the power… he could hold it in his mind. He hurled it towards where Cassie was racing away. There was a crack and a bolt of lightning hit a tree on the path Cassie was running on, missing her by inches. Cassie shrieked and ran even faster, disappearing from view.

Sam staggered back and sat down heavily on the deck chair, breathing hard, trying to calm himself. What was wrong with him? He had almost killed Cassie. If the lightning had hit her, she would have died. He had come that close to killing his own sister. What kind of a monster was he? No amount of anger excused what he had done. He got up to go after Cassie, to apologize, but he hesitated, wondering what he would even say? Her frightened face as she ran filled his mind. He couldn't sit anymore. He was livid at himself now for losing control. He got up and loped towards the beach. He needed to be alone for a while. He was running along the beach when the skies started darkening.

He found a quiet spot on the beach and sat down, looking towards the sea and the fast approaching thunder clouds, thoughts spinning in his mind. Was this it? Was this his power? He still wasn't sure how he had done what he did. He had to try again. He slowed his breathing, calming himself like how Mr. Harris had taught them, and concentrated. He could feel all the elements which made up the storm, the wind, the water, the energy. He tugged at the energy and held it again. He opened his eyes and looked at the waves crashing in front of him.

He got up and walked towards the water. He thrust the power he could feel in his mind, towards the waves, to push them. The waves seemed to hit a barrier and crashed, much before they hit the shore. He moved forward into the sea. The waves which should have crashed on him fell away, and crashed around him. He walked in deeper, where the land started sloping down into the sea. It was like he was in a bubble. The waves crashed angrily around him, but not a drop of water touched him. He was fascinated. He could control the water... and wind.

He remembered the day when he'd been lying on the hillock behind his house. He had imagined a wolf in his head while watching the clouds. That cloud had looked exactly like the wolf he had imagined. Maybe he had manipulated the cloud that day. He just hadn't realised it. He walked farther and farther into the sea, looking around in wonder, at the waves towering around him.

He felt a wave of exhaustion wash over him and he felt his hold, his attention, slipping away. He panicked and lost his concentration completely. The sea crashed around him and he went under. He kicked his legs and came up gasping. The storm hit as he went under again. He swallowed water, choking, panicking. He kicked and came up again, taking in big gulps of air as he broke through the surface of the water. The rain was coming down in sheets and the waves crashed around him. He couldn't see, he had no idea which side the shore was.

He held his breath, closed his eyes and calmed himself down. He stopped fighting the waves and let himself get tossed around. Some semblance of sanity returned. He took short, quick breaths, keeping his mouth open as little as possible, to prevent any water going in. He'd been so focused on the storm, and in pushing the water away, that he had no idea how far into the sea he had walked. He felt something hit him hard on the shoulder. He felt himself panicking again as he kicked and twisted around, to face the new threat.

It was a surfboard. He looked around trying to find the surfer, but he couldn't see anything through the rain. He twisted around again, looking for the surfboard now. It was being pulled away by the waves. His energy was running out, and he knew that the surfboard may be his only chance of survival. He struck out after it, but each time he neared the board, another wave pushed it away. He had almost given up hope, and had just decided to roll over onto his back and float for as long as he could, when he felt a sudden change in the current and on his next lunge, he landed on the surfboard.

He started slipping off it as soon as he landed, and he threw his arms and legs around the board quickly to hold on. Luckily, he had landed on the narrow end and so his arms went almost all the way around it, but he knew if he didn't get to the middle soon, he would tip over. Inch by inch, painfully, he worked his way down, till he could feel the board balancing itself on the waves. With his weight, the board had stopped flipping over, but he was still getting tossed about. He tightened his hold around the board, and clung on.

Cassie sat curled up on the window seat, in the room she and Sam were sharing. She had drawn the inner curtains so her parents wouldn't be able to see her if they looked in. She was still in her swimsuit, her beach towel wrapped around her. Shivering, she sat staring out the window. She could still feel the tingle of the electricity from the lightning. What the hell had happened out there? Did Sam do that? Could anybody do that? She could still picture him standing at the edge of the pool, his hands clenched; his face intense with concentration, as wave after wave of water had lifted off the pool and splashed over her. Her eyes filled with tears.

And the lightning? Another couple of inches and she could have died. She knew she wasn't the easiest person to live with, but killing her?

'Well,' she thought bitterly, 'I deserved it, didn't I?' Tears ran down her face, as she remembered how mean she'd been to Sam the last couple of days. Her mom being nasty to her wasn't his fault, but had that stopped her? No, it hadn't, she had viciously taken out her frustration at Sammy. She'd finally done it, hadn't she, pushed him to his limit. She had gone to the swimming pool to annoy him again because she'd been mad with her mom.

She'd been watching television after breakfast, when her mom had returned from her massage. Her dad was holed up in his room, working from morning. Five minutes after her mom walked in, she'd heard the fighting begin. She'd quietly switched off the television, and was trying to slip away to her room and hide, when her mom had come out of her parents' bedroom.

'Where do you think you're going? This is a great family vacation. You sit in your room, and your Dad sits in his. We could all have stayed put in Skallen; I could have worked overtime and earned my bonus. If I had known I wouldn't be spending the Christmas break with my family, I would have just gone to work. Do you know how difficult it is to keep a job these days? They judge you, if you take time off from work. There are a hundred other people, most of them much younger than you, waiting to fill your shoes. You have to constantly prove to them that you are a hard worker. And taking off for Christmas, doesn't exactly say hard worker. My job isn't like your Dad's. He can afford to sit at home or on vacation and still clock in his hours, from the comfort of his room. I have to be there, on my feet, all day long. Where are you going when I'm talking to you? Excuse me, don't you dare walk away from me.'

Cassie had heard enough, and she had turned and started walking away. Her mom had gone ballistic. 'How dare you walk away when I'm talking to you? Is this the respect I get around here? This is your fault. You give her too much importance. She thinks she can do anything she wants.' Her mom's voice had faded as she'd gone back into her room, to continue ranting at her husband. Cassie had felt bad for her dad. She hoped he hadn't been on a conference call. She'd run up to her room, pulled on her swimsuit, grabbed a towel and her book and had quietly slipped out of the cottage before her mom came out again.

She'd walked around aimlessly for a while. She'd gone down to the beach and teased a child, moving her giant beach ball away from her, each time she got near it. She'd been so mad she hadn't even been aware that she was doing it. She'd been thinking about her mom's tirade.

'So much anger…? At what? Did she want to work or not? Did she even know what she wanted? No one is making you work,' Cassie had wanted to scream at her, 'especially not Dad.'

It had seemed like a good idea to find Sam and bother him. Cassie had made her way towards their pool, to check if he was there and he was. She'd decided to throw the beach ball at him even before she sat down. It was dancing around in the water, waiting to be chucked. She'd been spinning the ball in the pool, as a prelude to chucking it at him, when the first wave had hit her. She hadn't understood what was happening. She remembered being terrified as she'd run around the pool, slipping and falling, picking herself up and running again. When she had looked around in terror, she'd seen Sam standing at the edge of the pool. And then had come the lightning. The electricity had surged through her. She started trembling again, as she remembered how scary it had been. She'd run back to the cottage and up to her room, and had been sitting here ever since.

'Aaaah!' she shrieked, as the sky was split by a bolt of lightning. It was followed a minute later, by a massive rumble of thunder. She peered out at the darkening day. She could see thunderclouds moving in from the sea, bringing sheets of rain. She was used to the tropical thunderstorms, after years of holidaying in the islands. She remembered happier times, when they were younger, and her mom and dad would come out and play in the rain with them. The storms here were spectacular, especially watching them from the beach. They weren't allowed to go out during a storm because getting hit by lightning was a possibility. The storms were also fierce and could uproot trees and roofs, and there were chances of getting hurt by flying debris. But Sam and Cassie had sneaked out many a time and had watched the storm, huddled under a tarpaulin on the beach.

It suddenly struck her. 'Sam didn't do it, at least not the lightning... there was a storm brewing. That's where the lightning must have come from.'

It seemed more plausible, the more she thought about it. It was definitely a better explanation, than Sam causing lightning. She could see people hurrying back to their cottages from her window. These storms passed soon, and she knew the skies would be clear again in no time. She bit her lip, thinking about Sam... she hoped he was okay. Their bedroom faced away from the pool and she didn't know if he was still there. She didn't want to step out of the room, in case her mom caught her. In her current mood, her mom would probably blame the storm on her.

Sam would be okay. He was old enough. He'd be able to take care of himself. She wondered how he had made those waves. He must have got a wave maker, she decided, and must have been waiting for her to show up. She wondered where he'd got the wave maker from. Probably from one of the pool boys. He got along famously with all of them, and Sam could be very persuasive. He was going to get into so much trouble if anyone found out. She yawned, and winced as there was another huge rumble of thunder. She felt better, now that she had an explanation for the lightning, though it was still scary when she realised how close she had come to getting killed. Her stomach rumbled. She was quite hungry. Breakfast seemed like it had been ages ago.

She had to leave the room at some point. She knew she wasn't going to get away with having walked away from her mom. Her mom would now bring it up, every time she yelled till she got a new bone to pick on.

Thinking about that was enough to drown her hunger. Maybe, if she waited a little longer, Sammy would be home. Then, she could get some food while her mom fussed over him.

CHAPTER 20

Maya was at the mall with Felicity and Mary Anne. Her two friends were back from their respective weekend trips, and the trio had decided to hit the mall, do some shopping, have lunch and maybe take in a movie. They had spent an entertaining couple of hours, browsing through the shops, looking for beach wear for Felicity, who was going away on a cruise in a couple of weeks. Maya had bought a pretty sweater for her mom for Christmas. She had decided to come later with her mom to pick up Christmas gifts for her friends. Mary Anne had taken a fancy to a pair of earrings and Felicity had liked a stole, and now Maya knew what to get them.

After shopping, they went to have lunch. They ordered pizza and while they waited, Mary Anne told them about her scuba diving experience during her trip, and how gorgeous the instructor was.

All of a sudden, Maya felt Sam in her head. She hadn't been thinking of him, but she could somehow sense him. She felt uneasy. Why had Sam popped into her head now? She frowned. As far as she knew, Sam was still in Tobago. Maybe they'd come back early. She blanked her mind to her friend's chatter and thought of Sam. For an instant, she had a vivid image of surging waves around her and pelting rain, and a sudden certainty that Sam was in trouble.

'Maya! Hey, Maya!' She opened her eyes and found her friends staring at her curiously. She stared blankly back at them. 'Hey! You okay? You kinda zoned out just now.'

'Excuse me,' Maya looked up, alarmed. It was only their waiter, with the pizza.

Maya lurched to her feet unsteadily and staggered back a few steps, tipping her chair over. It fell with a crash, and a few heads turned towards them. She took a couple of unsteady steps, swaying. She could hear her friend's voices. They sounded far away.

'Maya, what's wrong? Maya?' She staggered back again, as she felt waves buffeting her, and she caught the edge of the table to keep her balance.

She closed her eyes and shook her head, trying to clear it, and a few seconds later the swaying stopped. Now, she felt like she was being shaken like a leaf. She opened her eyes.

Her worried friends were shaking her. 'Maya! Darn it, Maya!'

She put her hands up and fended them off. 'I'm okay… I'm okay.'

Felicity straightened Maya's chair, and Maya sat down heavily. She felt a mounting sense of urgency. She had to speak to one of the other four. She got up from her chair. Her friends looked up at her, puzzled.

'Where are you going?' asked Felicity, frowning.

'Guys! Give me a minute… I'll be right back. Don't be hogs and eat up all the pizza,' she said, in what she hoped was a light-hearted voice. 'Save a piece for me,' she added, smiling, trying to act normal. She turned around and started walking away.

'Maya… are you sure you're okay? Do you want me to come with you?' Mary Anne called out.

'Yeah, yeah, I'm fine… I'll be back in a jiffy. I'll just splash some water on my face,' she said. She hurried through the crowd towards the elevator and rode down to the ground floor. She had no idea where she was going, but her feet seemed to be taking her somewhere. The mall had a central atrium, with arms stretching out on all sides, filled with shops. She walked to the centre of the atrium and stopped. She twirled around on the tips of her toes, looking around her.

'Maya!' She heard a familiar voice, shouting her name. She looked up at the second floor and saw Ryan peering over the rails. She felt a surge of relief when she saw his face, and she waved to him to come down. He turned and said something to Lisa, who had appeared beside him and was also looking down at Maya. She seemed to be protesting, but Ryan said something to her and left. Lisa looked down furiously at Maya, who turned away, feeling uncomfortable.

She was relieved to see Ryan. She knew something was wrong. She could feel it. Maybe she was being stupid, but she'd feel better once she'd told Ryan. She was sure he'd know what to do. She was looking around to see if she could spot Ryan, when to her surprise, she saw Sebastian coming out of a showroom on the ground floor. He seemed to be looking for someone. He spotted her and waved. He turned back and called out to someone in the showroom, before walking over to her. By then, Ryan was down and was making his way towards them. He too seemed surprised to see Sebastian.

'What's wrong?' asked Sebastian. Maya was surprised. She wondered how he knew something was wrong.

'It's Sam,' she said. 'I have this weird feeling that Sam's in trouble.'

'Did you call him?' asked Sebastian, frowning.

'No, I'll try now,' said Maya, flipping open her phone. She tried Sam's number several times.

'If you can't get through to him, try Cassie,' suggested Ryan. Maya tried Cassie's number, praying that Cassie had her phone with her.

Meanwhile, Sam was still struggling to stay on the surfboard. He was exhausted. The storm had passed, but he was too far from shore. He had tried to paddle, but the waves were still unruly, and he wasn't making any headway. His arms were too tired to paddle anymore. He could see the beach, and it was empty. No one would spot him if he lay down on the board. He sat up, balancing himself carefully. He knew if he slipped off, he would not have the strength to pull himself onto the board again. He hoped people would start coming back to the beach, and somebody would spot him before it became too dark.

As he waited, he could sense that he was drifting further away from the shore. He was also getting worn out, trying to keep his balance. He realised after a while that no one would be able to see him, even if they looked out to sea. He was too far away. As he drifted farther away from the beach, the waves became choppier, and he had to lie down again, so he wouldn't get thrown off, or overturned. It felt like hours had passed, and it was getting darker. He didn't know how long he'd be able to hold on. He knew if he didn't get spotted soon, he wasn't going to make it.

As he lay on the board, he thought to himself for the hundredth time about what a stupid thing he had done, to have walked into the sea like he did. Who did he think he was? Moses? Maybe that's all Moses had been. A normal human being with special abilities. He had manipulated water like Sam had done. Though he hadn't stupidly drowned in it, like Sam was sure he was going to. Moses had visions, had spoken to God.

'Maybe Moses was also a telepath,' mused Sam. 'God, if you can hear me, I sure could use some help here,' he whispered wearily.

As he said it aloud, he had a thought. He wasn't a telepath. But he knew one. It was a long shot, but he had nothing to lose. Earlier, as soon as the storm had passed, he'd tried to manipulate the water again, but nothing had happened. He'd been too tired to focus. Now, he clung to the board and closed his eyes. He shut down his thoughts, gradually, like he'd been trained and concentrated. He thought of Sebastian, Ryan, Cassie and Maya… especially Maya, and sent out a fierce plea.

'Help me!'

He concentrated harder and harder, sending out his cry for help repeatedly, like an S.O.S. He sat up in a bit and looked hopefully towards the beach. Maybe, Cassie had heard him. To his dismay, he couldn't see the beach anymore. He groaned and lay down again, his limbs starting to shake with the effort of clinging on to the board.

Cassie sat up bolt upright. She had dozed off at the window and had dreamt that Sam had shouted for help. It had felt so real that she was worried. She decided to go check on him. She pulled open the curtains, jumped off the window seat and went out. No one was there in the hall, and she slipped out of the door which led to the swimming pool. It had stopped raining and everything smelt clean and new. She peered over the hedge which ran around the pool. The poolside was empty. She turned and ran down the path to the beach. He wasn't there either. She checked the entertainment areas and the video arcade in the clubhouse, and some of the other places he may have gone to, but he wasn't in any of them. She asked some of the bell boys and waiters, but no one had seen him. She was getting more concerned, the longer she searched.

It wasn't like he would get lost, but she couldn't shake off the feeling that he wasn't okay. As she walked back to the cottage to check if he'd returned, she thought of Maya, Sebastian and Ryan. She should call them sometime. Maybe she'd call them now. She hurried, feeling an increasing sense of urgency. By the time she reached the cottage, she was running. She raced in and up to her room. She heard her phone ringing as she entered her room.

'She's not picking up,' said Maya, trying Cassie's number, over and over.

'What's going on?' asked Sebastian. 'There I was, in the showroom, looking at some watches and all of a sudden I felt Sam, and then I had you in my head. I walked out and saw you. Why were you in my head?' he asked suspiciously.

'I thought of Sam too, and then, I felt you. I looked over the rail and there you were,' said Ryan. 'Did you send a message? You know… here?' He touched his head.

'No guys, I wasn't in your head. I just had this bad feeling that Sam's in trouble and I thought of you both, and you turned up. Darn it, why isn't she picking up?' she cursed, trying again.

'How did you know we were here?' asked Sebastian, curiously.

'I didn't… Cassie, pick up the phone. Where is she? Maybe she'll pick up your calls. Try her,' said Maya.

The panic in her voice got to them. They took out their phones and tried Cassie, but it kept going to voice mail.

'What do we do… I don't know what to do. I'm trying once more, and then I'm calling Mr. Harris,' said Maya.

Her call was picked up on the second ring and Cassie's breathless voice said, 'Maya? Hey!'

'Cassie! Where's Sam?' asked Maya.

'Why?' said Cassie. Her sense of foreboding increased.

'Cassie, is he with you?' asked Maya.

'No, I don't know where he is. I've been looking for him for an hour, and I haven't been able to find him,' Cassie said, starting to panic.

'Cas! Are you near the sea?' asked Maya, thinking of the waves.

'Yes… we're in Tobago, at a beach resort,' replied Cassie.

'Listen. This may sound crazy, but do you have binoculars?' asked Maya.

'Y… es,' said Cassie, feeling confused.

'Take it, go down to the beach and look out to sea,' said Maya. 'Use the binoculars. Go now! As fast as you can. And take the phone with you.'

Cassie grabbed the binoculars as she raced out, and ran all the way to the beach. The vacationing families were back on the beach, now that the storm had passed. She searched among them but couldn't see Sam. She raised the binoculars to her eyes and looked out to sea. There were a few boats which were venturing out again. She swept the binoculars from one side to the other, adjusting the lens, trying to make it clear. She pulled the phone out of her pocket and called Maya.

'Maya, there's nothing to see. I don't know what I'm looking for. This is crazy,' she said.

'Cas! Cas! Listen! You can't give up. Look again,' Maya said, urgently.

Maya was trying hard to stay calm, but her heart was thumping with fear, and she was trembling. Ryan put his arm around her and she rested her head on his chest, biting her lip to stop herself from crying. She didn't know why she was so sure that Sam was in some kind of trouble, but she was certain he was.

Cassie sighed and picked up the binoculars again. This was so frustrating… Maya was mad. She swept the sea again. Nothing unusual. There was an empty lifeguard tower to her left. She walked over and climbed up on it. She sat down and looked through the binoculars again. There were the boats, chugging away. She moved her head around, straining to see as far as she could. There was the buoy. She and Sam used to swim around the buoy and come back to shore… when their mom wasn't around. Her mother would have had a cow, if she had known that Sam was swimming that far out.

There was another buoy, further out. It was new. She adjusted the binoculars again and gasped as she centred on it. The phone slipped out of her suddenly nerveless hands and fell down onto the sand. She jumped off the tower, picked up the phone and called Maya, as she raced towards the clubhouse.

'Maya! He's there... I can see him. He's way out in the water. But I'm sure it's him. I'm getting help. I'll call you back,' she said and hung up. She ran into the reception area and was relieved to find a manager she knew, on duty.

'Kenny! Kenny! Sam's out in the water... way out. You have to send a boat,' she cried urgently.

'What?' said Kenny, looking perplexed.

'It's Sam. He's out there... in the water... in the middle of the sea.'

Cassie wished he'd stop opening and closing his mouth like a goldfish, and do something.

'I don't understand? What do you mean?' Kenny didn't look like he was processing what she was saying. She ran around the reception desk and grabbed his arm, shaking it, talking slowly.

'Send a boat out! Call the lifeguards! It's Sam. He must have got caught in the storm.'

Kenny finally seemed to comprehend what she was saying, and he jumped into action. He grabbed the phone, called the pier and told them what had happened. He asked Cassie to explain to them, where exactly she had seen Sam. When they hung up, Cassie turned and ran back to the beach and climbed up the lifeguard tower, to see if Sam was still there. She felt relieved when she saw that he was.

She pressed the binoculars onto her eyes, trying not to lose sight of the tiny green dot in the distance. Ten minutes later, a lifeguard boat raced towards the dot. She couldn't see clearly, but guessed they must have pulled him on board, because the boat turned around. As it sped back, she jumped down and ran towards the pier. They were bringing Sam out on a stretcher

She ran over. 'Sammy! Sammy!' she called out, running towards him. One of the lifeguards gently pulled her away.

'Hey! Easy! He's okay!' She was weeping now, as she saw Sam. His face was pale, his eyes shut and his lips were blue.

'Let me go! Let me go! That's my brother.' She kicked back and connected with the lifeguard's shin and he let her go with a yelp. She was beside Sam in a second, patting his cheek. 'Sammy! Sammy!' His eyelids flickered open. He tried to say something, but no sound came.

'It's ok! It's ok! You're ok! Thank God! You're ok!' She was so relieved.

The lifeguard, whom she had kicked, came and pulled her away, more firmly this time. 'Where are your parents?' he asked.

'What?' said Cassie. She wanted to call Maya.

'Your parents,' he repeated, giving her a gentle shake. 'Call them,' and when she still didn't respond, he looked around and saw Kenny.

'Call the parents,' he shouted out. Kenny nodded and pulled out his phone to call Cassie's parents. Cassie stood there watching, till they loaded the stretcher into the ambulance and it left.

She called Maya. 'He's fine. They're taking him to the hospital, but he's fine.' She was sobbing now. Kenny came over and put his arm around and held her as she sobbed into the phone.

'Oh! Thank God, he's ok! He's ok!' Maya felt her knees buckling. Ryan put his arm around her, to steady her.

'He's fine! I'm ok!' She stepped back and looked up at the boys, who were looking thoroughly confused.

'Er… what's going on?' asked Sebastian

'Sam,' said Maya

'Yes! I got that,' said Sebastian, sounding exasperated. 'Where is he? What happened to him? What was all that about the binoculars?'

'Listen… I've got to get back to my friends. I'll call later and explain. I have to get back,' said Maya. She took a couple of unsteady steps. The boys looked at her and then at each other.

'Man! You gotta take her home. I'd take her, but Lisa will kill me if I don't go back. Will you take care of her?' asked Ryan

Sebastian looked put out. He glanced back at the showroom he'd been in. 'I'm here with someone too. I can't simply dump her and go.' He looked back at Maya's pale face and sighed. 'Fine… I'll take her. Give me a few minutes. I'll go fetch Anna.'

Mary Anne and Felicity rushed up, just then. 'Maya, where did you disappear? We've been searching for you everywhere. Are you ok?'

'I'm fine, guys. I'm ok. Ryan, Seb, the girls will take me home.' She saw the relief on Sebastian's face and gave a watery smile. 'Yeah, yeah, you can go back. I'll call you later.' She turned and started walking away with the girls.

'Are you sure, Maya?' called out Ryan. She just waved and kept walking. They had come in Felicity's car and as soon as they got in, the girls started plying her with questions.

'What was that all about? Maya, you're so pale? Are you okay? What were those boys doing there? Did you know they were there?'

Maya put up her hands. 'Guys, give me a minute.' She had to think fast. She owed her friends an explanation. 'I wanted to throw up and I was feeling dizzy. I went to the ground floor towards the restroom, and I felt faint all of a sudden. Sebastian and Ryan were there. They thought I was sick and they came over to help. I didn't know they were there. I don't know where they came from.' The last bit was not a lie. She had no idea from where they had appeared. 'They were only helping me, till you guys came.'

'Well, Ryan was more than helping you,' said Felicity.

'Yeah, you were draped all over him,' said Mary Anne, giggling.

'Lisa didn't look too pleased. She was standing on the second floor, glaring at you. I saw Ryan looking up sheepishly…,' said Felicity.

'As you clung to his big, burly body,' hooted Mary Anne.

'Girls, enough,' Maya protested weakly. She was feeling mortified.

When they reached Maya's house, Mary Anne asked, 'Do you want me to come up with you? I can ask Dad to pick me up later.'

'Thanks, Mary Anne. But I'm still feeling a bit woozy. I'll probably sleep for a while.' She waved goodbye to them and made her way in.

Cassie was sitting in the clubhouse, wrapped in a blanket when her parents came in. Her mom caught sight of Cassie and ran up to her. She grabbed her by the shoulders and shook her.

'Where is he? Where's my baby?' she said hysterically.

'Honey…,' Cassie's dad pulled her mom away. Kenny walked over to them.

'Mr. and Mrs. Johnson, Sam's at All Saints Hospital. If you come with me, I'll drive you there,' he offered. Cassie got up at once, the blanket slipping off and falling to the floor. She was still in her swimsuit. 'I want to come too.' She took two unsteady steps forward and when her dad held out his hands, she collapsed into them, sobbing.

'Cas! I'll take your Mom and go to the hospital now. I'll call you as soon as I see Sam. You go to the cottage and change. I'll come and pick you up,' he promised.

When she didn't reply, he asked again, 'Honey? Cas?' He put his hand under her chin, and tilted her face up to look at him. He saw her tear stained face and hugged her. 'Honey, they told me what happened. The lifeguards. They told me how brave you were. Just hang in there. I'll call as soon as I see him.' He bent down, picked up the blanket and wrapped it around Cassie.

Her mom tugged at his arm impatiently. 'Come on, let's go.'

Her dad gave Cassie a quick peck on the top of her head and said, 'Now go back to the cottage and get changed. I'll call.'

He hurried out with her mom and Kenny. Cassie turned and walked with leaden steps back to the cottage. The door was wide open. She went in, closed it, and went up to her room. She changed out of her swimsuit and sat down to wait. She wanted to call Maya, but she didn't want her dad getting a busy line, so she didn't. Her dad called in an hour to tell her that Sam was fine. He was awake and they were bringing him back home with them. When she heard that Sam was okay, she felt her eyes tearing up again. After her dad had hung up, she sat on the floor hugging her knees and rocking herself as she wept in the dark.

Maya pulled out her phone as soon as she had seen her friends drive away, to call Cassie. She tried the number as she entered the elevator. There was no signal. She cursed and waited impatiently. As soon as she walked into her house, she tried again and got through.

'Hello,' a voice croaked.

'Cas?' said Maya. 'Is that you?'

She could hear Cassie clearing her throat. 'Hey, Maya,' Cassie said.

'Have you been crying?' asked Maya, sounding concerned.

'Just a bit,' said Cassie. She sounded drained.

'I can understand. I was so worried here. I can't imagine how you must be feeling,' said Maya.

'He's fine, Maya. My folks are at the hospital now. He's awake and talking. They're bringing him back with them tonight,' said Cassie.

'Oh! What a relief, Cas. I was so worried,' said Maya, collapsing on the sofa.

There was silence for a few seconds and then Cassie asked softly, 'How did you know, Maya? If you hadn't called and insisted that I go look, I don't think... I don't think...,' she stopped and softly started sobbing again.

'I don't know Cassie,' said Maya. 'I was sitting in the mall and I could feel Sam in my head, shouting for help. I could see him... no, not see him, but I could feel him. I can't explain it. I could feel the waves, smell the sea... I don't know how, but I'm not going to question it. I'm just glad I did,' she said quietly.

'Me too,' said Cassie. 'Maya, if anything had happened to him, I don't know what I would have done. I've been so nasty to him... I...'

'Cas, stop it. Don't do this to yourself. It's over. What was he doing in the middle of the sea anyway?' asked Maya puzzled.

'I have no idea,' said Cassie. 'I'll know only after he comes home.'

'He's coming home tonight, right? Then, I'll call tomorrow and speak to him. I'll call Seb and Ryan and tell them Sam's fine,' said Maya.

'They know?' asked Cassie. 'You called them?'

'This is going to sound totally random, but they were there at the mall... apparently they heard Sam too or felt him... sensed him. Hey, I don't know. I've stopped trying to find reasonable explanations for anything that happens to us. I won't be surprised if Sam has learned to fly and dropped into the sea by mistake.' They both chuckled. 'You keep your chin up. You did good. I'll call tomorrow. Bye,' said Maya and hung up.

She was exhausted and she didn't feel up to talking to the boys, so she texted them to say that Sam was fine.

CHAPTER 21

'What the hell was that? I knew something was going on between the two of you,' yelled Lisa, as she threw her bag into the car, got in and slammed the door shut. Ryan opened the door on the driver's side and got inside. They were using Lisa's car as Ryan's pickup was at the service station. He'd left his bike at her place, and they'd taken her car to the mall. He shut the door and looked at her.

'What are you on about, Lis?' he asked. She looked at him, her face red with anger. He knew what she was upset about and had been waiting for the outburst the whole afternoon. He had thought she would chew his head off when he went back upstairs, but all their friends were there, and she hadn't said anything. The girls had been shopping, and the boys had hung out in the arcade, all morning. Lisa and Ryan had just met up to go for lunch, when Ryan had seen Maya and gone down. When he'd gone back up, Lisa and the others had already gone to the restaurant.

'What were you thinking, mate? You're in so much trouble,' Randy had whispered in his ear, when Ryan had squeezed in beside him.

'I know,' Ryan had replied, glumly. 'I wish she'd yell and get it over with. This waiting is driving me crazy.'

They were supposed to go for a movie after lunch, but as they had walked towards the cinema, Lisa had said, 'I have a headache. I don't feel up to a movie. I'll catch up with you guys later. Ryan, sweetie, will you take me home?'

Everyone had known what the headache was, and with a few sympathetic looks and murmurs, their friends had walked on to buy tickets, while Lisa and Ryan had come down to the car.

'You know what I'm talking about, Ryan Carter. Don't play the innocent with me. That girl was clinging to you. In the middle of the mall!

Did you do that just to embarrass me?' She was screeching now. She picked up her bag and swung it at him. It bounced off the side of his head. He winced.

'Lis, if I was hooking up with her, would I be doing it in the middle of the mall, under your nose?' asked Ryan, exasperated. 'It's not what you think.'

'Really? So, what is it? Tell me! I saw you.' His phone beeped. Before he could move, Lisa lunged forward, slipped her hand into his jacket pocket and pulled out his phone.

'Is that her? It is her, isn't it?' she demanded, shaking the phone under his nose.

Ryan sighed. 'It's probably Randy,' he said.

She opened his phone, and the sender's name popped up.

'Ha!' she said, waving the phone in front of his face. 'It is her,' she said, triumphantly.

Ryan was surprised. The five of them never texted each other. They hardly called or spoke to one another, outside training.

'He's fine? Who's fine? Who is she talking about? What does she mean?' yelled Lisa.

'What?' asked Ryan, looking confused.

'She's messaged, "He's fine". Who is she talking about? What does she mean?' Lisa's voice faded, as Ryan understood the message.

'Sam! Maya meant that Sam was okay. She must have spoken to Cassie again,' he thought.

'Are you even listening to me?' screeched Lisa.

Ryan wanted to shut out the noise. He hated it when her voice reached that decibel.

'Lis!' He put out his hand. She smacked it away and shook the phone at him again.

'What does she mean? What does she mean?' Ryan had no idea why he came up with what he did, but it had seemed like a good way to stop the screeching.

'She's talking about Sebastian. She means Sebastian's fine. You know Sebastian. You saw him. He was standing right there. Sebastian and she had a fight, and she was upset. I was looking over the rail while I was waiting for you, and I saw them fighting. You know we train together, and I know them pretty well. They're a nice couple, and they're my friends. Seb walked off, and she was looking upset. I thought I'd help smooth things over. You saw how upset she was. She threw herself at me and burst into tears. What could I do? Seb came back to apologize, but she was still too upset and wouldn't talk to him. And then her friends came, and she left with them. You must have seen her leave?' he asked innocently, thanking his stars he hadn't tried to be chivalrous and drop Maya. He hoped Lisa was buying his cock and bull story.

'Well, I guess Seb went after her, and they made up. So, she's just telling me he's fine… you know, they're fine,' he finished.

Lisa gulped. 'She's seeing Sebastian? Since when?'

Ryan shrugged. 'I don't know. I think since school started,' he replied.

'I see,' said Lisa, her eyes glinting.

'Yes, they were fighting and I only went to patch it up and ended up in the wrong place at the wrong time, and got you all mad at me. It wasn't my fault.' He looked downcast.

'Oh! Sweetie. I'm so stupid. I'm sorry. It's just that you spend so much time with her, I get so jealous,' said Lisa, throwing her arms around him. Ryan was used to her mood swings by now. He just accepted that he would never understand women.

After a while, as they were sitting there wrapped in each other's arms, watching the sky darkening outside, Lisa said, 'Ha! Sebastian's dating that Indian chick… from when school started… huh? How about that?'

Sebastian's explanation to Anna about the afternoon's incident was much simpler. She had come out of the showroom and seen Maya crying. She'd also seen Sebastian and Ryan hovering around and like any suspicious girlfriend, she'd asked Sebastian about it. He'd told her Maya had episodes. She would break down crying for no apparent reason. She was in his class and so he knew about it. He'd told her that, in fact, most of the school knew about it. She'd had one that afternoon in the mall, and he'd seen her in the atrium and had gone to see if he could help in any way. He told Anna with a straight face that Maya was on medication, and was seeing a doctor for her "problem". He not only allayed her suspicions, but earned a whole lot of brownie points for being such a sensitive person.

Cassie was still up at half past ten, when Sam and her parents returned. Sam walked in looking perfectly fine. He had some sticky plasters on his arms and legs and one on his cheek. Cassie threw her arms around him.

'Hey! Easy, huh? Ouch! Ouch!' Cassie released him from the tight hug. Sam smiled weakly at her. 'Sorry. Not taking hugs right now. Body hurts all over,' he said.

Cassie felt herself being pushed aside roughly. 'Careful! You're hurting him,' her mom said. 'Sammy! Why don't you go lie down? I'll get you some soup,' she said in a softer tone to Sam. Sam was still holding on to Cassie's arm.

'Mom, I'm fine… honestly,' he turned to Cassie. 'I heard what… you know… I… thanks… and, sorry about earlier,' he said.

Cassie punched him lightly on his arm. 'Shut up… I'm just glad you're fine.'

Their dad walked past them and switched on the T.V. 'Come on, kids. Let's put this behind us. It's a vacation, for heaven's sake. Let's watch T.V. and pig out. No soup, honey. We're ordering everything on the menu tonight.'

He threw the remote at Sam. 'Come on, Sammy!' He sat down and patted the space next to him.

Sam turned and held out the remote to Cassie. 'You'll take it anyway,' he said, but he was smiling.

'Ah! About that! I'm sorry too. I was an ass. And I know I'll regret saying this, but I'm not doing that anymore. Not to you, anyway.' She didn't take the proffered remote, but walked over and perched on the arm of the couch, leaning against her dad.

'We heard Sammy's story about how he went swimming, and the storm struck and how he got caught in it. But, how did you find him?' asked her dad

'It was the strangest thing. I was just sitting on that lifeguard tower after the storm passed, you know the one on the left, and I was trying to see if I could spot a whale or maybe some dolphins, and I see… this.' She pointed at Sam. Her dad and Sam started laughing.

'Well, I'm glad you did,' said Sam, not looking convinced at all. He knew she'd tell him what actually happened later, when they were alone. He didn't remember much of what happened. He had a hazy memory of the boat and the sound of the ambulance. His first clear memory was of his parents hovering around his bedside. He'd recovered fairly rapidly after that. Kenny had come in a bit later and told him about how Cassie had helped rescue him.

He was just glad to be home. His mom came and sat down next to him and he leaned his head on her shoulder, feeling drowsy. Anyway, the one good thing about the whole incident was that his parents seemed to have stopped fighting.

CHAPTER 22

Maya woke up to the insistent ringing of the phone. It had been ringing on and off for about a half hour, and she'd ignored it. She didn't feel like waking up yet. She'd gone to bed early the day before, even before her mom came home. She'd felt worn out after the chaos of the day. But she had felt restless and had been unable to fall asleep. She had twisted and turned in her bed, till the wee hours of the morning, when she had finally drifted off into an uneasy sleep.

The phone wouldn't stop ringing. She groaned and reached for it. It fell silent as she picked it up. She flipped it open and saw eight missed calls. She checked the time. It was past ten. She sat up groggily and checked the calls. There was one from her mom, two from Cassie, four from Ryan and one from Sebastian. She called her mom as she went to get coffee. Her mom sounded worried. Maya had gone to bed by the time her mother had returned the previous day, and she had still been asleep when her mom left in the morning. She assured her mom she was fine and promised to call later. She took her coffee and curled up on the couch with it. As she wondered who to call first, the phone rang. It was Cassie.

'Hey, Maya! Finally! Been trying you since morning,' Cassie said.

'Yeah, you and the rest of the world,' thought Maya. Aloud, she said, 'Hi, Cassie! I woke up late. How's Sammy? Is he home? How is he feeling?'

'Yeah, he's home. He's right here. I'll give it to him.'

Sam's voice came on. 'Hey, Maya... did she wake you too? She jumped up and down on my bed, till I woke up,' he said grouchily.

She was surprised at how happy she felt to hear his voice. He was like family now. They all were like family to her now, except maybe Seb, she couldn't care what happened to that ass.

'Cassie told me how she found me. I don't know how you did it, but thanks, Maya,' said Sam.

'Hey Sammy... I'm just glad you're safe,' said Maya.

Sam sounded sheepish, as he said, 'Did Cassie tell you about the stupid stunt I pulled?' he asked.

'What stunt?' asked Maya.

'How do you think I ended up in the middle of the sea?' he asked. He told her about what had happened. She couldn't believe he'd been so stupid, but she was also excited about what he had done. She told him how she and the others had heard his cry for help. They were silent for a few minutes, after exchanging stories.

'We're kind of brilliant, aren't we?' said Sam softly.

'Yeah,' agreed Maya, laughing, 'and so modest about it.' They spoke for a while and she hung up, promising to call later.

She called Ryan next. He seemed to be more frantic, judging by the number of calls. She had just started telling him what Sam had told her, when she got an incoming call. It was Sebastian. She put them on a conference. She told the boys what Sam had done. Finally, the events of the previous day made sense to the boys.

'When I get my hands on that idiot...,' swore Ryan.

'He has now officially become the coolest kid I know,' said Sebastian, sounding awed. 'Hey, Ryan,' he said, after a few seconds. 'Did you get my New Year's Eve invite?'

Sebastian's dad was throwing his annual New Year's Eve party, which was supposed to rock. Maya had to attend because her mom was the hostess, though Maya wasn't complaining. She was asked to invite whoever she wanted and she had invited her two friends. It had never occurred to her to invite Ryan. She was surprised at Sebastian's gesture.

'That is uncharacteristically nice of him,' she mused.

'I don't know, mate. I don't know what our New Year's Eve plans are. But I'll try and drop in for a while,' Ryan said.

'That's cool,' said Sebastian. He wasn't simply being nice as Maya thought. He was inviting Ryan because he wanted Lisa to come. He wanted Lisa to see his gorgeous girlfriend, attend his amazing party, and take a good look at what she'd passed up. Payback!

'Oh, do come, Ryan!' urged Maya, quite excited. Sebastian rolled his eyes. Maya's crush on Ryan was so obvious he didn't know how the big oaf couldn't have noticed.

'I don't know what my friends are doing,' said Ryan, hesitating.

'Bring them along. The more, the merrier,' said Sebastian.

'I'll ask them and let you know,' promised Ryan.

Sam was back at the poolside the next day, lying in the sun and listening to music. This time, Cassie was there too. She was lying on the deck chair next to him, reading her book. To Sam's amusement, Cassie seemed to be stuck to his side all the time… and that was when he could get away from his mom. She put her book down, leaned across and patted Sam's leg.

'Sammy?' Sam pulled out his earphones and looked at her. He raised an eyebrow. 'I just wondered. Have you tried again?' she asked. He knew what she meant.

'No, Mom was with me the whole of yesterday. She even waited for me to fall asleep, before she left. I was just thinking about it. Should I?' He looked around. They were alone.

'Yeah, I think you should. There's no one around. It's the perfect time.'

'Do you want to go away? I don't want to hurt you,' he said, sounding uneasy.

'No, you won't,' she asserted quietly. 'You were angry that day and that's why you aimed it at me. I doubt you knew you could make lightning strike, Moses,' she said. He groaned. She'd started teasing him by calling him Moses, after he had told her what he had done on the beach.

'Please, stop that,' he said.

'Fine… but go on. Try and do it now. You must be dying to see what you can do,' she said. 'I am.'

Sam turned around and concentrated his thoughts on the water in the pool. He thought he'd do his Moses thing. It was pretty amazing and Cassie would get a big kick out of it. He breathed deeply, calming himself and felt around in his mind for the mass of energy he'd felt before. He frowned. He couldn't feel it. He tried harder and harder, his face screwed up in concentration. At last he thought he felt something, but try as he might, he couldn't reach it. It felt like the surfboard in the sea the previous day. Every time he reached for it, it seemed to slip away. After five minutes of laborious effort, he opened his eyes. He was sweating and panting in exhaustion. Cassie was kneeling in front of him, staring at him in concern.

'Sammy? Are you ok?' she asked.

'Yeah! Yeah!' He felt dizzy. He shook his head to clear it.

'Are you sure? You're pale and you're trembling, and you look like you're about to faint,' she said sceptically.

'I'm fine,' he snapped at her in his frustration. 'Let's just go back to what we were doing.' He jammed his earphones back in his ears, lay back in his chair and closed his eyes. Cassie looked at him confused, for a moment. Then she shrugged, picked up her book and lay down too.

Sam wasn't listening to music. He couldn't understand what had happened. Why hadn't anything happened? He had done it so easily the day before. He hoped Cassie wouldn't bug him to try again. He knew he wouldn't be able to. It was like he had lost the key. He could feel the energy with his mind, but it was like he had lost the key which unleashed it. He was unable to reach it, grasp it, and manipulate it, like he had done the day before. Why couldn't he do it? What should he do? Should he try again? What if he was never able to do it again? Thoughts whirled crazily in his mind. He wanted to scream in frustration. He couldn't sit still. He jumped up to his feet. Cassie looked at him, puzzled.

'I'm going for a walk,' he said abruptly and trotted off down the path that led to the beach. Cassie sat up, undecided whether to follow him or to stay put. She realised he needed some space, so she lay back and let him go on alone.

'Don't do anything stupid,' she called out after him and picked up her book.

It was late afternoon when Sam returned. Cassie had gone back to the cottage and was now curled up in her favourite spot, the window seat! She looked up when he opened their room door.

'Thank God, you're back. I was starting to get worried,' she said. He ignored her and threw himself on his bed.

'Sam,' said Cassie, after a couple of minutes. He didn't answer. He hoped she would get mad and leave him alone. 'Can I say something, without you snapping my head off?' she started again, tentatively.

He turned over and faced her. 'It seems like you won't shut up till you do, so spit it out,' he said rudely.

His rudeness didn't seem to faze Cassie. 'I was thinking… do you remember how easily I broke the monster cup the first time? It was effortless. I just thought about it and it happened. But after that? I had to practice for almost six months before I could move anything. And I practiced real hard, for those six months. All I'm saying is, you're feeling frustrated because you're not able to do it again. I get that. You've no idea how frustrating it was to sit and stare at that pencil, hoping it would move, day after day. Maybe, you merely need to practice now. Mr. Harris will be able to help you.'

Sam looked thoughtful. After a few minutes when he still hadn't said anything, she prompted, 'Well?'

'You're right. Of course, you're right. I was stupid to think it was going to be that easy. It wasn't easy for any of you. I should be happy I have some kind of ability, right? I mean, I don't even know what it is, leave alone know how to control it. As you said, Mr. Harris will be able to figure it out.' He smiled. 'I feel better already… thanks.'

CHAPTER 23

There was light snowfall on New Year's Eve. Sebastian's dad had sent a limo to pick up Maya and her mom. Mary Anne and Felicity, who were going for the party with Maya, had gotten dropped off earlier at Maya's place. None of the girls had been in a limo before and were pretty excited. The three of them had spent the entire week getting ready for the party. They had all bought new outfits.

Maya wore a full length, shiny red gown, made of soft fabric which fell in waves, flattering her figure. It had a modest slit, showing a bit of leg. She had left her hair loose, and it swung gracefully down her back. She had gone for minimal and wore ruby earrings which dangled from her ears, complementing her ruby bracelet. Felicity was dressed in a blue figure hugging dress that just stopped short of being a mini. She had great legs and showed off quite a bit of it. Mary Anne was in a pink and black combination, with an overdose of frills and flounces. When she had come out of the changing room at the boutique, looking like she'd been gift wrapped, the other two had vetoed the dress. But, Mary Anne had gone ahead and bought it anyway. Now with black stockings and her hair piled up, she looked amazing. Unusual, but amazing! Only Mary Anne could have pulled off that outfit, thought Maya, looking at her friend affectionately.

Maya had only been to sleepovers and birthday parties. This was the first time she was going to a proper, grown up party, and she was elated. Her mom would be there of course, but she'd be busy playing hostess. She looked at her mom approvingly. She looked stunning, in a long black gown with a low back. Her mom had enthusiastically joined in their preparations for the party, taking them out and helping them pick out things to wear. Now she looked at the three girls, beaming.

'You look beautiful, girls. Come on, stand together. Let me take a picture.' She took her pictures and then they left to Sebastian's house. Maya had been to Sebastian's house a couple of times, but she still couldn't get used to the sheer size of the place. They could see the glow of lights, much before they reached the mansion itself. They had to present their invites at the gates, to verify that they were listed.

As they drove up to the house, they stared in wonder at the beautifully lit grounds. The grounds were festooned with blue, fairy lights. The snow reflected the bluish light, making everything look surreal. The house itself was decorated with red and green lights, giving it a charming, Christmas feel.

The limo pulled up at the portico, where Sebastian's dad, Daniel, was waiting eagerly, looking very smart in a tuxedo. He opened the door, even before the car stopped, and helped them out.

'So, what do you think?' he asked, holding out his hand expansively.

'It looks wonderful, Dan. You've done an incredible job,' said Neha, Maya's mom.

He beamed with pleasure. 'Come on, let me show you the hall.' He led the way inside.

Mary Anne's parents were archaeologists and she was extremely taken up with Daniel's collections of priceless paintings and sculptures.

'Guys! That's a Ming vase,' she said, reaching for a long, graceful vase which stood on a pedestal. Maya swatted Mary Anne's hand away.

'Don't touch anything. You're the one who's always telling us how expensive these things are,' she said severely. Mary Anne wasn't even listening to her; she was looking around enthralled with her mouth open.

Maya tugged at her. 'Mary Anne, come on,' she hissed.

When Daniel saw that they had stopped, he came back and stood in front of the painting Mary Anne was staring at, open-mouthed. 'Ah! I see you've found my Renoir. You have very good taste.'

Mary Anne's mouth opened even more. 'That's the original?' she asked, in wonder.

'Unfortunately, no! Much as I would like my original works of art decorating my home, where I can stare at them whenever I want to, it isn't safe. I do have the original of this Renoir, though, but it's in my vault. Most of what I keep around my house are replicas of the originals.'

Neha walked back towards them. 'Mary Anne's parents are Nora and Elliot James, the archaeologists,' she said, slipping her arm through his. 'You can imagine how interested in history and art, their daughter would be. She's been brought up on a diet of Da Vinci and Michaelangelo,' she said smiling.

Daniel's eyes lit up. 'But, that's marvellous. I'm a big fan of their books,' he said. 'Neha, we must have them over. They would appreciate the beauty of the pieces I have. I'm afraid most of the rich and famous coming in today, wouldn't know a Renoir from a Rembrandt.' He shook his head sadly. 'But the wooing must be done if I want to get more of this.' He waved his hand around the room. 'Now, come along,' he said and walked down a wide corridor which ended in front of two large double doors.

'Mary Anne, I'll bring you back. Dan won't mind. You heard him. Now, come on,' Maya said, dragging the reluctant Mary Anne away, and they hurried to catch up with the others. As they neared the doors, it silently swung open. Daniel stepped in and waved his arms with a flourish.

'Welcome to Ali Baba's den,' he announced.

They stopped and stared. Felicity gave a snort, and Maya dug her in her ribs. Neha seemed at a loss for words, as Daniel looked at her eagerly.

'Oh! Dan, it's lovely,' she managed finally, reaching over and giving him a kiss.

He looked thrilled. 'You're sure. It's not too… you know… over the top?' he asked anxiously.

'No, honey, this is you and I love every bit of it,' she replied.

Maya looked at them in amusement. When her mom had started dating Daniel, she couldn't understand what her mom saw in the brash, offensive man. Daniel would constantly embarrass her mom with inappropriately expensive gifts, and try to impress her by making every date as spectacular as possible. After one bizarre date, where he'd bought the tickets for the entire performance of a well known musical, her mom had put her foot down. She had sat mortified as the star-studded cast had performed exclusively for the two of them. When they'd got back home, she'd told him that if he pulled a stunt like that again, they were done. Daniel, to his credit had worked hard to tone down the extravagance.

Maya's mom was pretty conventional, and Maya was brought up that way. Her mom was simple in her wants and lifestyle. One day, she'd asked her mom how she could put up with Daniel's extravagance without cringing. Her mom had smiled and said, 'I love him. He's like a child. He's used to the idea that if you give things to people, they have to like you. He doesn't understand I like him anyway. Giving gifts makes him happy. I like making him happy.' Maya hadn't understood then. She knew most of the stuff he gave her mom stayed locked up in her cupboard.

But now, standing here in this huge circus tent and watching his look of utter devotion, as he waited for her mom's approval and seeing her mom's indulgent smile and answer, she thought she was beginning to understand. Happy with her approval, Daniel whisked her mom away to show her around. Left alone, the girls looked at each other and started giggling.

'What the hell is this?' asked Felicity, one hand pressed against her mouth to stop herself from laughing out loud. She gave another one of her snorts. 'Oooops, sorry... but... I mean...,' she waved her hand around the room.

'Did he tell your Mom that he was trying to tone it down?' asked Mary Anne. Maya nodded, also laughing as they surveyed the room.

The huge room was swathed in richly coloured cloth which stretched and crisscrossed each other near the ceiling, and fell in swatches down the walls. Light shone dimly through the cloth, bathing the room in a warm, soft glow. There were piles of fake gold coins in treasure chests, fake jewellery spilt out of decorative boxes, hookahs and charmingly embroidered cushions and throws were scattered around the place.

'It feels like we're in Sheherazade's dream,' giggled Mary Anne.

'Share what?' asked Felicity.

'You don't read, illiterate. You won't know what she's talking about. It's a book,' said Maya.

'Like you understand all her references,' shot back Felicity and they both laughed. Mary Anne was a walking encyclopaedia, and she'd come out with the oddest bits of information. The other two were used to it.

A waitress in loose pants and a bustier, with a transparent cloth covering her hair and the lower half of her face, came up and offered them a tray of refreshments. There were waiters in similar pants, paired with embroidered waistcoats and turbans also walking around. The effect would have been quite spectacular, if it hadn't been so ostentatious. The girls were still giggling, as they made their way across the space and found a sofa, partially hidden in an alcove behind some heavy curtains. They had a good view of the hall from there, but were mostly hidden themselves.

There was some kind of instrumental music playing softly, which added to the Arabian ambiance. The girls stuffed themselves with the delicious hors d'oeuvres being served as they watched the guests start trickling in. They entertained themselves by commenting on Skallen's rich and famous who were in full attendance. Suddenly, the curtain was pulled back and they looked up startled, and saw Sebastian standing there.

'Why are you hiding here? And, what is that rubbish you're drinking? And, by the way, I heard what you just said about the mayor's wife,' he said gleefully.

'What? Who? No, we didn't,' said Maya flustered.

'Don't know what you're talking about,' added Felicity innocently.

'Yeah! Yeah!' said Sebastian grinning. He seemed to be in a particularly good mood. 'I'm here to rescue you. The real party is downstairs, the fun party. Come on,' he said. The girls scrambled up and followed him. They went back along the corridor through which they had entered, and took the elevator to the basement.

'He has an elevator in his house,' squeaked Felicity in Maya's ear.

'Shh!' hushed Maya, hoping Sebastian hadn't heard. He thought no end of himself as it was.

The elevator opened onto another corridor. It had neon strips, lighting it from both sides. The boom of the music hit them as the elevator doors opened. They followed Sebastian along the corridor, and through the door at the end. They were at the indoor swimming pool. The swimming pool was covered and had a platform with a D.J. at one end. The rest of the pool had been turned into a dance floor. There were quite a few people already gyrating to the music.

It was a young crowd and the party seemed to be in full swing. Sebastian had disappeared. They made their way along one side to a dark corner, where they wouldn't be noticed. Sebastian soon returned with drinks for the three of them.

'Here you go. Have fun. Tell me if you need anything.' He handed them their drinks and disappeared once more. The girls shrank into the shadows, sipping their drinks. They didn't know anyone and most of the kids there seemed much older than them.

After a few minutes Mary Anne said, 'I miss upstairs.'

'Me too,' said Maya.

'I don't know. It seems quite fun here,' said Felicity, jigging to the music. 'Not like we were doing much upstairs either,' she added.

Maya and Mary Anne looked at each other. 'Fine, we'll give it ten minutes and if we still don't like it here, we'll go back upstairs,' said Mary Anne.

Sebastian was being a good host. He was circulating, Anna by his side. His dad had told him to make sure that Maya and her friends were having a good time, and he had made sure of that. He greeted a friend who had just come in and then looked around to see what the trio was doing. He couldn't see them in the corner where they'd been trying to hide. He searched for them and spotted them on the dance floor. Good! He beckoned a waiter and asked him to get the girls another round of drinks. He had added vodka ice to their first drink, to loosen them up and it seemed to be working. They seemed to be having fun.

He turned around, as another couple came in. Anna and he went up to greet them. Anna looked ethereal, in a clingy, shiny white gown, her blonde hair spilling to her waist. He knew they made a striking couple, and he was enjoying showing her off.

The indoor swimming pool was at a lower level of the house, and had side doors which opened out into a garden. A wrought iron staircase wound up from the garden to ground level. From there, a gravel path led to a road that wound around the side of the house, meeting the main driveway. It made it easier for guests to get to Sebastian's party. They got dropped off at the side entrance.

As Sebastian and Anna were making small talk with the couple who had just entered, Sebastian spotted Ryan coming in. He went over. 'Hey, big guy,' he said, banging fists and giving him a half hug. 'Glad you could make it.' He'd noticed with delight that Lisa had tagged along. She looked extremely sexy in a short black dress, but she wasn't a patch on Anna.

'Hey, man!' said Ryan. 'Sorry, I can't stay long. We're heading to another party. Thought I'd drop in for a bit.'

He hadn't wanted to come. But Sebastian's dad's parties were a big deal in Skallen, and Lisa had wanted to go for it. He knew why she had wanted to go. This was the biggest party in town, and she could tell her friends later that she'd been to it. But if it made her happy, he didn't mind.

'Of course. Have a drink before you go,' said Sebastian, calling a waiter. 'What will you have? Beer?'

'You're serving alcohol?' Ryan asked, surprised. He looked around. None of the kids looked old enough to be drinking. Hell, he knew Sebastian wasn't old enough to be drinking, let alone serving alcohol to others.

'Only the best at my party,' said Sebastian. 'By the way, this is my girlfriend, Anna. Anna, this is my pal, Ryan, and his girlfriend, Lisa.' He saw Lisa looking up at Ryan with a puzzled expression. 'Suck it,' he thought to himself. Someone called out to him, and Anna and he excused themselves.

As soon as Sebastian and Anna walked away, Lisa turned towards Ryan. 'You told me he's dating Maya,' she hissed.

Ryan had forgotten the lie. Now, he fumbled, 'Er... they broke up? I think... I mean... you saw them that day. It wasn't going too well. You know, fighting all the time. Anyway, I'm glad he's found someone. She seems like a nice person.'

'Ryan! Hey, you! It's so good to see you.' Maya hurled herself on Ryan. 'I was just dancing over there…,' she said, pointing to the dance floor, '… on that thingy and I told my girls… I said… hey, that looks like Ryan. I'm going to say hi to him and I came right over… and here I am.'

'Yeah! Yeah!' Ryan was trying to get her off him. He could see Lisa's face turning red with anger. 'Nice to see you too.'

Maya was three drinks down and feeling very happy with the world. When she had seen Ryan, it had seemed like a good idea to go across and drag him to the dance floor. Ryan was trying to push her off him, but Maya wasn't having any of it. She clung tighter. He turned towards Lisa, with Maya still clinging to him.

'I didn't know she'd be here,' he said.

'Of course you knew, dummy. I told you that I'd be here that day, over the phone. Remember, when you called me,' Maya said, now holding Ryan's arm and dragging him. 'Come on, let's go dance.'

Ryan hastily disentangled himself and turned to Lisa. 'It's not what you think, Lis.'

Lisa raised one hand. 'Ryan Carter, I have only one question. Did you call her?'

'Lis, I can explain. The thing…,' began Ryan, but Lisa cut him off.

'A yes or no would do,' she said sharply.

'Yes, but…,' he was talking to her back, as she strode away furiously. He looked down and found Maya draped all over him again.

'Get off me, girl. Are you drunk?' He bent down and sniffed. 'Damn, I'll kill Sebastian,' he swore. He found a chair, pushed her into it and asked, 'Where are your friends?'

She pointed vaguely somewhere and grabbed his arm. 'You know what? There's Ali Baba's cave upstairs, with lots of treasure. Let's go on a treasure hunt.' She jumped up and raced away. Ryan watched her go, wondering what to do. He saw her trying to drag her two friends off the dance floor. All three fell back on the floor, giggling.

'Damn!' he swore again and looked around for Sebastian. He saw Sebastian standing with Anna and talking to a group of friends. He waved, trying to attract his attention. Sebastian saw Ryan waving, excused himself and walked over. 'We've got to get these girls home. What did you give them to drink? You are such an idiot, Seb,' said Ryan.

'What girls?' asked Sebastian.

Ryan pointed to the three girls, still rolling on the floor. 'Maya and her friends, you ass. Look at them.'

'I gave them one drink,' protested Sebastian. He had given them only one spiked drink. But the girls had decided to try out some of the fancy sounding cocktails after that.

'Well, that doesn't look like one drink,' Ryan replied, watching the three tottering to their feet.

Sebastian swore and turned to Anna, who had just walked up, and was watching the girls in amusement. Some of the other guests were also staring at the girls now.

'Babe, I'll go leave them somewhere, where they can sleep this off. I'll be back in a few minutes. Will you take care of things here?' he asked.

Anna didn't look too pleased, but she nodded. Ryan and Sebastian rounded up the girls and herded them upstairs. Ryan looked around, but he couldn't spot Lisa anywhere. He decided to deal with her later. They ushered the girls back upstairs to Daniel's party, and into the alcove they'd been sitting in earlier. They pulled the curtains around them.

'You sit right here. Don't move,' said Sebastian. The three nodded, and fell over each other, giggling.

'Maya! Quiet, and no more drinking. I'm serious,' hissed Ryan.

'He's serious,' said Maya, turning to her friends, 'and I'm humorous.'

The stale joke set them off again.

'Seb, we can't leave them here. They're making a scene and people will soon notice,' said Ryan.

'Fine, let's take them up to my room,' said Sebastian.

They somehow managed to get the three girls out to the hall and upstairs to Sebastian's suite without mishap, though Mary Anne kept trying to steal things on the way. She was holding a delicate Dresden piece, as they walked into Sebastian's room, and he had to pry it away from her reluctant hands. He turned on the T.V. and switched to a music channel.

'Ooh! I love this song,' said Felicity, and started swaying to the music. Maya and Mary Anne also seemed to think this was a great idea. They joined her, and the three were soon singing at the top of their voices and dancing. Ryan and Sebastian looked at them helplessly.

'Do you think anyone will hear them?' asked Ryan.

'I doubt it,' said Sebastian. 'My rooms are far enough from the party, and anyway, no one will hear them with all the noise below.'

'Now stay here and watch T.V., till I come back for you,' said Sebastian. The girls didn't answer. They were too busy hitting a high note, in the chorus of the song.

'Do you think they'll stay put?' asked Ryan.

'We could lock the door,' suggested Sebastian.

'No, no,' said Ryan, looking shocked. He turned around and looked at Maya. 'Maya?' he called out.

She looked up, fluttering her eyelashes at him. 'Yes, Ryan?' she simpered.

'We'll be back in a bit. Don't come down till we come to get you, understood?' he ordered sternly.

'Okay, Ryan,' she said, looking coy.

'Man, you're passing up a big opportunity here,' Sebastian said laughing, indicating Maya.

'Please, that's all I need now,' muttered Ryan, as they turned to leave.

Ryan went straight down to the basement, but Sebastian got off a level above, to find Neha and tell her that Maya was with him. He didn't want her to find Maya in her drunken state. He was already feeling bad about having gotten the girls drunk, and Neha made him feel worse, by giving him a hug and thanking him for taking such good care of Maya and her friends.

He returned to the basement, back to his party. The dance floor was packed, and everyone seemed to be having a great time. He looked around for Anna and frowned as he caught sight of her. She had her coat on and was leaving out the side door. He hurried over to the exit and stepped out after her. She was climbing up the stairs which led to the drive. He called out to her, but she didn't answer. He ran up the stairs, taking two steps at a time and caught up with her before she reached her car, which was already waiting for her, the chauffeur holding the door open.

He grabbed her arm. 'Hey? What's going on?' he asked.

She twisted her arm out of his grasp and shouted, 'Leave me alone, you pig.'

'Where are you going?' he asked, confused. He had no idea why she was angry. She'd been fine when he had left her.

'Home, and I never want to see you again. Don't bother calling,' she yelled, as she reached her car.

'Fine, but just tell me what happened,' he asked.

'I know about Maya and you, you two-timing creep. Maybe she has no problem about you being a cheat, but I do.'

Sebastian was bewildered. 'What are you talking about? I've never dated Maya,' he said.

'Lisa told me, you jerk, and she also told me how you hit on her.'
She got into the car and slammed the door shut. Sebastian was too
stunned to even protest anymore. Maya? Seriously? Why would anyone
think he was dating Maya? He couldn't stand the girl. He watched
helplessly, as the car drove away.

He turned around, fuming. He was going to find Lisa and ask her
what was going on. He was saved the trouble of going back in as Ryan
and Lisa came up the stairs pulling on their coats. They seemed to be
arguing.

He marched towards them, furious. 'What the hell is going on? My
girlfriend just left. She was mad at me because, for some reason, she
thinks I'm dating Maya. She said you told her that,' he accused Lisa.

'I didn't tell her that you are dating Maya. I told her, you were dating
her. Of course, after tonight, I'm not sure who she's got her claws hooked
into,' spat Lisa, looking at Ryan.

'Why would you lie to my girlfriend? You simply couldn't stand to
see what you passed up?' asked Sebastian.

'I didn't lie. You're a liar. You hit on me, while you were dating Maya
and then…,' started Lisa.

Ryan interrupted, 'He hit on you?' He turned to Sebastian. 'You hit
on my girlfriend? When was this?' he asked Sebastian, incredulously.

'That was ages ago. That's not the point. She told my girlfriend that I
was dating Maya. I've never hooked up with Maya,' yelled Sebastian.

Lisa turned towards Ryan, enraged. 'You told me they were dating,'
she accused.

'You told her I was dating Maya? Why would you make up a story
like that?' asked Sebastian, looking at Ryan with anger.

Ryan could feel the rage building up in him. He caught Sebastian by his collar and lifted him right off the ground.

'You hit on my girlfriend?' he bellowed furiously.

One of the kids from the party, who had stepped out for some air, saw a fight brewing. He raced back in to alert the others, and a small crowd started pushing and shoving their way up the stairs. Sebastian and Ryan were oblivious to the spectators.

'Ryan, put him down!' Lisa was screaming as she grabbed his arm and shook it. 'Let him go.' She could feel the situation getting out of hand. She didn't want a scene in front of all these people. 'Let's get out of here. He's not worth it,' she said, trying to calm him down. The look on his face frightened her.

Sebastian was as mad as Ryan and he didn't care if Ryan clobbered him, but he wasn't going to back down. He looked Ryan straight in the eye and said, 'Why don't you ask your girlfriend, how she flirted with me and even accepted a date with me?' he taunted softly.

Ryan gave a roar and swung Sebastian, flinging him away. Sebastian went flying into the air and fell on a pile of snow, almost twenty feet away. He had missed hitting a tree by inches. Ryan set off after him, his blood pounding in his head, pushing all reason out.

'Ryan! Ryan! Listen to me, Ryan! Calm down!' he heard Maya's voice in his head.

He shook his head, trying to get her out. He saw Sebastian staggering to his feet. Luckily, Sebastian had fallen on a snow drift and was mostly unhurt, but he was shaken. He looked up, dazed, and saw Ryan charging towards him. He knew Ryan would beat him black and blue if he caught him. He was no match for Ryan's strength. He did what he knew best. He ran. He knew Ryan wouldn't be able to catch him. He dashed away and quickly doubled back, so that he was behind Ryan, who was looking around wondering where Sebastian had disappeared to.

There was a thick, broken branch on the ground. Sebastian quietly picked it up, raised it high and brought it down with a solid thump on Ryan's head. He felt pain shoot up his arm as he made contact. The branch split in two. Ryan swayed forward with the impact, but it didn't seem to affect him much. He turned around. Sebastian turned to run again and tripped over another broken branch. He went sprawling in the snow. Before he could jump up and run, Ryan threw himself on Sebastian.

'This is it,' thought Sebastian, his breath leaving his body in a whoosh, as Ryan's entire weight landed on him. 'I'm going to die.'

All of a sudden, Ryan uttered a shriek, rolled off Sebastian and curled up into a ball, holding his head in his hands. Sebastian saw his chance. He jumped up and picked up another branch, to whack Ryan again. As he raised it over his head, he felt a sharp jolt of pain shooting through his head. The pain was unbearable. He clutched his head as he fell to the ground.

CHAPTER 24

'How are they progressing, Blane?' Mr. Harris looked up, when he heard the melodious voice. Iola was walking down the path to where he was sitting under a tree. This was one of his favourite spots in Pha-yul, with a spectacular view over the vast lake, and the snow-capped mountains beyond. The kids would not have recognized "Blane" as their unkempt Mr. Harris. He was wearing long, plain, rust coloured robes. His hair had grown longer and was curling around the edges, and his stubble was threatening to become a full blown beard. He was sitting cross-legged on the grass. Iola sat down next to him and looked into the distance.

After a few moments, she prompted him again, 'Well?'

Mr. Harris turned and looked at her. 'Iola, they're progressing as well as can be expected. They're young. They need time,' he said.

Iola sighed and looked at him. 'Time is a luxury they may not have,' she said.

Mr. Harris looked up sharply. 'What do you mean?' he asked. 'What do you know?'

'There are rumours that you have found the five.'

'Do they know who my five are and where they are?' asked Mr. Harris, looking concerned.

'Everybody seems to think they have the five. So, to answer your question, no, I don't think they know where your five are. Even if they did, they wouldn't make a move till they are absolutely sure they have the right ones.'

'Hm! I hope we're doing the right thing,' he muttered.

'Should we just bring them here now, Blane? I feel we're taking a big risk by leaving them exposed. Here, they'd be safe. Marcus has his five here,' she said softly.

Mr. Harris looked at Iola. 'And how is that going for him? I may not live here all the time Iola, but I know what's going on most of the time. Bringing Sam and the others here would be a mistake. You know how I feel Iola, and you also know why. They're not ready to come here, yet. Once they get here, everyone will want a piece of them. I don't want to put them through that, till they're ready,' said Mr. Harris. 'That's how... I feel, but you know I will follow whatever you think is best,' he added softly.

Iola reached out and squeezed his hand. 'I trust your instincts, Blane. It has never led us astray,' she said.

Mr. Harris grimaced. 'I wouldn't say that. I've been wrong before. I could be wrong again.'

'We were all wrong. It wasn't only you. You can't keep blaming yourself.'

'Maybe the others believe that, Iola... but you and me, we know what happened... sometimes, I think, the others know too.'

'Blane, it's done, it's over,' Iola said firmly. 'You have to let it go, sometime.'

'When we're through, when we find him, and stop him... then, it will be over,' said Mr. Harris.

Iola shook her head and looked at him sympathetically. She knew she couldn't help him. This was a burden he would have to learn to let go. They both sat in silence, looking at the mist rolling over the lake towards them.

'What about the little one?' Iola asked, after a while.

Mr. Harris shook his head. 'Nothing.'

Iola looked at him. 'Maybe we're wrong. Maybe, it isn't them?' she asked.

'Iola, don't you think it was too much of a coincidence that the five ended up living in the same city. Only one of them was born there. They all came together on the same day when they had detention, under me. They manifested their abilities around the same time, all these signs… it cannot be a mere coincidence. Something is pulling them together,' he looked up at her, 'and I think that something is Sam.'

Iola pulled at a weed on the ground. She sometimes wondered if Blane wanted to find the five so badly he was not willing to entertain the possibility that he may be wrong.

'Sybil and Marcus are not convinced they are the five,' she said.

'I don't care what Marcus and Sybil think. I live with these children. I see the power Sam holds over the others. They turn to him… they look at him for guidance, though he's the youngest. I don't think they're even aware of it and neither is he. It's the way we felt about you, Iola. He holds them together, like how you held us together,' he said softly.

She looked sad, as she said, 'I didn't do a very good job, did I? I hope he does a better job.'

'Enough of maudlin about the past. Let's talk about pleasant things. So, who are you betting on?' Mr. Harris asked.

'Why, us, of course,' replied Iola smiling.

'Iola, we have two teams participating. Which one?' he asked again.

'Blane, you know I could never choose from one of our teams,' she said. 'But you've been watching them practice. What's your opinion?'

Mr. Harris considered. 'Kylie's team looks as good as they did last year, but I think they'll be facing stiff competition from Marcus' team this year. His five are strong and very talented. They've got a good chance at the "Gran-sdur". Of course, I don't know much about the competitors from the other communities,' he replied.

'I thought you'd enter your five,' said Iola.

'Mine aren't ready yet. Marcus has set his five up for failure by entering them this year. They aren't ready yet. I also think it is better that we keep my five under wraps, for a while more,' said Mr. Harris.

Iola got up gracefully, in one fluid motion. 'Come on, let's go and get some breakfast. I'm particularly keen on watching today's competition.'

Mr. Harris got up too, and they started walking up the path. 'What's so interesting today?' he asked.

'Today is fencing. Wait till you see young Carl. He would have made a great musketeer.'

'Carl?' muttered Mr. Harris. 'Wasn't he born on the same date as Sam?'

'Yes,' said Iola, 'and he's in Marcus' team.' Mr. Harris followed her up the path, looking thoughtful.

CHAPTER 25

Maya received a message from Mr. Harris a couple of days after New Year's Day, asking them to report for training at the gym. There was still a week to go before school started. It was too much to hope they'd get off till then. She hadn't spoken to Sebastian or Ryan after New Year's Eve. She sighed when she saw the message. She thought she'd better call the boys and decide on what they would tell Mr. Harris. They all had to stick to the same story. She still wasn't sure exactly what had happened that night.

She remembered the evening in bits and pieces. After Ryan and Sebastian had left the three of them in Sebastian's room, she and her friends hadn't stayed there long. They had found the room boring and had decided to go back downstairs. They'd wanted to dance and had made their way down to the basement. They'd lost their way a couple of times on the way down, and they'd had to keep putting back the things Mary Anne kept trying to steal.

When they'd finally reached the basement, and were winding their way to the dance floor through the crush of moving bodies, someone had grabbed the microphone from the D.J., and yelled, 'Fight! Outside!'

There was an exodus to the door, and the three girls had also jostled and pushed their way out. It was only once they'd climbed up the stairs and out on to the drive, that Maya had realised it was Ryan and Sebastian who were fighting.

She'd come out just in time to see Ryan pounding after Sebastian through the snow. She had tried to call out to them with her mind, but they hadn't seemed to hear her. As she'd watched, Sebastian seemed to vanish and had appeared seemingly out of nowhere, behind Ryan. There'd been a low gasp from the crowd.

'Mate! Did you see that?', 'Did he just disappear?', 'How'd he do that?'

She'd heard the murmurs and exclamations around her. That had sobered her up fast and the fuzziness in her head had cleared instantly. She'd looked at the kids milling around her. She had seen shock and amazement on their faces. She knew that she had to do something fast.

Sebastian and Ryan hadn't responded to her calling out to them, so she'd done the next best thing. She'd sent out a sharp jab at Ryan. Ryan had buckled down and curled up, holding his head. A minute later, Sebastian had also crumpled. She'd jabbed them over and over, keeping them down.

'Stop! Stop it, you witch!' Maya had opened her eyes, to find Lisa holding her by the shoulders and shaking her.

'Wha…?' Maya had stumbled backwards, feeling dizzy. Someone had pulled Lisa away.

'She's doing something to them. It's her,' Lisa had screamed.

Maya had ignored her and peered over the crowd to check on Sebastian and Ryan. They'd both staggered to their feet and were looking dazed. She'd hoped they weren't about to start fighting again.

Lisa had pointed at her and continued screaming. Some of the other kids had turned to look at Maya. Maya realised that she was still holding her head in her hands. She'd backed away, muttering, 'She's mad. I had a bit too much to drink. My head hurts.' Some of the kids had smiled hearing that. But that wasn't the worst part of the evening.

She'd turned, to push her way back inside, when she'd heard her mom's voice, 'Drunk? Did you say drunk?'

Maya had cringed as her mother had bundled her friends and her into the car and taken them home. She'd had to listen to a dozen lectures about drinking, the next day. She now flipped her phone open and called

Ryan. He picked it up on the second ring.

'Hey!' he said. 'Got the message, huh?' He didn't sound pleased either.

'Yeah!' said Maya. 'I thought we should get our stories straight before we see Mr. Harris. I'll call Seb and put him on a conference. We should all stick to the same story.'

'No!' Ryan snapped. 'I don't want to talk to that jerk.'

'Er... ok.' Maya was quiet. She wasn't sure whether she should ask him why he was mad with Sebastian. She was saved the trouble.

'Do you know that he hit on my girlfriend?' asked Ryan.

'Oh? At the party? Was that why you were fighting?'

'No, not at the party... before that. And then he made it sound like Lisa had flirted with him,' said Ryan, angrily.

Maya thought to herself that Lisa was quite capable of having flirted with Sebastian, but she didn't say anything.

'Anyway, forget that. What do we tell Mr. Harris?' asked Ryan.

'We have to come clean. A lot of people saw you. Once school starts, he's bound to hear about it. I suggest you leave the explaining to me,' she said.

'Whatever,' said Ryan.

He'd had people asking him about New Year's Eve and what had happened, and he'd decided on a simple answer, "Adrenaline rush!", and had stuck to it. He knew in no time, something more exciting would come up and people would forget about this. He knew Sebastian and he had been stupid, and if Mr. Harris gave them an earful, they deserved it. But if he had to do it again, he was sure he'd do the same thing.

'Fine... I'll tell Seb then,' said Maya and rang off. 'Boys are so stupid,' she thought, as she called Sebastian.

Sebastian surprised her with an apology, as soon as he picked up.

'For what?' asked Maya.

'The booze. I thought one drink would loosen you up. I didn't mean to get you drunk or into trouble. And, thanks for not getting me into trouble.'

'I didn't even know you had spiked our drinks,' said Maya, surprised. 'And, you didn't get us our second drinks or our third. We managed to do that and make fools of ourselves quite well, on our own. So, forget it. Look, I was just talking to Ryan,' she started.

Sebastian cut her off. 'Do me a favour. Don't mention that jerk's name to me,' he said, sounding furious.

'What are you mad about? I thought you hit on his girlfriend and that's why you were fighting,' she asked, confused.

'Is that what he's telling everyone? He told Lisa that I was dating you, and she told Anna this at the party, and now Anna won't talk to me anymore.' Maya was stunned.

'Why would he do that?' she asked 'What's wrong with him?' Maya was mad now.

'I don't know. I haven't spoken to him since that night and I don't intend to,' replied Sebastian.

'I don't understand,' said Maya. 'I spoke to him just now. He didn't say anything.'

'Like he would tell you. What did you call for, anyway?' asked Sebastian.

'To get our stories straight for Mr. Harris,' said Maya.

'Why do we have to tell him anything?' asked Sebastian.

'Because a lot of people saw you, and people are talking about it. He's sure to hear about it. It's better we tell him,' said Maya.

Sebastian had also been bombarded with questions about the fight. His answer to everyone was as simple as Ryan, but not very modest. He usually grinned and told them, 'I was born amazing'.

'I still think we can get away with it,' he said.

'I don't think so. I'll do the explaining. You simply have to keep your mouth shut. And if he yells, we take it and say sorry. We were stupid and he has every right to yell at us.'

'I don't understand why we have these cool abilities, if we can't use them,' Sebastian muttered grumpily.

'Seb? Did you hear what I said?' asked Maya impatiently.

'Yes, I did, mother. Fine! I wish I could train alone. I don't want to see that oaf's face again. I think I'll ask Mr. Harris if I can train alone,' said Sebastian

'Right now, I don't want to see him either. So if Mr. Harris agrees to train you alone, let me know,' said Maya.

The next day, Cassie and Sam were at the gym first. They'd returned the day before and had both received messages an hour later from Mr. Harris about training. Their mom was obsessive about unpacking as soon as they returned from a vacation, so they hadn't had a chance to call the others. They couldn't wait to see them. When they went into the gym, Mr. Harris was already there, waiting for them. They were happy to see him. Cassie ran across and threw herself at him, giving him a big hug.

'Happy New Year, Mr. Harris,' she said.

He gently disentangled himself, saying, 'My, my, it's nice to know I was missed. A very Happy New Year to the two of you. How was your holiday?' he asked.

'Mr. Harris, it was great. We've so much to tell you. You know…,' started Cassie.

Sam interrupted. 'Let's wait till the others come, and we can tell them all together,' he suggested.

Cassie looked put out, but she kept quiet. A few seconds later, Maya walked in. She practically flew across the room and threw herself at them.

'Sammmeeee! It's so good to see you! And you too, Cas.' She hugged them both and then punched Sam.

'Sammy, you gave us such a scare. That was so stupid. We were so worried.' Sam looked sheepish.

'Worried? About what?' Mr. Harris asked, looking concerned.

Ryan and Sebastian walked in, just then. They ignored each other. Cassie and Sam greeted them enthusiastically and were surprised at the lack of enthusiasm on their part. They both looked grim.

Mr. Harris greeted them and turned to Sam again. 'What did you do to make them worry?' he asked.

Sam told him about all that had happened on his trip, with Cassie adding her two-bit now and then. Mr. Harris's face lit up. He looked ecstatic.

'This is great news,' he said.

'Well, not really,' said Sam, looking glum. 'I've tried to do it again and I don't seem to be able to,' he said.

'Nonsense,' said Mr. Harris. 'You only need to practice. From now on, I want you to stay back for an hour every day, Sam. You've got a lot of catching up to do,' he said, indicating the others.

'Mr. Harris,' said Maya, with hesitation. He looked at her. 'There is something else.' She looked at Sebastian and Ryan. They were both looking at the floor.

'What is it?' asked Mr. Harris, looking from one to the other.

'We got into some trouble during the holidays.' She related what had happened over New Year's Eve. Mr. Harris listened to the story without expression. The boys continued staring at the floor, leaving Maya to do the explaining. Maya told the story from her point of view, leaving out the reason for the fight and her drunkenness.

When she'd finished, all Mr. Harris asked was, 'Are people talking about it?'

Sebastian answered this time. 'A bit, but most of them have forgotten the incident already,' he offered.

'Let's hope it hasn't reached the wrong ears,' said Mr. Harris cryptically. 'Let this be a lesson to you. How important it is to control your ability and not stupidly misuse it, when you don't know how to control it,' he was looking at Sam, 'or what could be the consequences of abusing it,' he said looking at Sebastian and Ryan. They all looked sorry for what they had done.

'Now, shall we start?' They nodded. Sebastian and Ryan looked relieved to have gotten off so lightly.

'Did you really do that?' Sam asked Maya, looked awed as they took their places. Maya smiled. At least someone thought she was cool.

CHAPTER 26

They got back into routine in no time, and the days once again became a blur, of training, school, training and more training. They were all getting better at controlling their abilities. Maya was now practicing projecting thoughts into people's minds and was having a lot of fun. Mr. Harris had specifically told her to project thoughts into the minds of the other four. She did that gleefully, much to their annoyance. She kept getting them into trouble or distracting them, by projecting weird and funny thoughts. When the others complained to Mr. Harris, he'd told them that they had to learn to block her projections, by blanking out their thoughts and pushing her out.

They learned to do that quite fast and soon, when she projected a thought into their mind, they'd push her out, with a "Get out, Maya". They were able to push her out once she got in, but they were still not able to anticipate it fast enough, to stop her getting in.

Sebastian's new challenge was jumping. In reverse! Mr. Harris had him jumping hurdles, the high jump and doing the pole vault, as part of his training, and Sebastian found he enjoyed it. He also had Sebastian jumping up the stands in the stadium. He started with just one step and then he'd increased it. Sebastian was up to five steps at a time now. His muscles protested every day, and he missed and fell very often, but he persisted and kept practicing.

The first few weeks after they got back to training, Sam was like Mr. Harris's new toy. Other than setting out new challenges for them and giving them a tip or two, he left the others alone and directed all his attention to Sam. Sam tried his best, but was unable to do anything. When he tried hard, he could feel the energy deep in his mind, but he couldn't reach it. It was very frustrating.

One day, after hours of trying, he flopped down wearily and said, 'No, that's it! I'm not doing this anymore. I cannot. I'm useless.'

Mr. Harris sat down next to him. 'Sam, nothing comes easy. You have incredible power in you. You cannot give up this easily. You know what? I think I'm putting too much pressure on you. Let's ease up, shall we? You practice hard, but at your pace. What do you say?'

Sam nodded, but he was not convinced. He felt very frustrated and depressed, especially when he saw how well the others were progressing. One day, after a particularly exasperating evening, Sam was sitting on the field, tired and feeling sorry for himself. The other four had gone home long back. He looked up and saw Mr. Harris walking towards him

'Sam!' said Mr. Harris. 'I've been thinking. The other day, when you and Cassie were telling me the story of how you controlled the water on your vacation, I got excited. I feel that I didn't pay enough attention to your story. Explain it to me again, in detail.'

Sam explained again, right from the beginning, his parents fighting and Cassie's annoying behaviour, to how he had manipulated the energy he had felt within him, and ended up stuck in the middle of the sea. Mr. Harris nodded, like something made sense.

'Sam! I think, your power manifested that particular day, because of the storm, and what triggered it must have been the anger you felt against Cassie,' he said.

'What do you mean? That I can use my powers only if there is a storm and I'm angry?' asked Sam.

'No, what I'm trying to help you understand is that the energy is in you. You will learn to reach the power within you, soon. But that day, it happened because of the storm. You say that you felt the storm around you, the electricity and the power of the storm. You were able to do all that you did that day, because of the storm. But soon, you will be able to do it anytime you want. Don't give up hope. Maybe you have had to wait longer than the others to find your gift, but I have a feeling your gift will be well worth the wait. Believe in yourself!' he said and patted Sam on the arm. 'I think that's enough for today. Go home,' he added, in a kind voice.

Ryan's control over his strength had increased dramatically. He could now break and crush most things. He was able to feel the weak spots in objects, and by placing his fingers on the pressure points, he could shatter even large boulders. He'd learnt by experience that even the large boulders had pressure points. Some weekends, Mr. Harris would ask him to go to the local quarry, instead of coming to school for training, and practice breaking boulders there.

He also had Ryan breaking glass. This was proving more difficult for Ryan than breaking boulders. Mr. Harris asked him to find the pressure point and exert just enough pressure to crack the glass. Mr. Harris had demonstrated with a wine glass. He had held the glass in his hand and had felt around and pressed. The glass had broken into two neat pieces. After a few days of practice, Ryan was able to find the pressure point, but he always seemed to exert too much pressure than what was needed, and he ended up shattering the glass. His arms were full of nicks and cuts. He wore gloves for protection, but that protected him only up to his wrist. He didn't mind. He actually liked the pain. It stopped him from thinking of other things.

His training and football were his whole life now. The rest of his life was in shambles. His dad had thrown him out of the house. After their confrontation six months back, which had ended with him breaking the console, things had grown steadily worse. It was like Ryan's stand had pushed his dad over the edge. His dad had started being aggressive and abusive often.

One day, when Ryan was out, he'd hit Tammy, and she'd packed up and left. She was now staying with her boyfriend. Ryan didn't blame her. If it hadn't been for Joey, he would have left long back. Luckily, his dad wasn't showing his temper at Joey yet, but Ryan knew it was simply a matter of time. He had tried to stay out of his dad's way as much as possible, leaving home before his dad woke up and returning as late as possible.

A couple of weeks back, when he'd returned home from work, he'd found his things strewn on the drive. He'd tried the front door, but his dad had changed the locks. He'd shimmied up the trellis and found the balcony door locked too. He'd knocked and rung the bell a few times, but no one had answered. So, in the end, he'd called Randy and had asked him to come around. Randy and a couple of other friends had driven up, and helped Ryan load his stuff. Randy's mom had insisted he stay with them, and Ryan had accepted gratefully.

Ryan had gone to Joey's classroom the next day, to check if Joey was fine and Joey had clung to him, weeping. Ryan hoped now that he wasn't around his dad wouldn't start in on Joey. He wished he could take Joey away with him, but he was sure if he did that, his dad would call the cops. Joey had begged Ryan to take him back to Randy's. He'd explained to Joey the consequences of running away and Joey had understood, but it hadn't helped Ryan's feelings of guilt. He checked on Joey every day at school and tried to spend as much time with him as possible. If his dad wasn't home, Joey would call, and Ryan would go over. He had enough time to spend with Joey now since Lisa had broken up with him after the New Year's Eve fiasco. Only the routine of training and football helped him hold onto his sanity, as his life crumbled around him.

CHAPTER 27

Cassie's skills were honing beautifully. She could now move two or sometimes even three things at the same time, in different directions. But she only had to master one task, before Mr. Harris had a harder challenge lined up for her. Being a hard worker, she enjoyed the challenge. She was also thrilled with how well she was progressing in her studies. The results were out, and she had done extremely well. She had topped in almost all her subjects. She had scored the highest in Physics, and she was ecstatic, as she had worked hardest on that subject. She had wanted to live up to Ms. Cabot's expectations.

When Ms. Cabot had given out their papers, she had told Cassie, 'Well done, Cassandra. Great job!' Cassie had almost exploded with happiness.

A few weeks later, Cassie was putting away her things into her satchel at the end of class when Ms. Cabot called out to her softly, 'Cassandra, I would like to have a word with you. Please stay back after class.'

Cassie felt her heart skip a beat. Since the time that Ms. Cabot had confided in her, Cassie had hoped she would get to spend more time with Ms. Cabot. But to her disappointment, Ms. Cabot hadn't asked her to stay back or shown any particular interest in her.

'Yes, Ms. Cabot,' she said, flushing with pleasure.

She hoped neither Maya nor Sebastian were going to make nuisances of themselves, by staying back. She turned around and pretended to be packing her bag, watching Maya and Sebastian through the corner of her eye. Luckily, they seemed preoccupied and left without waiting for her. Once all the kids had left, Cassie approached Ms. Cabot's desk.

'Cassandra, I found a very nice series on famous scientists and philosophers. I was wondering… maybe, you'd like to watch it sometime?' she asked.

'Yes, Ms. Cabot, I'd love that,' said Cassie, enthusiastically.

'I thought we could watch it after school sometime one of these days, and discuss it. I haven't seen it yet. I felt it would be more interesting, watching it with someone who would enjoy it as much as I,' said Ms. Cabot.

'Yes, Ms. Cabot,' trilled Cassie.

She couldn't believe Ms. Cabot wanted to hang out with her and watch… whatever it was she had said. She hadn't paid attention to that part. She was willing to watch anything, if it meant spending time with Ms. Cabot.

'Maybe tomorrow, you could stay back after school?' asked Ms. Cabot.

Cassie's face fell. 'I… I'm sorry, Ms. Cabot… but I can't… I'd love to. But I have practice,' said Cassie, feeling disappointed.

'Oh right… with Mr. Harris. How's that going?' asked Ms. Cabot.

'It's alright,' said Cassie, in a bored voice.

'Maybe, you could tell him you have some extra classes and take off?' asked Ms. Cabot, with a wink. 'I promise I won't tell.'

Cassie was sorely tempted. She couldn't believe Ms. Cabot had become so close to her, and liked her so much she was willing to keep a secret for her. Like how a best friend would. For a minute, she got carried away with her fantasy. She imagined discussing fashion and boys with Ms. Cabot, going shopping or taking in a movie with her, or… she came down to earth with a crash, when Ms. Cabot said, 'Well, Cassandra?'

Cassie sighed. She knew there was no way she could lie to Mr. Harris. She had a feeling he'd know right away.

So, she sadly shook her head. 'I wish I could Ms. Cabot, but I simply can't miss practice.'

'You're a good girl, Cassandra. I admire your discipline. I was merely testing you. I would never think of helping you bunk practice. You are so much like me. Well, I guess I'll have to watch the show by myself. It would have been nice to watch it with you, though,' said Ms. Cabot, with a sigh.

Cassie felt horrible for disappointing Ms. Cabot, and she walked out of class feeling dejected. She tried even harder in the following weeks to please Ms. Cabot, to make up for having turned down her offer. To Cassie's delight, a couple of weeks later, Mr. Harris became busy with the football team and their upcoming game that he hardly bothered with their training. Thinking that this may be the only chance she would get to spend time with Ms. Cabot, Cassie decided to ask her about the documentary she had mentioned.

She hung back after Physics period the next day, and waited for the rest of the kids to leave. After the last one left, she hesitantly approached Ms. Cabot's desk. Ms. Cabot looked up and saw her waiting.

'Yes, Cassandra,' she asked smiling. Cassie was relieved. Ms. Cabot wasn't angry with her, for having said no.

'Mr. Harris is busy with the football team and he's eased up on our training. I think I could get away this week, Ms. Cabot. I was wondering, if we could perhaps watch the documentary you were telling me about. That is, if you feel like it,' she asked hopefully.

'That'll be lovely, Cassandra. I haven't watched it yet. It would be nice to watch it with you. I'll tell you when.' Ms. Cabot looked genuinely delighted.

The next day Cassie didn't have a class with Ms. Cabot, but she received a note from her, asking Cassie to come to the audiovisual room after school. When school ended that day, Cassie told Maya that she was feeling unwell and wouldn't be coming to practice. She asked her to tell Sam that she would be going home straight after school. Maya didn't suspect anything as they were all taking turns playing truant, with Mr. Harris not paying much attention to them. Cassie waited for Maya and Sebastian to leave class, before hurrying over to the audiovisual room.

Ms. Cabot hadn't come in as yet, so Cassie sat down and waited. The audiovisual room was on the second floor of the main building. It was a long room with a screen at one end. The projector hung down from the ceiling, about halfway up the room. The room had no windows, so Cassie had turned on the lights when she'd come in.

Ms. Cabot came in soon after, with a box of CDs. 'Hi Cassandra! You're already here. Good! Would you please come and help me?' she said, setting the box down on one of the tables which stood against the wall. 'That CD is somewhere in here. Here...' She gave a stack of CDs to Cassie. 'You go through that. I'll go through these.'

As they looked through the CDs, Ms. Cabot asked her, 'How did you manage to get away from practice today?'

Cassie looked nervous and said, 'I told them I wasn't well.'

She waited for Ms. Cabot's reaction. She hoped Ms. Cabot wouldn't think badly of her, for having lied. But Ms. Cabot didn't say anything. They continued to search through the CDs.

'Ah! Here it is!' exclaimed Ms. Cabot, pulling out a disc.

She slipped it into the player and pressed play. They sat down in the front row to watch. Cassie had thought the documentary would be deadly dull. She had only agreed to watch it, to spend time with Ms. Cabot. Putting up with some boring show was well worth it. But to her surprise, she found herself enjoying the documentary. Ms. Cabot added a few comments here and there, explaining some of the things Cassie couldn't understand. They spent a very pleasant hour. After it was over, they discussed the documentary for a while. Cassie had many questions and Ms. Cabot patiently answered them.

'How are things at home, Cassandra?' asked Ms. Cabot, after a while.

'Oh, still the same, Ms. Cabot. Mom angry all the time, Dad hides behind his work and Sam and I tiptoe around the place,' she said, with a grimace.

'Has Sam gone home?' asked Ms. Cabot. 'Don't you go home together?'

Cassie wondered how Ms. Cabot knew that. 'I don't know. He's probably at practice. Not that we practice much nowadays. Mr. Harris is fully occupied with the football team. They're very good,' she added enthusiastically. 'Do you think we'll win, Ms. Cabot?'

'I think we have a very good chance, especially with Ryan on the team,' replied Ms. Cabot.

'He is brilliant,' said Cassie, proudly.

Ms. Cabot lowered her voice. 'It's not only his skills at football they're talking about, you know. It seems that something strange happened over the holidays. You train with him. You don't know anything about it, do you?' She looked at Cassie and then shook her head. 'How stupid of me! Of course, you wouldn't know.'

Cassie felt affronted, and so she said, 'Oh, about the New Year's Eve fight. I know all about that.'

'Really?' Ms. Cabot raised her eyebrows. 'Well, what did happen? I heard such strange stories. How do you know? Who told you?' asked Ms. Cabot.

Cassie was thrilled she knew something important that she could share with Ms. Cabot. She told her about the fight.

'Oh! I heard all this,' said Ms. Cabot dismissively. 'It's just that I heard a rumour, about Sebastian disappearing. But I guess that's all rubbish,' said Ms. Cabot, getting up.

'He didn't disappear,' blurted out Cassie. 'He just runs very fast.'

As soon as she said it, she realised she'd been indiscreet. She looked down, feeling annoyed with herself. On top of that, Ms. Cabot must think she was mad. Cassie looked up at her, but Ms. Cabot didn't look surprised.

'So, speed is his ability, huh?' she said smiling. 'What's yours?' she asked, sitting down again.

Cassie felt frightened. 'You know?' she whispered, her mind in a whirl.

'Cassandra, do you think Iola would allow you to be under the supervision of only one person?' Ms. Cabot asked gently. 'I'm here, to keep an eye on Mr. Harris. You are very special children. We have to make sure you are well protected, at all times. I need you to promise me that you won't tell Mr. Harris that I'm here, keeping an eye on him. You seem to be the most sensible of the five of you, and that's why I decided to confide in you. What Ryan and Sebastian did was very foolish.' She shook her head. 'But, I guess, boys will be boys.'

Cassie was thrilled that she could finally share her secret with Ms. Cabot. She answered all the questions Ms. Cabot had. She told her how much they'd progressed and what they could do now. She couldn't believe Ms. Cabot was part of this.

'That was why I felt such a connection with her,' thought Cassie.

Ms. Cabot knew so much, so much more than Mr. Harris. Maybe they could get Ms. Cabot to coach them, instead of Mr. Harris.

'I'll work hard and she'll be so proud of me,' Cassie thought dreamily.

Ms. Cabot interrupted her daydream. 'What about your brother? What can he do?' asked Ms. Cabot.

'Nothing much,' giggled Cassie. She saw Ms. Cabot's face fall and quickly added, 'Though he did do something incredible while we were holidaying in Tobago.' She told Ms. Cabot the whole story.

'That's remarkable,' said Ms. Cabot. Cassie felt a little piqued at that. Ms. Cabot placed her hand on Cassie's arm and looked at Cassie, with her bright, blue eyes and said, 'but personally, I think you are much better at controlling your ability than he will ever be.'

Cassie was thrilled. For the first time in her life, someone thought she was better than Sam. 'You said he tried again and he couldn't do it?'

'Yes,' said Cassie gleefully. 'He's been trying, over and over. Mr. Harris has been trying all sorts of things to help him, but it doesn't seem to be working.'

Ms. Cabot looked thoughtful. 'What does Mr. Harris think?' she asked.

'He acts like Sam's the chosen one or something. He seems to think Sam will do something miraculous,' said Cassie, wishing they'd get off the topic of Sam.

'Cassandra, keep me posted on what's happening there. You mustn't tell Mr. Harris about me being here to keep an eye on him. It undermines him, you see. I think it's also better that you don't share this with your friends either. They don't seem to be as sensible as you,' she added. 'This has to be our secret. Yours and mine. Can I trust you?' she asked.

'Yes, Ms. Cabot, of course,' said Cassie fervently.

'You are a brave girl, Cassandra, and I know you will outshine the others,' said Ms. Cabot.

She looked down at her watch. 'Oh dear! Is that the time? We've had such a lovely time I didn't realize it was so late. You'd better hurry and get home, before it gets too dark,' she said.

Cassie looked down at her watch. She was surprised to see that it was almost six. She picked up her bag.

'Thank you Ms. Cabot. I'll see you on Monday,' she said, as she left.

Ms. Cabot called out after her, 'Remember Cassandra... our secret!'

CHAPTER 28

Holy Trinity had now reached the finals of the Raiken Trophy. Sixteen towns, including Skallen, vied for the football trophy every year. The first round of matches was between the various schools, within the town, and then the school that won the finals represented their town. Skallen had only three schools which had football teams, and Holy Trinity's was easily the best. They usually won the finals in their town and went on to represent Skallen. The tournament had been initiated by Skallen and their neighbouring town, Firsten, decades back. For years, the two towns had clashed for the trophy. Soon, other towns nearby had started participating, and now it was one of the major events on the region's calendar.

Skallen hadn't made it to the finals in twenty years. They hadn't even made it past the first two rounds for the last couple of years. They were playing the Purple Silks, of St. Jessop's School. The Purple Silks were from the town of Roberton. Roberton had won the trophy for the last two years, and were hoping for a hat trick. But the Skallen Raiders were in top form, and looked like they had a very good chance of breaking their losing streak. The whole school was on a high, awaiting the finals.

A big blow to the team morale was the absence of Devon, the captain of Skallen Raiders, who had taken a bad fall in their quarter finals against Belmont and broken his ankle. He had missed the semi-finals and wasn't fit enough for the finals either. Ryan was promoted to captain. But it hadn't stopped the Skallen Raiders from thumping their opponents, Skerritas, in the semi-finals.

The Principal and the Skallen council had made sure the finals would be held in Skallen. It wasn't only the kids at school who were excited. The whole town was waiting with bated breath. The yellow and orange Skallen Raiders' colours were up all over town. There were buntings crisscrossing streets and adorning the front of houses. There were "Go Skallen Raiders" posters stuck on shop windows. There was even a huge billboard with "Go Skallen Raiders" and the team logo on the highway, as it entered the town.

The championship match was being played in the Holy Trinity football stadium, which could seat 3000 people, and the tickets were all sold out on the first day. As the big day neared, the excitement was palpable. Ryan had completely stopped training with the other four and was concentrating solely on football. Mr. Harris also spent almost all his time with the football team. Sebastian, Cassie, Sam and Maya were left to practice on their own. They practiced on the football field and though none of them were football fans, the tension and excitement of the match infected them too. They had taken to hanging back after training, to watch the team practice for a while. Sam had suddenly found himself very popular in school as he was on first name terms with all the players.

The match was scheduled for the first week of February. Skallen had experienced a snowstorm in the beginning of January, and sporadic snowfall for the first two weeks of the month. To everybody's relief, it stopped snowing in the middle of the month, and by the first week of February, the weather was cold but clear. Finally, the first Saturday of February arrived.

Ryan woke up on the day of the match feeling nauseous, as his gut seemed to twist in anticipation of the day. He'd found that being captain was a big responsibility. He felt the weight of the town riding on his shoulders. He'd closed his mind to the pressure and was trying to keep his thoughts only on the game.

He sat up and stretched, knocking over the lamp which was on Randy's bedside table. He was sleeping on an air bed in Randy's room.

Randy's room was tiny and was just about big enough for one person, let alone two burly football players.

'Wha...?' Randy sat up with a start.

'My bad!' said Ryan, and tried to twist around in the tiny space to reach the lamp.

'Leave it. Let's get ready. We don't need to straighten up our room. There's no way my Mom will yell at us today,' said Randy, grinning.

He leapt out of bed. 'Man, I'm on fire. Let's go! Let's go!'

His enthusiasm infected Ryan, and his nervousness disappeared, as he lifted his hand up for a high five.

'Go Raiders!' he yelled, as Randy high-fived him.

They got ready and were on the field by seven. Mr. Harris had asked them to come later than usual as he wanted his boys well rested before the game.

The stadium was packed with spectators that morning. The number of people who came by to watch them practice had steadily grown, over the past month. At first it had only been students of Holy Trinity, but soon other residents of Skallen had also started dropping by, to watch their team in action. Cassie, Sebastian, Maya and Sam had been on the football field, training since five, as usual, and were almost done when the players started arriving. Now, they too were sitting in the stands watching the team practice.

'So, tell me again,' Maya asked. 'What's that guy called? The one who keeps falling down?'

Sam groaned. Once he'd gotten invested in the game, he'd read up everything about it. He was like a walking football encyclopaedia. He knew almost everything about the game, names of school players, national players, international players, present and past. He knew the stats, the history of the game and even football gossip. He couldn't understand why the others couldn't simply read up on it. He'd sent them links, but it didn't look like they'd read any of it.

'Striker! He's a striker! The ones standing on this side of that line,' he said, pointing, 'are usually the strikers.'

Maya nodded. 'Right.' After a few minutes, she asked, 'Do you think we'll win?'

'We're looking pretty good. We've got a good chance of winning,' said Sam.

'I think I'll try out next year,' said Sebastian. 'I'm so fast, I'll be running circles around them.'

'Yeah, right, like Mr. Harris will let you display your powers out there, in front of the whole stadium. Keep dreaming,' said Cassie.

'Well, I won't run very fast. But, just think about it. I'll be so cool. Chicks dig this, you know. I didn't realise that. Otherwise, maybe I'd have started playing earlier,' said Sebastian.

'Maybe, being the operative word,' said Maya drily.

'I thought you'd got back with your girlfriend,' asked Cassie.

'I did,' said Sebastian, 'but I like keeping my options open.'

Sebastian had made up with Anna before she'd gone back to school, and they'd promised to keep in touch. Sebastian had known that wasn't going to happen. They'd promised to write and to call each other, but he hadn't heard from her since she left. To his surprise, he found he didn't care much. He usually moved on pretty fast, but he thought he'd feel bad about Anna because he'd liked her. But it seemed like he was super resilient. He watched Ryan intercept a pass, with fluid grace. He had more or less mended fences with Ryan over the New Year's Eve fight, though he didn't think they were going to be best buddies anytime soon.

'Ok, I'm out of here,' said Maya, interrupting his thoughts. 'Are you coming this evening?'

'Try and stop me,' said Sam.

'We've made posters and stuff,' added Cassie.

'Oh, I don't know. Maybe I will, maybe I won't,' said Sebastian, in a bored voice.

'Then maybe I'll see you or maybe I won't,' said Maya, shaking her head at Cassie and Sam and mouthing, 'What an ass!' as she picked up her bag and walked away. The others left soon after.

The match was scheduled to start at seven. By five, the players were in the locker room. Mr. Harris had only made them practice for a couple of hours in the morning. The kids were under a lot of pressure, not only from school, but from the whole town. It was getting to them, and it showed at practice, in the morning. They had fumbled, missed passes and were losing their temper. So he'd asked them to stop.

He'd gathered the boys around and spoken to them, calming them down. He'd sent them home after that and had asked them to avoid the company of friends or family, as much as possible. He didn't want anyone to stress his boys anymore today.

He was on the field the rest of the day, overseeing things. He went to the locker room at six sharp. The boys were changed and sitting around, exchanging friendly banter, trying to stay calm. In spite of his talk that morning, they all still seemed wired up. He went around the room talking to the boys individually, trying to ease the stress. Ten minutes before they had to go out, he went to one end of the room and blew his whistle to attract their attention. There was immediate silence and they all looked at him, expectantly.

'Okay, boys, this is it! I'm not here to give you any last minute instructions. We've gone through the plays enough number of times, for them to be imprinted in your brain... or at least, I hope it is,' he added smiling. He held up a football. 'See this? This... is all that you have to focus on, for the next two hours. I know the last few weeks haven't been easy. Carrying the hopes and expectations of an entire town can be a heavy burden. I want you to leave that baggage, here. When you go out on the field today, this ball is the most important thing. This ball... and your team. Nothing else and no one else matters. You will win today, for yourselves... not for me, not for the school, not for Skallen... but for yourselves. Now... the present... it's your time!! So make the best of it. You are winners. You are the Skallen Raiders. You've won your last fifteen matches. You are unbeatable. You are the best! So, go out and win this game!'

By the end of his speech, most of the players were bouncing on their toes, raring to go. They could hear a low rumble start outside, "Skallen! Skallen!"

'Put it here,' shouted Ryan, stretching his hand out, palm facing down. Other hands came smacking down, on top of his. 'Let's go win it, boys,' he bellowed, pumping his fist.

They jogged out of the locker room and onto the field. There was a thunderous roar as they went out. They ran onto the field and stood in a straight line, for the anthems. The opposing team, in their purple and black colours, had jogged out too, and they were now standing in line, beside the Skallen players. The school anthems were sung first, and then the town song. The whole stadium stood up and roared out the Skallen anthem, along with the players. Then, Skallen's mayor walked down the line, greeting the players and saying a few words of encouragement, here and there. The captains greeted each other, exchanged flags and waited for the referee to join them for the coin toss. The referee tossed the coin, as the Roberton captain called it. Roberton won the toss, picked the side, the whistle blew and the match started.

For the first fifteen minutes, the two teams seemed evenly matched.

The players on both sides passed the ball, dribbled and feinted, without giving the other side an inch. Skallen scored the first goal. It was a clever pass, from Ryan to Randy, who slipped past the Roberton goalkeeper with ease. The crowd went ecstatic.

Maya was jumping up and down as she screamed with the rest of the crowd, "Go Skallen!" Her throat was already hoarse from screaming. She was there with her mom, Mary Anne, Felicity and their parents. Daniel had asked Maya and her mom to join Sebastian and him in the V.I.P. box, but Maya had wanted to watch the match with her friends, and so her mom had declined the invitation. She looked around at the packed stadium. It looked like the whole town was here. She tried to see if she could spot Cassie and Sam, but she couldn't.

Sam and Cassie were way over on the other side. They had come by themselves since their mom was working late and their dad was out of town. They were also jumping and screaming, waving the posters they had brought along.

Sebastian was there too, watching from the V.I.P box with his dad and some friends. Gone was the air of boredom with which he had answered Maya's question in the morning. He was holding the Skallen flag and shouting as enthusiastically as the rest of the stadium, at the top of his voice.

The crowd was still rejoicing over their first goal, when Roberton evened it by scoring a goal. Sheldon had seen the Roberton player approaching with the ball and had run out as usual from his goalpost, leaving it wide open. The Roberton player had neatly sidestepped Sheldon, and sent the ball flying into the unguarded goalpost.

There was a collective groan around the stadium. Roberton capitalized by scoring two more goals in quick succession. The first was a penalty stroke given to the Roberton side. They were awarded the penalty because of Ryan. In frustration, he had elbowed a Roberton player, while trying to get the ball from him. Ryan had clearly heard the crack of breaking bone as he had connected. The Roberton player had gone down, howling. The medics and the Roberton football coach had rushed onto the field to help him. He was carried out on a stretcher, and Roberton was awarded a penalty stroke. The replacement, who had come in for the hurt player, had converted the penalty into a goal. Just before the whistle went for half time, Sheldon had again left his goalpost unguarded, giving away the third goal.

Mr. Harris walked grimly up and down the locker room, at half time. The mood in the locker room was sombre. Mr. Harris spoke quietly to Sheldon about leaving the goalpost.

All he said to Ryan was a curt, 'Behave yourself!'

He walked to the front of the room. The boys were panting, exhausted and looking very sorry for themselves.

'You've trained too hard and too long to let this slip away. Believe!' he said, raising his voice. 'Believe in yourselves! Believe in your team! Believe that you can win! This is your time. Don't let it slip away,' he added, in a softer tone.

He saw the players looking glumly at one another. He could see that his words weren't motivating them. They seemed to have given up. They already looked beaten. There was another five minutes to go, before they had to go out. Ryan was sitting on a bench, staring down at the floor. He hadn't even looked up when Mr. Harris had spoken. He got up now and looked around at his teammates.

'I don't know about you guys, but the game isn't over for me yet. I'm not a loser… and I don't plan to lose tonight. I intend to win this, with or without your help. If it means kicking that ball all by myself to their goalpost, I will. You look like you've given up. So, there doesn't seem to be any point in me even asking for your help. But, I'm asking anyway! I need to know who I can depend on. Who is going to win this game with me?' They all simply stared at him. 'Who is going to stand with me?' he shouted again, louder.

Randy grinned at him as he stood up. Ryan put out his fist and Randy fist bumped him. One by one, the players picked themselves off the bench or the floor, and fist bumped Ryan. All except Sheldon, who stood leaning against his locker, chewing.

Ryan looked at him. 'Shel?' he asked.

Sheldon spat out the piece of paper he'd been chewing on. 'I don't know, Ryan. I mean, I plan to win this game all by myself, with or without your help. Even if it means, hitting the ball all the way from my goalpost to theirs. So, I'll be damned if I'll come and stand by you,' he said grinning.

'Yeah, man!', 'Way to go, guys!', 'Let's wrap this up!' With whoops and cheers, they jogged out onto the field again.

Skallen began cheering for their boys, as they ran out. The Roberton players looked smug, like they already had the game in the bag. Five minutes into the second half, Skallen scored their second goal. The Roberton players realised that Skallen was putting up a fight and bucked up their pace. Both sides played great football, neither giving the other team an inch.

Skallen scored again and equalized the game. It looked like the game would end in a penalty shootout. Half a minute before the final whistle, Ryan had the ball. He was halfway down the field. He looked around for another player to pass it to, but they were all covered. He looked down the field at the Roberton goalpost, and saw that, except the goalkeeper, no one was near. He knew he wouldn't be able to make it to the goalpost in time. It was a long shot, but he decided to take it. He gave the ball a mighty kick. It flew straight as an arrow, into the waiting arms of the goalkeeper. The ball slammed into the goalkeeper, lifting him off his feet. The goalkeeper and the ball flew backwards into the net, and hit the back of the goalpost. There was a second of stunned silence, as the final whistle blew. Then, it sank in. Skallen had won.

The crowd surged up as one, erupting in cheers. Streamers, flags and confetti rained down on the field, as the Skallen players hugged one another, collapsing to the ground. The mountain of bodies grew, as one by one, the players threw themselves on the mounting pile.

Maya would have screamed if she could, but her voice was hoarse. All that came out were strangled croaks. She and her friends were clutching one another and jumping up and down, in excitement. On the other side, Cassie and Sam were doing the same. Cassie had bitten her fingers raw, during the last ten minutes of the game. Sebastian was busy in the V.I.P box, collecting money from all his friends who had bet on Roberton.

The bodies which were piled on the ground disentangled themselves, and Ryan was hoisted up on the shoulders of the other players. They did a victory lap. Sam yelled and waved at Ryan, as the players jogged past them. Ryan was waving at the crowd and he caught sight of Sam and Cassie. He waved back at them and gave them a thumbs up, much to Sam's delight.

Cassie looked around the stadium after the group of players had passed them. She saw quite a few people leaving. After a match, it took hours to get the cars out, and many people left early to avoid the rush.

'Come on Sammy, let's go. We can ask someone to drop us,' she said. There was still the trophy to be handed out, surely a speech or two. It would take another half hour, for things to wrap up. She caught sight of the Greenes, who lived on their road. She was sure they wouldn't mind dropping Sam and her back home. If Sam and she hurried, they would be able to catch up with the Greenes outside.

'No, I want to stay and congratulate Ryan,' said Sam.

'Sam! It's past ten. Mom told us to be home by nine. We're in trouble, as it is. Come on. Get up,' urged Cassie.

'I'm not coming. You leave if you want to,' said Sam obstinately. 'There are so many people I know here. I can get a lift with anyone.'

'That actually sounds like a better idea,' thought Cassie. Her mom couldn't get mad at her for coming late if Sam came in even later.

'Fine! I'll see you at home, then,' she said. She picked up her bag and hurried out to the car park, looking for the Greenes. She saw Colin Greene and called out to him. He and his mom were waiting for his dad to bring their car around. They readily agreed to drop her.

'But, where's Sam?' asked Mrs. Greene.

'He wants to watch till the end. He said he'd find someone to drop him home,' said Cassie.

'Dad, can I go back and watch with Sam?' asked Colin eagerly.

'I'd let you go if I thought for a minute that you would actually go watch with Sam. You'd only go find that nasty gang you hang out with,' said Mr. Greene.

'But, Dad… I promise,' protested Colin.

'No, Colin. We're going home,' said Mr. Greene firmly.

Mrs. Greene looked mortified, that this exchange had taken place in front of Cassie and she hastily changed the subject. Cassie was dead beat by the time she got home. Her mom wasn't home yet, and all Cassie's worrying had been for nothing. She changed, crawled into bed and was asleep in minutes.

CHAPTER 29

Maya woke up and reached out for her bedside lamp. She switched it on and looked at the clock. It was almost five in the morning. She felt a vague sense of anxiety. She wasn't sure why she had woken up. It was still dark outside, so she lay down again and pulled the covers over herself. She'd been dreaming about something; she didn't remember what it was about. She yawned and tried to go back to sleep. She tossed and turned for a while, restlessly.

She finally got up, padded over to the armchair near the window and curled up in it, staring at the darkness outside. She tried to remember what it was she'd been dreaming about. Sam? Something about Sam! The feeling that something was wrong wouldn't leave her. She got up from the chair, went to her bedside table and picked up her phone. She debated whether to call Sam or not. He must be fast asleep. He wasn't going to be pleased if she woke him up because of a crazy dream. It was just a dream, and she didn't even remember much of it. She decided that it was stupid to wake him up. She walked back to the armchair with her phone. She sat there looking at the instrument for a while, undecided on what to do. She finally decided to call. She knew she wouldn't be able to go back to sleep till she'd spoken to him.

She flipped her phone open and called him. His phone kept ringing. He didn't pick it up. He was probably sleeping too soundly to hear it. She went back and lay down. She pulled the covers over herself again and tried to go back to sleep. After half an hour, she gave it up as a lost cause. She just couldn't shake off the feeling that something was not okay. Her stomach felt queasy with anxiety. She decided to try Cassie's number. It rang for a bit before Cassie picked it up and said a sleepy hello.

'Cas! It's Maya!'

'Maya! Do you know what time it is? What's wrong with you? We don't have practice today. Go back to sleep,' said Cassie, sounding sleepy and irritated.

'I know, I know. I'm sorry for waking you up, Cas. But, I had this weird dream. It's probably nothing, but is Sam okay?' she asked nervously.

There was a pause. 'Why?' asked Cassie, sounding more awake.

'I just told you. I dreamt about him and…,' Maya hesitated, '… also, I have this bad feeling,' she added. 'He's home, right?'

'He should be. But, one sec! Let me check.' Maya waited, while Cassie got out of bed and went to Sam's room. She knocked on the door, but there was no reply. She opened the room and switched on the light. Her heart leapt to her throat when she saw the empty bed.

'Cas?' She heard Maya's voice over the phone, sounding concerned. For a moment, it felt like it was coming from far away as Cassie went cold with fear.

'He's not here. His bed hasn't been slept in. Maya, he's not here.' There was silence, as both girls panicked.

'Do you think he might have crashed out in some other room or in the living room, maybe?' asked Maya.

'I'll check.' Cassie raced through the house, checking all the rooms, trying to be as quiet as possible.

She knew it was a futile exercise, as Sam never slept anywhere else but in his own room. She even peeked into her parent's room, but only her mom was there. Cassie felt a growing sense of apprehension.

'Maya, he's nowhere in the house,' she whispered, as she made her way back to her room.

'Could he be at a friend's place? Maybe it became late and he slept over at someone's house,' suggested Maya, hopefully.

'No way!' said Cassie. 'First and foremost, he doesn't have any friends, definitely none he'd stay over with. And even if he had plans of staying over, he would have informed my Mom.'

'Maybe he called and told your Mom,' said Maya.

'Maybe. Should I wake her up and ask her?' Cassie asked nervously.

'I think you better. Call me back as soon as you can,' said Maya, hanging up. She sat by the phone, trying to stay calm as she waited for Cassie to call back.

On one hand, Cassie was filled with anxiety about Sam and on the other, she felt scared to go and wake her mom. If Sam hadn't called her mom, Cassie knew who was going to get blamed for Sam's disappearance. She hesitated outside her mom's door, but then she thought of Sam and she went in.

As she had foreseen, her mom went crazy. She raved and ranted at Cassie for leaving Sam alone at the match and coming home without him. Finally, she realised that yelling at Cassie wasn't going to help in finding Sam. She called the police and told them that her son was missing. They said they'd send someone around. Then, she called her husband and asked him to get back home. By this time, Cassie was going through the school book and was calling Sam's classmates, one by one.

By eight, the house was crawling with people. The police had arrived and a few neighbours, who'd seen the police car outside, had come over to see if they could help. Her mom was busy with all of them and Cassie slipped away to her room, to call Maya. She had texted Maya earlier, telling her that her mom didn't know where Sam was, and promising to call as soon as she could get free. She brought her up to speed with what was going on.

'Get ready,' said Maya. 'I'm coming to pick you up. And, call Seb and Ryan. Tell them we're meeting at Seb's place. Tell Ryan to come there,' she instructed.

'My Mom will have a cow if I go missing now,' said Cassie.

'Doesn't matter! We'll deal with that later,' replied Maya.

Cassie got ready. To her relief, when she went back down, her dad had arrived. She told him, quietly, that she and some friends were going to check out the usual places Sam hung out at, and see if they could find him. Her dad was so preoccupied she didn't think he even heard her. He simply nodded absent-mindedly. That was enough for Cassie. She scooted.

Maya dressed swiftly. As she dressed, she tried to remember her dream. She could recall fragmented bits. It had been dark and frightening. She'd felt something cutting into her wrists and ankles. It was all so hazy... she wasn't sure she remembered it right. But the one thing she remembered clearly was that she had felt Sam's presence strongly. There had been a voice, saying something. Someone else's voice, not Sam's. There was something vaguely familiar about the voice, but she couldn't place it.

She left a note for her mom and hurried out. She was at Cassie's place in twenty minutes. Cassie was standing outside her house, on the kerb, stamping her feet and shivering in the cold. She got into the car, carrying a thick book.

'I brought the school book along. I've already called some of his classmates. I thought we could divide the rest and call them from Seb's place,' she said. 'Why are we going to Seb's place, anyway?'

'Your house is crawling with people. My Mom will be curious if we meet at my place. I've no idea where Ryan stays. At Seb's house, no one will even notice us,' said Maya. 'By the way, did you call them?'

'I tried, but neither of them picked up.' She turned towards Maya, a frown creasing her forehead. 'Maya, do you think Sam's in trouble?'

'I've got this bad feeling, Cassie. That's why I called,' said Maya.

She was driving fast, way above the speed limit, but she couldn't care less. It was early morning on a Sunday and there was hardly any traffic. They were at Sebastian's house in no time at all. The gate was remote controlled and had to be opened from the house. But luckily, their butler, Fred, recognized Maya when she pressed the button and stuck her face in the camera. He opened the gate for her. He already had the front door open for them, when they drove up.

'Master Sebastian is in his suite, Miss,' he said. 'Shall I bring up some coffee?' he asked courteously.

'Thanks Fred, we'd appreciate that. Could you tell me again, how to get to Sebastian's room? You know how I get lost here,' said Maya.

Fred smiled and gave them directions. Maya and Cassie hurried up. Cassie had never been to Sebastian's house and she looked around in wonder.

'Maya... this place...,' she started.

'I know. It's overwhelming,' Maya snapped, 'but we don't have time to sit and gawk. Come on.' They followed Fred's directions and found Sebastian's room. Maya knocked on the door, but he didn't answer.

After five minutes of knocking, Maya said, 'To hell with it,' and she opened the door and peeped inside. The T.V. was on and Sebastian was sleeping on the couch. He had spent the night partying away, celebrating Skallen's win. Maya strode over and looked down at him. He looked rather angelic in his sleep. She shook him roughly.

He opened his eyes and looked at them, groggily. 'Wha... ? Maya? What are you doing here?' he asked. 'What time is it?'

'It's Sam,' said Maya urgently. 'He's missing.'

Sebastian groaned and sat up, rubbing his eyes. 'Oh no, not again. What's with that kid?' He looked up at them. 'But why are you here, though? He isn't here.'

'Yes, we can see he isn't here. We're trying to find him,' said Maya.

Sebastian still looked confused. 'I don't understand. Maybe, he's at some friend's place. Have you tried calling his friends?' he asked.

'Yes, I've called quite a few, there are still some more to call. I've got the numbers here,' said Cassie, holding up the school book. 'We thought, we'd divide it up and call everyone. It'll be faster.'

'Couldn't you find someone else to disturb? Why couldn't you do this from one of your houses?' asked Sebastian grumpily.

'My house is crawling with people,' said Cassie.

'And my Mom will want to know what's happening, if we go to my house,' said Maya. 'Where's your Dad? I don't want him to find me here. He may tell my Mom and that's a whole load of questions, I don't want to answer.'

'Don't worry, my Dad's not here. He's off on some work, to France or somewhere. But why can't you tell your Mom? I mean, it's not a secret that Sam's missing, right?' said Sebastian. 'I came home at five this morning, and I've only had a couple of hours of sleep. So, maybe my brain isn't awake yet, but again… why are you here?'

'Listen,' said Cassie. 'Sam's not the type of kid who crashes out in other people's houses. It's not something he'll do. I'm still going to call all the names in this book, but I know he's not going to be in anyone else's house.'

'Just because he hasn't done it before, doesn't mean he'll never do it,' said Sebastian. 'He's growing up. People change. I think you're making a big deal out of nothing.'

Cassie's phone rang, just then. It was Ryan. Cassie told him what had happened and asked him to come to Sebastian's house. Ryan had slept over at a friend's place after celebrating their win and was getting home with Randy. He said he'd get Randy to drop him off at Sebastian's.

'You called that moron too? What is this? A free for all? Why is everyone landing up at my house?' whined Sebastian.

'Seb… I had a dream, about Sam. I have this feeling he's in some kind of trouble,' said Maya, in a quiet voice.

That got Sebastian's attention. 'Like last time?' he asked, looking worried.

'Yup,' said Maya, 'and that's when I woke Cassie. She checked Sam's room and we found he was missing.'

'Ok, so what do you want to do?' asked Sebastian.

'I thought we'd try all his friends first,' said Cassie, putting the large book on the centre table. 'If all three of us divide it, we should finish fast. Then, we could make a list of places he usually hangs out at, and go looking for him.'

They started on the calls. They were almost done with the calls, with no result, when the intercom buzzed. Fred's disapproving voice came on the line. 'There's a boy here… what was your name again… Ryan? He says he's a friend of yours, Master Sebastian.'

'Yes, yes, send him up, Fred,' said Sebastian. Fred entered the room a few minutes later, bringing the coffee, biscuits and Ryan with him. Maya still hadn't forgiven Ryan, but she decided to forget it for now. She hoped Ryan and Sebastian would also be cool with each other.

'Hey guys? Any news?' asked Ryan.

They shook their heads. 'Have you called Mr. Harris?' he asked.

Cassie's phone rang just then. It was her mom. Cassie looked anxious as she took the call. Her mom was screaming into the phone. They could all hear her, clearly.

'Where are you? We're sick with worry about your brother, and now you disappear too, without a word to any of us,' her mother screamed.

'Mom, I told Dad that I was going out to look for Sam,' said Cassie, looking close to tears.

'This is your fault, Cassandra. You should have brought him back home with you, last night. It was so irresponsible of you.' Cassie burst into tears.

'Mom, that's not fair. I asked him to come home with me. He refused,' sobbed Cassie. Sebastian took the phone from Cassie's hand. He looked furious. They were all shocked at Cassie's mom's accusations.

'Mrs. Johnson, this is Sam's friend. We're all out, helping Cassie search for Sam. If we find him, we'll call,' Sebastian said curtly, and cut the line. Maya was holding Cassie as she continued weeping.

'Don't pick up the phone if she calls again,' said Sebastian, looking at the phone in disgust.

'Shouldn't we call Mr. Harris?' asked Ryan, again.

Sebastian was looking at Cassie. 'Cas! Would you calm down? You breaking down now isn't helping in any way. Now, think! Where did you leave Sam? And did he say anything about how he was getting home.'

Cassie gulped, trying to control her tears. 'I wanted to leave as soon as the match was over. But Sam wanted to wait and congratulate Ryan, so he hung back. He said he'd hitch a ride home with someone. That's why I left.' Her eyes teared up again.

'Hey! Wait a minute! I saw him after that. He was waiting outside when I came out of the locker room. He came to congratulate me. There was an after match party at Darren's place that I was going to. I was hitching a ride with Randy and we were heading the other way, towards your house, Maya, so I couldn't offer Sam a ride home. But I did ask him how he was getting home, and he said... he said... um,' Ryan screwed up his forehead, trying to recollect. 'I think... I think he said he was going home with Ms. Cabot.'

Cassie felt a wave of relief sweep over her. Ms. Cabot would have seen Sam hanging around alone, after the match. She would have thought it wasn't safe and would have given him a ride.

'That's the sort of nice thing Ms. Cabot would do,' thought Cassie. Then a thought struck her, and she asked aloud, 'But why didn't she drop him home? Where did she take him? Do you think he's still with her?'

'One way to find out. Let's ask her. Her number will be in the book too,' said Sebastian, pulling the book towards him.

Maya had been quiet. Now, she said softly, almost to herself, 'It was her voice I heard.'

'Who? What?' asked Ryan.

'Ms. Cabot. She was there. In my dream. She was talking to Sam,' said Maya.

'What's she talking about?' asked Ryan, looking at the other two.

'She dreamt Sam was missing and that he's in trouble,' explained Cassie.

'And I just remembered... Ms. Cabot was there too, in my dream, talking to Sam or yelling... I'm not sure... it's all very fuzzy,' said Maya.

'Maya, try and recollect your dream. The last time when Sam got into trouble, you knew where he was. Maybe, you could figure out where he is now too,' said Ryan.

Maya leant back against the couch and closed her eyes. She tried to recollect as much of the dream as she could.

'It was dark. I couldn't see Sam, but I could sense him. I couldn't see anything, actually.' Her face was scrunched up in concentration. 'I think he was tied up. His hands and legs were tied up. The rope was cutting into his wrists and ankles.'

Maya moaned softly, like she was in pain. 'It hurts... feeling dizzy and nauseous. I... I... I think... I'm tied to a chair. Sitting on a chair.

There's light now. I can see the room better. Ms. Cabot is there, smiling. She says it'll all be okay. It'll be over soon.' Maya sighed and became quiet.

The others waited for a minute and when she still hadn't moved, Cassie shook her gently. Maya opened her eyes, looking dazed. 'I saw him… in fact, it was like, I was him. I can't explain it. But, that's all I can remember.'

'Was Sam hurt in any way?' asked Cassie

'I don't know. I couldn't see Sam. I could sense him, but I couldn't see him. But, I think he was in pain,' said Maya.

'Why would Ms. Cabot have Sam tied up?' asked Cassie.

'She's such a bad word, I wouldn't put anything past her,' said Sebastian, savagely.

'You don't like her, Seb. I can't think of any reason why Ms. Cabot would tie Sam up. I don't think I'm recollecting it right,' said Maya.

'Well, she did give him a lift, so she's the last person who saw him,' said Ryan.

'Stop it! You make it sound like he's dead,' cried Cassie.

'Sorry, Cas. I didn't mean to. I was just thinking aloud,' said Ryan.

'But why would Ms. Cabot have him?' said Maya, once more. 'It doesn't make sense.'

'Don't you think it's time we called Mr. Harris?' asked Ryan, once again.

'What's wrong with you now?' asked Sebastian, looking at Cassie, who had gone as pale as chalk.

Maya went and sat beside Cassie and put one arm around her. 'Shut up, Seb. Can't you see she's upset about Sam? Don't be a moron!' she said, glaring up at him. She turned to Cassie. 'Cas, don't worry. He'll be okay.'

Cassie pushed her away and stood up. 'What have I done? I didn't mean to... I didn't realise...,' she looked around wildly, '... it's all my fault.'

'Cas, what is it?' said Ryan, starting to feel scared now. 'What is your fault?'

'Cassie, it's not your fault. Don't let what your Mom said bother you. How could you know he wouldn't come straight home,' consoled Maya.

'Shut up, Maya,' snapped Ryan. 'Cassie, what did you do? And please don't waste time crying, for heaven's sake.'

Sebastian and Maya looked at Ryan crossly. The girl was clearly upset and Ryan was making it worse, by shouting at her. But Ryan's words seem to have had an effect. Cassie took a deep breath and pulled herself together.

'I told Ms. Cabot everything,' said Cassie, in a small voice.

'Everything? What everything?' asked Ryan.

'About our powers. What we can do, what Sam did, everything,' said Cassie, looking ashamed.

'Cas,' said Maya, shocked. 'Why did you do that?'

'She said she was part of Pha-yul. She said she's senior to Mr. Harris... kind of his boss. And that she'd been sent to keep an eye on him. But...,' she gave her friends a perplexed look, '... she knew about our powers. She said they were not sure if Mr. Harris was doing a good job and she was sent here to supervise him. She also told me not to tell him or you, anything.' She closed her eyes, still pale, but she wasn't crying. 'I believed her. I'm so stupid. I believed every word she said.'

'Maybe... maybe, there's a simple explanation. Maybe, Mr. Harris can sort this out. Let's call him and find out,' said Ryan. They all looked at each other, waiting for one of the others to make the call.

'Fine, I'll call,' said Maya, picking up her phone.

CHAPTER 30

Sam struggled against the ropes which bound his wrists and ankles. His throat was parched, and his lips were dry, and his head felt fuzzy. He looked around the room that he was in. It swam in and out of focus. Not that he could see much, anyway. It was too dark. He could make out dim outlines of things, but he couldn't see more than that. Where was he? He shook his head to clear it and immediately felt like throwing up. He controlled the nausea with difficulty, breathing deeply.

Memory came back in bits and pieces. The match! Skallen had won the match. He had wanted to congratulate Ryan. He'd bumped into Ms. Cabot as he had made his way to the locker rooms. She'd asked him where Cassie was, and when he had told her Cassie had left earlier, she'd asked him how he was getting home. He had told her that he was hoping to hitch a ride with someone, and she'd offered to drop him.

She'd asked him to wait out in front while she brought her car around. As soon as she'd walked away, Sam had gone racing to the locker room. Luckily, he hadn't had to wait as Ryan was on his way out. He'd congratulated Ryan and raced back out. Ms. Cabot was already waiting in her car, impatiently, when he'd come dashing out. Sam had climbed in with a mumbled apology.

He'd given her directions to his house. He remembered they'd spoken about the game and how well Skallen had played. Right after they passed the War Memorial, she'd pulled up to the side and stopped the car. From then, his memory was hazy. He remembered wondering why they'd stopped, but he'd thought it would be rude to ask. She had after all been doing him a favour. She had pulled a bag from the back, taken something out and poked him with it.

It had all happened so fast, he hadn't even had time to react. She had poked him with something sharp. She'd just jabbed it into his thigh. He didn't remember much after that. She'd said something, but it was all fuzzy. Had she drugged him? But why? She was a teacher in his school. Why would she kidnap him?

'Oh dear God! She kidnapped me?' That was why he was tied up. As the reality of his situation sank in, he felt more confused than anything else.

He tried to remember more, but he couldn't. They'd been on the way back to his house, but he had no idea where Ms. Cabot had taken him. He'd woken up in this room, feeling dazed and dehydrated. After he'd regained consciousness, he'd tried to focus, to send out a plea for help to Maya and the others. But he had found it difficult to concentrate, and he wasn't sure if he had succeeded. He shivered. It was cold and damp. He didn't know how long he'd been here, unconscious.

The room he was in felt like a cellar. His granddad's cellar had smelled like this. A musty, stale smell. As he squinted, trying to see if he could make out anything in the room, he heard the sound of a bolt being pulled back. Light spilled in from behind him. He craned his neck around and found that the chair he was sitting on was placed with its back to a flight of steps. The staircase led up to a door through which the light shone. From where he sat, he couldn't see the door even if he twisted his neck. He looked around at the room he was in. He was right; it was a cellar. He heard footsteps coming down the stairs. He twisted around again to see who it was, but what little light which came in through the door, was obscured by the person descending. He couldn't make out who it was. He heard the footsteps pause and the sound of another switch being flipped on. The cellar was bathed in light.

He looked up as the person came around the end of the staircase and stood in front of him. It was Ms. Cabot. He stared at her, literally, with his mouth open. Nobody in Holy Trinity would have recognized this person, as their Physics teacher, Ms. Cabot. Gone was the long, thick hair, swinging down to the waist. No demure skirt and starched blouse. She towered above him, clad from head to toe, in a figure hugging, black leather outfit. Her hair was closely cropped, like a soldier's. She still looked stunning, Sam had to admit, though maybe the catwoman outfit was a bit much.

'Good! You're up,' she said, with a bright smile. She pulled up a chair, turned it around and straddled it the wrong way. She folded her arms and rested them on the back of the chair.

'Where am I? Why have you brought me here? You drugged me,' said Sam accusingly. He could hear his voice slur as he spoke.

'Sammy,' she said, in a surprisingly affectionate voice. 'Would you have come quietly if I had asked nicely?'

'Maybe I would have, depending on why you wanted to bring me here,' said Sam.

She seemed delighted by his answer. 'You're a tough cookie. Most boys would be cringing and crying for their Mommy by now.'

'I'm not most boys,' said Sam. He was terrified, but he wasn't going to let her know that.

'No, you aren't... in fact, you are a very special boy,' she said.

'What are you talking about?' asked Sam, small tendrils of fear creeping into his mind. She couldn't know. How could she know? No one knew.

'Your sister told me, all about your... special gifts? She told me about the amazing things you did,' said Ms. Cabot. 'I think you're brilliant,' she added.

'Oh no, Cassie! What did you do?' thought Sam, his fear growing. Aloud he said, 'I've no idea what you are talking about? Did Cas tell you one of her stories? She's very good at it. It's a problem. She's seeing a doctor. She's on…'

Ms. Cabot cut him off, as he rambled on. 'She didn't just tell me one story, Sam. She told me several. And the one I found most fascinating was yours. I can't believe I found you. Of all the people who Lucas sent out, I'm the one who found you. Lucas will be so pleased.' She gave a sigh of pleasure.

'Who's Lucas?' asked Sam. As he spoke to her, he was quietly struggling against the ropes which bound his wrists. He felt them loosening.

Ms. Cabot looked at him in surprise. 'You're kidding, right?' Then, she smiled. 'Nice try! For a minute there, I almost believed you.'

'I honestly have no idea who Lucas is, whether you believe me or not. And to tell you the truth, I don't really care. What I'm more bothered about is, why you've brought me here, and why you have me tied up?'

Ms. Cabot looked at Sam uncertainly. 'You really don't know who Lucas is?' She looked at him in wonder. 'Blane hasn't told you,' she whistled, a soft, low sound. 'What a stupid, little man.' She shook her head. 'Lucas, is just the most gifted man on Earth. He is the head of Dzog chen slob grwa . And the so called Elders at Pha-yul are dust under his feet.'

Sam looked at her, confused and scared. 'She knows everything,' he thought in panic. 'Who are you?' he asked.

'Finally got your attention, have I? Till now, I was just one of Lucas's students, but now since I've found you, I'm certain I'll be his favourite. My life is about to become one rollicking party.'

'Students?' asked Sam. He had no idea what she was talking about. 'What do you mean, students?'

'Lucas is the head of our community, Dzog chen slob grwa . That's the community, I belong to. Like Pha-yul, we've been searching for you, for years.' Searching for him? Sam was lost again.

'Why were you searching for me?' he asked.

'Because you are special, Sam. You're the one who can unlock the secrets of the Book,' she said dramatically, throwing her arms out with a flourish.

'What book?' Sam felt like Alice, falling through the rabbit hole. He wondered if Ms. Cabot was mentally unstable. Maybe, she had a personality disorder. That would explain the strange clothes.

She was staring at him. 'He hasn't told you about the Book? But, you're almost sixteen.' She got up and paced up and down, looking worried. 'Am I wrong? Have I made a mistake?' she muttered. She stopped her pacing abruptly and turned to look at him.

'There is only one way to find out. Use your power,' she ordered.

Sam blinked, as he looked up at her. 'I don't have any powers,' he said irritably.

Even here in the middle of the mess he seemed to be in, it still rankled that he didn't know how to use his powers.

'You're lying! Your sister told me about what you did,' yelled Ms. Cabot.

'That's true. But did she also mention that I haven't been able to do anything, since that time. What I did seems to have been a fluke. You think if I could use those powers, I would be sitting here, helplessly tied up? So, I guess you've got the wrong guy and I'm sure this Lucas, whoever he is, isn't going to be very pleased with you,' said Sam, with a smug smile.

Ms. Cabot took two steps forward, drew her arm back and punched Sam, hard on his face with her fist. Sam felt a flare of pain and a crunch, as his nose broke. He passed out.

Sam opened his eyes, spluttering, as water splashed on him. Ms. Cabot put down the bucket.

'Use your powers,' she commanded again.

Sam's face throbbed with pain. He could taste his own blood as it trickled down his nose and into his mouth. He saw two Ms. Cabots. He shook his head to clear it. Big mistake! His head exploded with pain.

'Use your powers,' Ms. Cabot repeated. 'If you don't, I'll break your little finger next,' she said, in a calm, cold voice, which sent a shiver up Sam's spine. He knew she meant it.

He looked up at her, trying to focus. 'Listen,' he slurred. 'You've pumped me full of some heavy duty drug and then, you punched me in the nose. Definitely not the best combination for my brain. I'll show you what I can do. Breaking pieces of me isn't going to help. Maybe, if you give enough time for the effects of the drug to wear off, I can show you.'

Ms. Cabot looked at him suspiciously for a moment, but what he said seemed to make sense to her, and she nodded. 'Fine, I'll give you some time. But when I come back, you better be ready,' she threatened and walked away.

He heard her footsteps going up the stairs and the sound of the door being shut and bolted. As soon as he heard the bolt slam home, he pulled himself together. He breathed calmly, trying to shut out the pain. He felt the pain gradually fading out. He breathed evenly, trying to bring his thoughts under control. At first, he found it difficult as the pain kept intruding, disturbing his concentration, but bit by bit, he brought his mind under control. He directed his thoughts on Maya. She was the one who was most receptive to his thoughts. He focused hard and sent out an image, of the cellar and Ms. Cabot. As he did, his head exploded in pain with the effort and he lost consciousness.

He awoke to the sound of voices. He kept his eyes closed.

'He's still breathing, you oaf! He's not dead. Come on, let's get him out of here,' he heard Ms. Cabot say.

'Why?' asked another voice.

'Thomas called. He said that he saw Blane hurrying out of his house. It may be nothing. But, I don't want to take any chances. It is better we take him to the farm. No one will be able to track us there,' said Ms. Cabot.

Sam peeked through half-closed eyes. There were three men and another woman there. The men were burly in leather jackets and faded jeans. All of them had long, dirty looking hair, tied in ponytails. One had a big snake tattoo, winding around his arm. The woman was also strong and hefty. She was holding a shotgun, and she looked like she knew how to use it.

'Come on, let's not waste time. We're leaving now,' said Ms. Cabot. 'Carry him to the car,' she ordered and then he heard her run lightly up the steps.

Two of the men untied him from the chair. He thought about making a break for it and opened his eyes slightly. The woman with the shotgun was standing right there. He knew he wouldn't be able to take two steps, before they brought him down. So he pretended to be unconscious and slumped to the floor when they untied him. The men swore and lifted him up. They tied his hands and feet again, carried him up the stairs and bundled him into a car. Every jolt, caused Sam's nose to flare in pain again and he bit his lip, willing himself to not shout.

After a few minutes, he heard the car start and they were moving. He took a chance and peeked. He was in the back seat of a car, half sitting and half lying down. Ms. Cabot was sitting beside him, but she was looking out the window, on the other side. She looked nervous. He looked at the front seat. He could see two of the men from the cellar.

He didn't know where they were going. His nose still hurt, but the overwhelming pain had gone. The effects of the drug had also worn off and his head was less fuzzy. He looked out of the window on his side. The landscape was familiar. They were driving out of town. His hands and feet were still tied, and so jumping out was not an option. They soon passed the billboard which said, "Go Skallen Raiders", which meant they were almost out of the town limits.

'Take this left,' he heard Ms. Cabot say and as the car turned, he saw a sign. It said, "Green Acres Farm – 4 miles", with an arrow pointing ahead. Twenty minutes later, the car stopped. Sam could see trees out of his window.

'Get him inside,' Ms. Cabot ordered.

He heard car doors opening and he closed his eyes tight again. He was dragged out of the car. He felt himself being carried up a flight of stairs, and flung down on something hard. He kept his eyes shut, till he heard a door close. Then, he peeked through half-closed eyes. There was no one around. The room was devoid of any furniture. It had a single window. He struggled and sat up. He didn't know how much time he had, before whoever Lucas was, made his appearance, or before Ms. Cabot started in on him again.

He focused on Maya again. He sent a mental picture of the "Go Skallen Raiders" billboard, and the sign which read "Green Acres", that he'd seen as they had driven here. This time, he was able to hold the thought longer and it was stronger. He hoped that it worked. He wondered what the others were doing. He knew it was daytime, as he could see light spilling in through the window. He struggled against the ropes binding him, in vain.

CHAPTER 31

It was two hours since Maya had called Mr. Harris. She'd told him Sam was missing. She had also told him everything else that had happened, including what Cassie had told Ms. Cabot. He had no idea who Ms. Cabot was, other than a teacher at school. He'd sounded worried and had told them to stay put, till he had tracked down Sam.

The kids spent a restless couple of hours. They were still at Sebastian's house, waiting for some news. Sebastian had asked for breakfast to be brought up, but no one had felt like eating anything. They'd turned on the local news channel, but there was nothing on it about Sam's disappearance. The press hadn't gotten wind of it yet.

Cassie's dad had called, worried about her, and she'd told him that she and some friends were still out looking for Sam. He'd said that nearly everyone in their neighbourhood was out looking for him too. He had added that her mom was worried about her, and to come home soon. Cassie had said she would.

The kids discussed Ms. Cabot's involvement at length. They still couldn't figure out why she would have taken Sam.

'Did Mr. Harris say anything about her?' asked Ryan.

'No,' said Maya. 'He said that he just knew her as a teacher at Holy Trinity.'

'Didn't you ask him why she may have taken Sam?' asked Ryan.

'I did. You heard me,' snapped Maya. 'He didn't answer me. He just asked us to stay put.'

'He never tells us anything,' said Ryan, looking annoyed, 'and he expects us to follow what he says blindly, without asking any questions.'

They discussed all kinds of possibilities about why Ms. Cabot would have taken Sam, and came up with nothing remotely plausible. They soon subsided into silence, each immersed in their own thoughts.

Abruptly, Sebastian stood up. 'I've had enough of sitting around, doing nothing,' he said. 'Let's go and do something.'

'Like what?' asked Ryan. 'We've no idea what's going on. Do you have any idea where Sam could be?' he asked, looking up at Sebastian.

'We could check out Cabot's house, for one,' said Sebastian. 'Her address is bound to be there, in the school book.' He went across to the coffee table and picked up the school book.

'She won't be stupid enough to take him to her house,' said Cassie.

'Frankly, I never thought she was particularly bright. But even if she doesn't have Sam there, we could poke about and see if we can find something useful,' said Sebastian.

'I'm sure it's the first place Mr. Harris would have gone looking,' said Cassie.

'Maybe, but at least it gives us something to do. I feel useless, sitting here, doing nothing,' retorted Sebastian.

Maya was standing by the window, looking out onto the balcony. She hadn't said anything for a while. All of a sudden, she staggered back, like someone had pushed her and she almost fell. The others turned towards her, startled. She reached out and grabbed the back of one of the armchairs to steady herself, her face screwed up in concentration.

'Maya?' Ryan stepped forward, but she put out her hand, motioning him away and Ryan stopped.

He looked at the others, bewildered. They couldn't understand what was happening. For almost half a minute, she had her eyes closed, concentrating.

'I know where he is,' she said, when she opened them. 'I mean, I don't know exactly where he is, because I don't think Sam himself knows. But I think, he must have glimpsed something on the way, to wherever they were taking him. I know it sounds crazy, but I think I just saw what he saw.'

'Are you sure, Maya?' asked Ryan.

'I don't know… I could sense him, so yes, I do think it was him,' said Maya, but she sounded uncertain.

'We should tell Mr. Harris,' said Cassie.

'No,' said Sebastian. They all looked around at him. 'What if Maya's wrong and we send him on a wild goose chase? We'd just be wasting his time. I think we should go check it out.'

'I still think we should tell Mr. Harris,' said Ryan, looking troubled.

'Are you chicken?' taunted Sebastian.

'I may be chicken, but I'm not stupid,' said Ryan.

'Ryan's right. We don't know what we're up against,' said Cassie.

Sebastian looked around at them. 'Listen, we all have incredible powers. Don't you think we can handle anything?'

'We may be good, Seb,' said Cassie nervously, 'but we've no idea who these people are. They could be better.'

Sebastian considered this for a couple of seconds. 'Fine, I'll give you that. But, I'm not saying we should go up against these people. What if Sam's not there? What if Maya's wrong? All I'm suggesting is that we go check the place out. And then we'll call Mr. Harris.'

'Mr. Harris told us not to go anywhere,' said Cassie.

'You know, I think Seb has a point. We will simply be wasting Mr. Harris's time if Maya's wrong and Sam's not there. There's no harm in going and checking the place out,' said Ryan. Sebastian looked surprised to get support from Ryan.

'If we're going by ourselves, we're wasting time talking about it,' said Cassie, getting up and picking up her phone. Sebastian wanted to take his dad's Lamborghini, as it was the fastest car they had, and it took them a while to convince him that attracting attention with a car like that, wasn't a very good idea.

In the meantime, Sam was desperately trying to loosen the ropes binding him, but they were too tight. His back hurt and he felt sore all over. His arms and legs were stiff, from being in the same position. His nose was throbbing in pain again. He'd lost track of time. He'd slid to the floor sometime back and didn't seem to have the strength to pull himself up again. So he just lay on the cold floor, shivering. He wondered what new horrors Ms. Cabot had lined up for him, when she figured out he couldn't use his powers. He wasn't looking forward to having his finger broken.

He closed his eyes as the door opened, hoping that whoever it was would think he was still unconscious. He heard footsteps approaching him.

'Get up!' It was Ms. Cabot.

She gave him a hard kick in the stomach, and he doubled over coughing, as pain flared through him. She caught him by his hair and pulled him up, to a sitting position.

'I know you're awake, you little worm. I've had enough of these games,' she yelled in anger. 'John,' she called out. One of the pony tails peered in. 'Get us a couple of chairs, will you?' she said.

Ponytail came in a few minutes later, with two chairs. He pulled Sam to his feet and pushed him down on one of the chairs, violently.

'It's been long enough for the drug to have worn off. What is wearing thin right now, is my patience. Do your thing,' she shouted.

Sam looked up at her, wearily. 'I'm sorry if Cassie gave you the impression that I can do stuff. But I can't. It's not that I won't. Believe me, if I could, I will. I don't want to get hurt again. I'm in enough pain already.' He gave her a pleading look, hoping she'd believe him.

She stared at him for a long time. Then, without another word, she walked towards him. She put her thumb against his broken nose and pressed down. Sam felt a fresh spurt of blood erupt from his nose and a blinding pain which seemed to envelop him. He screamed.

CHAPTER 32

'There! There's the billboard,' screeched Cassie.

'I see it, Cassie. I'm not blind,' said Sebastian. He was driving, and Ryan was sitting in front with him. Maya and Cassie were at the back.

'Maya, are you ok?' asked Cassie.

Maya was lying back, quite still, with her eyes closed. She opened them at Cassie's question. 'I can feel him… like, all the time now. I don't know why I couldn't feel him earlier. He seems to be in a lot of pain,' she said, looking worried.

'Try and tell him we're coming,' said Cassie.

'I did, but I'm not sure that he hears me,' replied Maya.

'If you can hear him, why can't he hear you?' asked Sebastian.

'I don't know. You think I haven't tried. I've been trying to reach him all morning,' said Maya. They drove in nervous silence for a while.

'Wait! Seb! Go back! I think I saw a sign,' said Ryan. Sebastian turned the car around and they drove back the way they had come, slower.

'There!' said Ryan, pointing.

The sign that said, "Green Acres Farm – 4 kms", was barely visible from the highway and it wasn't even a road. It was more of a dirt track, between the trees. Sebastian turned in and drove at a snail's pace, up the lane. There didn't seem to be any signs of habitation. The trees towered above them, blocking the sunlight and the undergrowth was dense. Sebastian had to switch his dim lights on, to see the path. They hoped that the lights wouldn't give them away.

The path wound between trees and soon became narrower. Twigs and branches scratched the sides of the car.

'My Dad is going to kill me,' said Sebastian.

'Seriously, Seb? Now?' said Cassie, annoyed.

Sebastian shut up and continued driving. They soon reached the end of the lane. The path ended. There were just trees in front of them.

Sebastian looked at the trees and turned around. 'Maya, you loser. You screwed up,' he swore and banged his fist against the steering wheel, in anger.

Ryan turned around too. 'Maya, are you certain that was the sign you saw?' he spoke mildly, but Maya could hear the doubt and worry in his voice.

'It looked like it,' she said, but she sounded unsure. There was no place to turn, so Sebastian started backing the car along the path.

'Wait!' said Ryan. 'The sign said, "Green Acres Farm".'

'Er... yes... I think we all noticed that,' said Sebastian sarcastically.

'So, where's the farm?' They looked at him confused. 'They would have put the sign up there because there was a farm here at some point. So, where is it?' asked Ryan.

'Ah! I see what you're getting at,' said Sebastian.

'Well, I don't. Can we get out of here? This place is creepy,' said Cassie.

'Seb, do you have a torch here?' asked Ryan. Sebastian opened the glove compartment, rifled through and pulled out a torch. He gave it to Ryan. 'Ok, I'll just go and have a look around. You wait here,' Ryan said.

'No,' said Sebastian.

'What do you mean, no?' asked Ryan, his eyes narrowing.

'No offense, big guy, but you'll make one hell of a noise, blundering through the trees and you're not exactly difficult to spot,' said Sebastian. 'Me, on the other hand, I can get through this whole lot,' he waved his hands at the trees surrounding them, 'in like five minutes, tops. Much faster and less noticeable. That's all I'm saying,' said Sebastian.

'You're right. Here!' Ryan gave him the torch.

Sebastian took the torch and got out. He seemed to vanish right in front of their eyes. He was back as he had promised, five minutes later, not even a bit out of breath.

'You're right. There is a farm on the other side, in a clearing. If we cut straight through here, through the trees, we should reach it in less than ten minutes,' he said. 'There is a turning, just after we entered this lane, to the right, which leads to the farm. We missed it when we were coming in.'

'Should we check it out before we call Mr. Harris, or shall we call him now?' asked Ryan.

Maya suddenly screamed, clutching her head and curling up on the back seat. 'Maya, what's happening?' asked Cassie, shaking her. Her screams sounded like she was in terrible pain and were horrible to hear. They watched helplessly, as she continued writhing and screaming.

'Hey! Do you think they'll hear?' whispered Ryan to Sebastian.

Sebastian shook his head. 'They're way that side. They won't be able to hear. But, what's wrong with her?'

Maya finally stopped, but she just lay there holding her head, panting. She seemed to pull herself together with tremendous effort and sat up. She was trembling.

'Guys! There's no time. You better hurry. They're doing something to Sam. He's in a lot of pain. Go, go and do something. Distract them, till Mr. Harris comes. I'll stay here and try to call Mr. Harris. I'll be of no help to you in this state. Hurry!' she urged.

The other three nodded. Cassie got out of the car, went around and joined the boys. The three of them hurried away through the trees, Sebastian leading them. Maya lay back and rested her head on the back of the seat. She shuddered to think what they were doing to Sam, to cause such incredible pain. She wanted to go with the others, but she knew if she started screaming again, the game would be up. She had to block Sam's pain if she was going to be of any help. She picked up her phone and called Mr. Harris.

Sebastian, Cassie and Ryan reached the edge of the clearing, where the farm was. It must have been a reasonably large farm at one time, but the trees had reclaimed the land and only the cottage itself, and an outhouse, remained of the original farm. The lane which Sebastian had told them about led to the front door of the cottage. There were three cars parked out front. Two men leaned casually against one of the cars, talking. Both held shotguns.

'Let's see. Say four people, per car. That's twelve. What's our strategy?' asked Sebastian, looking at Ryan.

Ryan blinked for a couple of seconds. He realised the other two were looking to him for a plan. He needed to come up with something fast. He was silent for a few seconds, thinking.

Then he nodded to himself and said, 'Right! Er... um... Seb I need you to do a recon. See if you can spot anyone else and where they are. If we know more or less where the rest are, we can figure out a plan. Also, check if Sam is in any of the rooms.'

Sebastian nodded and took off. He was back in five minutes. He squatted on the ground and picked up a twig.

'Ok, this is more or less how many rooms the cottage has, and the number of people in each room... er... more or less.' He drew a rough outline of the cottage and its rooms, and told them approximately how many people were in the different rooms. He hadn't spotted Sam anywhere, nor had he seen Ms. Cabot. 'I also have no idea how many people there are on the first floor or where they are.'

'If there are twelve, that will leave only three unaccounted for,' said Ryan.

'We're just assuming the number of people based on the cars. What if there were some here already?' asked Cassie.

Ryan looked glum. 'I didn't think of that. Let's just hope Mr. Harris makes it here soon. Ok, this is what we'll do. Cassie, hit the guys standing in front near the cars with something. Hit them hard. We don't want them to get up anytime soon. As soon as they're down, we sprint to the side door, here,' he said, pointing at Sebastian's drawing. 'I'll break it. Seb, you be ready to rush in, as soon as I break it. If anyone is there, take them down. We've got to take them by surprise. Cassie, you stay behind me. If we're lucky, no one will be there. Then, Seb you head to this room and Cassie to this one. I'll take this one,' he said, pointing at the rooms, where Sebastian had seen people. 'Hopefully, that's all there are. If there are more, we'll need to wing it from there,' he said. They looked unhappily at one another.

'Should we wait for Mr. Harris?' asked Cassie. She was terrified.

'I would, if they weren't hurting Sammy,' said Ryan. 'We can't just wait here doing nothing while they hurt him.'

'Right, so what are we waiting for? Let's go! Shall we set our watches to the same time?' asked Sebastian.

'Why?' asked Cassie, looking puzzled. 'We're not blowing up anything.'

'Yeah, I know, but I've always wanted to use that line,' Sebastian replied, smiling. The other two laughed.

'You're such an ass, Seb,' said Cassie, punching his arm.

'Yes, you are… but I'm glad you got my back, mate,' said Ryan. 'Ok, get those two goons, Cassie,' he instructed.

Cassie had spotted some logs lying next to the front door and she directed her mind towards them. She sent a couple of them flying at the two men and they crumpled, without a noise. Sebastian was beside them in a flash and back again, with the two shotguns. They crept out of the undergrowth and raced towards the side door, bent low. Ryan moved his fingers over the door, looking for weak points while Sebastian stood next to him, waiting to rush in. Ryan finally pressed down on two spots and the door broke open with a resounding crack. The side door led into a corridor, which joined another passage, perpendicular to the first.

A man was passing along the perpendicular corridor when the door broke open, and he looked around in alarm. Before he could lift the shotgun that he was carrying, Sebastian had disarmed him. Ryan barrelled through the broken door and straight into the man, pushing him against the wall. The man hit his head against the wall and slid down to the floor, unconscious. The kids didn't wait. They raced towards the rooms down the corridor. A man peeped out of the first door, on the left. Ryan didn't break stride. He ran full tilt into the man who was peeping out. He pulled back his arm as he neared him, punched the man in his face, and continued into the room that the man had come out from. Sebastian and Cassie raced ahead. Sebastian turned into the next door on the left, and Cassie raced on to the last door, which was on the right side of the corridor.

As she neared it, the door opened and a man stepped out. Cassie pushed at the man with her mind, and he staggered back into the room. As she turned into the room, he pulled out a gun from a shoulder holster. With a flick of her mind, she sent the gun flying across the room. There were three more people in the room, but luckily Cassie had the element of surprise. She sent a vase which stood on the mantel over the fireplace, whizzing towards the man who had pulled out the gun, and it hit him on the head, shattering on impact. He crumpled to the floor.

There were three more people in the room, two women, who were rising up from the couch they had been sitting on, and another man. The women were pulling out guns as they got up. Cassie gave a mental shove at one of them. She fell back against the other and they both went down. There was an iron poker by the fire. She aimed it at the second man who was levelling his gun at her. It spun through the air and embedded itself in his thigh. He dropped his gun and fell on his knees, holding his leg and howling in pain.

One of the women, who had fallen down, was getting up again and was reaching for the shotgun which was on the table. Cassie looked around. She spotted the gun she had knocked out of the hand of the man that she had hit with the vase. She reached for it with her mind and it flew into her hand. She raised it and levelled it against the two women. She had no idea how to use it, but she was hoping the women wouldn't realise that.

Sebastian walked in, just then. 'Whoa!' he said, when he saw the gun. He looked around the room. 'Cool,' he added approvingly.

Cassie ignored his comment. 'How many of you are there? I can read your mind. So, don't try to lie,' said Cassie.

'Twelve,' said one of the women.

'Should we tie them up?' asked Cassie.

'There's a closet in the corridor. I saw it as we ran in. We could shove them all in there,' said Sebastian. Ryan walked in, just then. 'How many in your room, Ryan?' asked Sebastian

'Two,' answered Ryan.

'There were two in my room too. So including the two outside, it makes ten. That leaves two more, besides Cabot,' said Sebastian.

As they discussed what to do, they heard Sam scream. It was a terrible, drawn out howl of pain. All three cringed at the noise. Noticing their distraction, one of the women lunged for the gun she had dropped. Ryan was on her in two strides. He picked her up and flung her out through the window. The window pane shattered as she went through. He turned around and glared at the other woman, who looked terrified.

'Where's the boy?' asked Ryan.

The woman pointed upstairs. As she pointed, they heard Sam scream again. All three went pale as they heard the dreadful scream. They herded everyone into the closet as fast as they could. They got the ones who were conscious to pull the unconscious ones in. The man with the poker sticking out of his leg was screaming in agony. The kids hoped whoever was upstairs couldn't hear all the noise from below.

'They're just common thugs. They have no powers,' said Sebastian, looking at them in distaste, as they prodded them into the closet. They heard another agonizing howl of pain from Sam, and they swiftly locked the closet door and raced to the stairs.

They tiptoed up the stairs. At the landing, Ryan told Sebastian, 'Run up and check where they are.'

Sebastian took off. Sam was screaming again. Cassie covered her ears and moaned. Ryan put his arm around her comfortingly, though he was as scared.

CHAPTER 33

Maya groaned and tried to blank her mind as another wave of pain hit her. But it was getting easier to push it out. She'd tried Mr. Harris's number, over and over, but he wasn't picking up his phone.

'Darn it! Pick up your phone,' she thought, in aggravation.

She could sense how weak Sam was becoming. She wished she had gone with the others. She felt useless, sitting in the car. She considered going after them, but she was sure she'd just get lost in the trees. It was very dark, and they had taken the torch.

She had an idea. She got out of the back of the car and climbed into the driver's seat. She could try and find the lane Sebastian had been talking about. When she switched on the car, the GPS came on. She tried Mr. Harris again, but there was still no answer. She checked their position on the GPS and messaged it to Mr. Harris. Then, she put the car in reverse and started backing up the lane.

'Ooh! Seb's dead!' she thought, as she heard and felt the fender scrape against a tree.

It took her almost ten minutes to find the lane. She turned into it. She had switched off the headlights as she didn't want to be spotted, and had to peer through the gloom to see the path. But the path here was wider than the one they had driven through earlier, and she was able to drive more easily. She hoped she wouldn't unexpectedly come upon the farm. The lane curved away in front of her, and she could see sunlight up ahead.

She pulled the car up to the side of the lane and walked the rest of the way. She walked through the trees and not up the lane. The curving lane curved, ending in a clearing, where a cottage stood. She couldn't see anyone, but there were three cars parked out front. She bent low, raced across the clearing and hunkered down behind the last car. It hid her from the cottage.

She peeked around the other side of the car. There were two men sprawled on the ground. Sebastian, Ryan and Cassie must have gotten in, she thought with relief. She hoped they had found Sam. She peered around again. She could see the front door, but it was shut. They wouldn't have gone in through the front anyway. She was wondering whether to risk it and run around to the side of the house or stay put, when another wave of pain hit her. She heard the scream accompany the pain. She breathed out, pushing out the pain.

There was a crash of breaking glass, and she peered around the car again. A woman flew out of a broken window and fell on the grass, a couple of feet away from her. The woman sat up dazed, looked around and caught sight of Maya. Maya immediately jabbed her mind and the woman curled up, holding her head. Maya got up swiftly and grabbed one of the logs which were lying near the fallen men. She went over to the woman and gave her a hard thump on her head with it. The woman lay still. Maya hoped she hadn't killed her.

She heard Sam scream again. She ran over to the window through which the woman had flown out and peered inside. It was empty. She pulled herself up and climbed in through the window, carefully avoiding the jagged edges of the broken glass. She darted over to the door of the room and peeped into the corridor. She heard thumps and crashes and the sound of breaking glass. It seemed to be coming from upstairs. She picked up one of the shotguns lying in the room and ran along the corridor, towards the stairs.

Ryan and Cassie didn't have to wait long on the landing. Sebastian was back, less than a minute later.

'There's no one in the corridor. There are three doors along the corridor. But I heard Sam scream. It's coming from the last door on the right, towards the front of the house. It must be over the room Cassie went into,' whispered Sebastian.

They winced, as they heard another scream. They crept up the rest of the steps, and Ryan peeped around the corner, into the corridor.

'Cassie, you stay here,' said Ryan. 'Seb, you come with me. I'll break the door. You be ready to burst through. There should be three people there, including Cabot.' Sebastian nodded. The two boys crept along the corridor. Cassie peeped around the corner and watched them.

At Sebastian's nod, Ryan threw himself against the door. It gave way and he tumbled in with the force of his push. Sebastian nipped in behind him as quick as a flash. A second later, he flew back out of the room. He hit the opposite wall of the corridor and crumpled in a heap on the floor. She heard sounds of a scuffle in the room and then the sound of glass shattering.

She ran along the corridor silently, pressed against the wall. She hesitated for a fraction of a second outside the open door, before peeping in. Two men were sprawled on the floor, but Ryan was nowhere to be seen. Sam was tied to a chair. She gasped when she saw her brother and rage filled her. He was a mess. His face was black and blue and his nose was bleeding. He was barely conscious.

'Ah! Cassandra! I was wondering where you were, my darling girl.' Cassie stared. She couldn't believe this evil looking witch, standing behind Sam's chair, was her sweet Ms. Cabot.

'You tricked me,' she shouted angrily, walking into the room. 'What have you done to him?' She ran towards Sam, crying, 'Sammy! Sammy!'

Cabot flicked her wrist and Cassie was flung back against the opposite wall. As she slid down the wall, she summoned all her energy and pushed back at Cabot. Cabot staggered back a few steps.

She recovered her balance and said with delight, 'That was very good, Cassandra. Now, maybe you will be able to get your brother to show me what he can do.' She stretched her hand towards Sam, her hand in a tight fist and made a twisting motion. Sam doubled over and screamed in pain.

'Stop it! Stop hurting him!'

Cassie and Cabot turned towards the door. Maya was standing there, looking at Sam, horrified.

'The girl who can read minds,' said Cabot softly. 'The whole circle of five! I've got you all. Lucas will be so pleased with me.' Maya lifted the shotgun she had in her hand and aimed it at Cabot.

'Let him go now, or I'll shoot,' said Maya.

Cabot smiled and flicked the gun away from Maya's hand, with a wave of her hand. Another flip of her wrist, and Maya went flying across the room. Cassie had staggered to her feet by then.

'Who are you? Why are you doing this?' she demanded.

Cabot walked forward, towards Cassie. 'Cassandra, believe me, this is not how I wanted it to be. I didn't want to hurt Sam. But, he's so obstinate. He just won't use his powers. And unless I'm sure he's the child that Lucas has been searching for, I dare not call him. You do understand, don't you?' She looked at Cassie, her blue eyes, wide and pleading. 'Will you please tell him to show me what he can do? I don't want to hurt him.'

Cabot was standing with her back to Sam, and she didn't see him straightening up. Cassie did. She thought if she kept Cabot talking, she could distract her.

'Who's Lucas?' she asked.

'Just the most remarkable man in the world. Once you meet him, Cassandra, you will understand why I did this. To please him. All we're trying to do is make a better world.'

Sam was in such pain, he was finding it hard to stay conscious. Through the fog of pain, he could hear Cabot talking. He looked around the room. He couldn't see much as his eyes were puffed up. He squinted, trying to see clearer. He'd seen Sebastian come in. Cabot had flung him out with a push of her mind. Ryan had managed to get the two pony tails down, before Cabot had lifted him, like he was a feather and thrown him out of the window. Without touching him! She was very powerful and enjoyed using her power to hurt.

He made a tremendous effort and reached out to Maya, prodding her awake. She stirred and slowly opened her eyes. She looked across at Sam. Cabot was still earnestly trying to convince Cassie that she should urge her brother to listen. She didn't notice Maya stirring.

Sam reached out with his mind to Maya. 'Stay down,' he said. Maya lay still. 'Maya, I know you can sense me. Can you feel my energy?' he asked.

Maya didn't understand what Sam was trying to tell her. 'Look into my mind,' said Sam. Maya probed Sam's mind. He opened his mind to her and let her in. And suddenly, she sensed his energy. She could actually see it. It was like a bottomless pit of pure, white light. She almost gasped in wonder. 'Send the energy to Cassie,' said Sam, urgently. 'Now!'

'Tell your brother to do one little trick for me,' Cabot was telling Cassie, smiling sweetly.

'You can go to hell,' yelled Cassie.

Cabot's smile faded. She turned and held out her hand towards Sam, making a fist. 'Do you want to see him suffer?' she asked in a tight, furious voice.

Cassie felt rage course through her. 'You leave him alone,' she cried and pushed with all her might.

Cabot was lifted off her feet and thrown backwards. She looked surprised for a second and then, her face twisted in anger. She staggered to her feet. As Cassie braced, for whatever Cabot was going to do to her, she heard Maya's voice in her head.

'Cassie, you can do this. Sam will help you.' Cassie didn't understand what Maya was saying and then, she felt it. Energy, pouring into her, in waves.

'You will pay for that, you little maggot,' said Cabot and held out her hand, pointing her fist at Cassie. 'You are a fledgling. My power is so much stronger than yours. I'll crush you,' she said.

Cassie held out her hand, pushing against the force which was emanating from Cabot. 'You may be more powerful than I am, but I have something you don't. I have Sam,' Cassie yelled back. 'You wanted to know what Sam can do. Well, you got your wish. Are you liking it?' taunted Cassie, as gradually she gained the upper hand.

She could feel Cabot weakening. Cabot looked surprised at first and then, her face twisted into an evil grimace, as she tried to push back. Abruptly, with an incredulous scream, Cabot went flying back, crashing into the wall behind her. She fell down, senseless. The kids looked at each other, stunned. They couldn't believe it.

'Come on, let's get out of here before she wakes up.' Maya scrambled to her feet and ran to Sam.

'Where's Ryan?' asked Cassie.

'He went out the window,' said Sam.

They could hardly make out what he was saying, through his swollen and bloody lips. He was barely able to speak. His entire face was swollen. Maya quickly untied him, as Cassie supported him. He slumped forward, onto Cassie.

'Oh no! You don't!' They looked around in fright. Cabot was staggering to her feet again.

'Don't you dare touch my kids again,' said a loud voice from the door.

They all turned around. Mr. Harris was standing at the door, a gun in his hand, levelled at Cabot. He shot her. She held her hand to her neck with a surprised look, staggered forward drunkenly and flopped down. Cassie and Maya looked at her supine body in horror. Mr. Harris had shot Cabot.

Mr. Harris saw their looks of horror. 'Don't worry. I didn't kill her. It's just a tranquilizer dart. She'll be out for a couple of hours. We'll get you to safety, by then.' He looked at Sam. 'Though, now I wish I had killed her,' he said, in a voice filled with fury. 'Come on. I need to get him help immediately.' He had his usual satchel and he pulled out two belts from it. 'Strap this on him.'

He handed one of the belts to Maya. Cassie held Sam while Maya strapped the belt on. Mr. Harris had strapped on his belt, by then. He put his arm around Sam, who had passed out again.

'Press his button, the green one. On my count of three. One, two, three.' Cassie pressed the button and both disappeared.

'Let's go find Ryan. I hope he's okay. Sam said he flew out of the window,' Maya said, looking concerned.

'What about these?' asked Cassie, pointing to Cabot and the two men lying on the floor.

'Let's drag them to the next room and lock them in,' said Maya. The two men didn't stir, as the girls dragged them.

'What happened to them?' asked Maya.

'Ryan happened to them,' said Cassie, starting to giggle.

The tension and stress of the day was just hitting them. Maya too started giggling. Once they'd started, they didn't seem to be able to stop. Both giggled hysterically, as they came back to drag Cabot into the next room.

'Did you see her face when Mr. Harris shot her?' asked Maya, between giggles.

They went into peals of laughter. They left Cabot in the next room, came out and shut the door. It was only then that they realised that the room had no lock. This set them off again. They clutched each other and giggled helplessly.

'Dragged them... all the way here... and those two... so heavy... simply... oh God, I can't,' said Maya, clutching her waist, as she tried to stop laughing.

'What the hell is so funny? I almost died.' They turned around to see Sebastian staggering to his feet, glaring at them.

'Oh dear, you should have seen Seb. He flew into the room and flew out a second later. He just went flying through the air... like in one second,' giggled Cassie, tears streaming down her face. 'It was like Wile Coyote or... or Daffy Duck... you know, like a cartoon.'

'I got hurt, you morons,' said Seb, but he was smiling too. Then, his smile faded. 'Where are Ryan and Sam?' he asked.

This sobered the girls up. 'Mr. Harris finally landed up. He's the one who zapped Cabot. Well, he didn't zap her. He shot a tranquilizer dart at her. He's taken Sam with him. I guess he'll come back. Did he say he'll come back?' Maya looked at Cassie. Cassie shrugged.

'And Ryan?' asked Sebastian

'Apparently, Ryan went out the window,' said Cassie and she bit her lip, trying not to laugh.

'It's not funny, Cas,' said Maya, also trying not to smile. 'He could be hurt.'

Sebastian shook his head. 'You girls are mad. Let's go find him.'

They turned to go downstairs, when Ryan appeared at the head of the stairs and limped up the corridor. He was holding one arm at an unnatural angle.

'Where is she? I will tear her from limb to limb. She'll wish she'd never been born. Let me at her.' He stopped and stared at them. 'What are you laughing about? You think this is funny?'

'No… no, Ryan,' said Sebastian, who was also laughing. 'Only you can fall from the first floor of a building, get up and come back to fight again,' said Sebastian, between snorts of laughter.

Ryan was still looking at them like they were mad, when Mr. Harris arrived. The laughter died immediately.

'How's Sam?' asked Cassie anxiously.

'He's with a healer. We don't know as yet how bad his injuries are. Come on, put these on. I'll get you out of here,' said Mr. Harris, handing out belts.

'What about Cabot and her thugs?' asked Sebastian.

'Once I get you out of here, I'll get back and do some cleaning up. Suffice to say that they'll be in a cold and dark place for a very long time. Come on! Hurry up! Strap on your belts!'

They swiftly strapped it on, and Mr. Harris said, 'The green button. On the count of three. One, two, three!'

CHAPTER 34

Mr. Harris was looking out of the window, at the magnificent view outside. He was in Iola's bedroom. One side of the bedroom had large, glass French windows which led to a balcony. It faced the lake and the mountains beyond. The view was breathtaking. But Mr. Harris wasn't enjoying the view. He was deeply immersed in his own thoughts.

Sam was lying on Iola's bed and a wizened, old man, was ministering to him. Iola was helping the old man.

Presently, Iola called out to Mr. Harris. 'Blane?'

He turned around and walked towards the bed. He couldn't control his feelings, and that annoyed him. He, who prided himself on how calm he was in any situation, was filled with a rage he couldn't control, as he saw the child lying on the bed, pale and weak. He couldn't believe Sam was still alive. The boy's inner strength amazed him. Very few adults could have withstood the abuse he'd been put through... and survived.

Iola sensed his emotions. She walked over and laid her hand on his folded arms. 'Blane, he'll be fine. Imran says so.'

The old man was putting away his things. He looked up, as Mr. Harris approached the bed. 'He'll be fine, but he needs plenty of rest.' The old man's voice was a wheezy croak. He continued explaining Sam's condition. 'His heart was squeezed, and there was bleeding, but I've fixed that. It should heal by itself now. His physical injuries can be fixed in any hospital.'

Mr. Harris nodded, not trusting himself to speak. He walked Imran to the door and opened it for him. He managed a soft, 'Thanks.'

Imran nodded. 'So much power in the little one. He's weak right now. But, I could still feel it. Look after him well,' he said and hobbled away.

Sebastian, Cassie and Maya were waiting outside, looking anxious. Mr. Harris told them, 'Sam will be fine. He's still unconscious though. We'll leave as soon as we can.' He stepped back and shut the door.

When Mr. Harris had come back to the cottage, given them the belts and instructed them to press the green button, they'd landed in the white room with the domed ceiling. They had stepped out of that room, into the long room where they had first met Iola. From there, Mr. Harris had taken them through a side door and through long, winding, stone corridors till they had reached the room they were presently in. It was some sort of a sitting room. It had exquisite antique furniture and richly woven carpets and tapestry.

Mr. Harris had asked Cassie, Maya and Sebastian to wait there and had left with Ryan, to get Ryan's wounds administered to. When he returned ten minutes later, he had ignored the three of them and walked straight into the room Sam was in.

They had all stood up when Mr. Harris had come out with the healer, hoping they could go in and see Sam, but now they sat down again, glumly. The main door to the sitting room opened, and Ryan walked in. They looked at him in surprise. Mr. Harris had examined Ryan on the way to the sitting room and had said it looked like Ryan had not only dislocated his shoulder, but had broken a couple of ribs as well. But Ryan now walked in, with just a bandage around his arm and a few sticky plasters.

'Why isn't your arm in a cast?' demanded Maya.

'Evidently, I heal very fast. They did push my arm back into my shoulder, and that was bloody painful, but my ribs seem to be healing, and so, they've just put a bandage around it. I don't feel any pain now.'

Iola was sitting in one of the armchairs by the window, when Mr. Harris went back into the room. He walked up and sat down in the other armchair.

'How many people know?' he asked quietly.

'Just you and me and the healer,' said Iola.

'I should have been more careful. How could I have failed to notice her? So consumed with my own importance.' He shook his head in disgust.

'Blane, enough with the self-pity and self-hate,' Iola spoke sternly now. 'It's been contained. Cabot and her henchman are in a place where no one can reach them, without me knowing about it. I've also leaked out the story that she thought this was the child, with no evidence to suggest it, and had taken him to manipulate him for her own ends. And that she kidnapped the others too, because they happened to be with him, tortured them and that Pha-yul rescued them. I've told her that this was the story that would be spread. She knows when the story reaches Lucas, she would be safer with us, here, than out there. She knows Lucas will find her, wherever she tries to hide.'

'Lucas!' Mr. Harris snarled the name, with hate. 'What's he doing with people like Cabot?'

'To be fair to him, I don't think he would have known how unstable Cabot was,' said Iola. 'If Cabot had called him, believe me, he would have killed Cabot, right there, when he saw what she had done to Sam.'

'Iola, still the same. Still believing the best of everybody, even when they've hurt you and let you down,' sighed Mr. Harris.

'Maybe, we all need to have some faith, Blane,' she snapped at him. 'I've also taken the liberty of spreading the word that these kids did not have the powers to get themselves out of trouble. So, you can expect some nasty comments and sneers, for the time you've been wasting on them,' said Iola, smiling now.

Mr. Harris smiled too. 'I can live with that. I've been through worse.'

Iola looked serious again, as she asked him, 'I need to ask you again, Blane, in the light of these recent events. I urge you to bring them here, where they'll be safe.'

'Do you know who it is, Iola?' asked Mr. Harris, looking at her gravely. 'Do you know who has been spying on us, for Lucas? He has his spies here. We have ours, there. Do you know who is faithful to us and who is faithful to Lucas? We don't know where the other communities stand on this. With so much uncertainty, I think they're safer in Skallen, at least for now. They've also shown themselves to be more than capable of looking after themselves.'

Iola nodded. 'They did prove themselves. But the next time, the people who go after them may be much more powerful. But, I bow to your better judgment where they are concerned. For now,' she added, in a sterner voice. Mr. Harris nodded.

After a while, she asked, 'Did he actually do that? Send out energy?'

Mr. Harris nodded, smiling. 'He did. Maya described it as a bottomless pit of white light.'

They looked at each other, hope shining in their eyes. Then, Iola looked away and stared out the window. 'I guess, by now, we should have learnt not to count our chickens before they're hatched.'

'True… but there is no rule which says we can't hope that they hatch,' said Mr. Harris.

Iola turned around. 'You're right as usual, Blane. And so wise! Call them in. They must be anxious to see Sam.'

'Yes,' he said, moving towards the door. 'I should also get them home. Half the town is out, searching for Sam.' He opened the door and looked at the four, waiting anxiously outside, and said, 'Come in!'

They trooped into the room after him. They had so many things they wanted to ask Mr. Harris, but when they saw Iola in the room, they felt tongue-tied. They stood there in silence, looking down at the floor, like naughty children waiting to be punished.

No one spoke. Finally, Maya couldn't take it any longer. 'We know we were stupid to go, when you told us not to and we really didn't mean to disobey you. It was just that Sam was in pain, and...'

'Maya, we know,' interrupted Iola, in her musical voice. 'We think you showed enormous courage given that you've still not mastered your abilities. Yes, I do think it was a bit foolish of you to have taken such a big risk, but I think if you had not done what you did, we might have lost Sam.'

All four looked at her, flushing with pleasure. 'Don't you go thinking that just because Iola said that, you're off the hook with me. I'll deal with you later,' said Mr. Harris, but his eyes were twinkling. 'Now, we better get you home. Your parents must be crazy with worry.'

He looked at Iola, who went to a cupboard and opened it. She took out some of the belts Mr. Harris usually had about him. Iola started carefully buckling one around Sam.

'Ryan, I'm setting yours and Sebastian's to reach the farm,' said Mr. Harris. 'Your car is there. You can pick it up and drive back home. Cassie, I have Sam's, Maya's and yours set to the copse of trees behind your house. Hopefully, they've finished scouring that area, and you won't land on someone. Once you get there, Maya and you take him in and tell them you found him in Blackburn Alley. He looks like he's been mugged, so go with that.'

'Aren't you coming?' asked Maya, going around and sitting next to Sam, to press the button on his belt.

Mr. Harris shook his head. 'No, there'll be too many questions if I turn up with you. I'll see you later.'

They nodded and pressed their buttons. Maya pressed Sam's button along with hers. They landed in a heap between the trees, behind Cassie's house. They looked around to see if anyone was there. No one was. Good! They struggled to hold Sam up. He was still unconscious. Cassie and Maya half dragged, and half carried him, up the path and through the wrought iron gate, into the backyard. They went around the side to the front of the house. They didn't bump into anyone as they hobbled up. The front door was wide open and as soon as they entered, bearing Sam, there was utter confusion. Two policemen lifted him off the girls and carried him inside.

Cassie's mom screamed in horror, when she saw the state her son was in. 'What happened to him? Where did you find him?' She and Cassie's dad helped the policemen lay Sam down gently on the sofa. One of the policemen called an ambulance.

Cassie's mom knelt down next to Sam and held his hand, weeping. 'Sammy! Sammy! Why won't he answer? What happened to him?' She jumped up, turned around and yelled at Cassie, 'What have you done to him?' Maya stepped out, in front of Cassie. 'What's wrong with you? Why would she do anything to him? She helped find him, didn't she?' she said hotly.

'Let it go, Maya,' said Cassie wearily. 'She's like that.'

She was so exhausted she just wanted to go to sleep, for a hundred hours. One of the policemen came and called Cassie's mom while a policewoman questioned the girls.

'Where did you find him?' she asked, in a gentle voice.

She could see how worn out the girls were. They told her the mugging story they had concocted, while they were dragging Sam into the house.

The cop took it down and said sympathetically, 'You both look beat. Why don't you sit down for a bit?'

'I think I'd better get home,' replied Maya. 'My Mom must be worried.'

She too was exhausted. Her car was at Sebastian's place and she didn't fancy walking home. So she called Sebastian and told him to swing by Cassie's house on the way back and pick her up. For once, Sebastian didn't give her any cheek. He sounded a bit tired himself. He said he'd drop off Ryan and come around to Cassie's. Cassie and Maya slipped out the front door and waited on the kerb, for Sebastian to turn up. They just stood there, waiting in silence, too weary to even talk.

CHAPTER 35

It was almost a week later, on a Saturday, after things had quietened down that they all met at the hospital, in Sam's room. Sam was looking much better, though he was still weak. He had suffered broken ribs and a fractured jaw. He was unconscious for two days, and the doctors had been rather worried. But now he was healing rapidly, much to the surprise of the doctors. He'd been shifted from the Intensive Care Unit to a private room, a couple of days before.

His mom hadn't left his side. The mugging story was accepted and the police had come around, after Sam had regained consciousness, to get the details from him. He had told them it had been dark, and he'd been unable to see the assailants properly. He gave vague descriptions and hoped it didn't match anyone.

The local press had gotten hold of the story and had made a nuisance of themselves at Cassie's house. It had been impossible to get in or out of their house, without having cameras flashing and microphones thrust in their faces. In the end, the police had decided to hold a press conference and had given an account of what had happened, as the newspapers were printing wild stories, from serial killers to an alien invasion. Once they knew it was a mugging, the press had soon lost interest.

The other four had gone back to school, the following Monday as usual. There had been a buzz about Sam's disappearance and Ryan's injuries. But that was soon overshadowed by the apparent disappearance of Ms. Cabot. There were several rumours about her disappearance, and she seemed to have left behind quite a few broken hearts. But the rumours were laid to rest, when her landlady and the school received letters from her, apologizing for her sudden departure. It appeared that she had an ailing mother who had taken a turn for the worse, and she'd had to leave unexpectedly over the weekend. She had added that her things would be collected and they were, in due course.

Cassie, Sam and their dad had finally convinced their mom to take a break and she'd gone home on Friday. On Saturday, Cassie and her dad had gone to the hospital to keep Sam company. After a while, Cassie had sent their dad back, telling him that she'd stay with Sam and would call, when she was ready to go home. She and Sam had then called Maya, Sebastian, Ryan and Mr. Harris and they'd all turned up, one by one.

Ryan's arm and ribs had healed in a week. He didn't even have a scar to show for it, much to his disappointment. The kids had visited Sam almost every day, but his mom had always been there and usually there were other visitors too, so they'd never gotten a chance to talk. Mr. Harris had also dropped in a couple of times and checked on Sam. They'd been waiting for a chance to get together alone, and were happy that they were finally able to.

They chatted for a while and joshed around, teasing each other and joking. Finally, as usual, it was Sam who said what was on all their minds. 'Mr. Harris, you owe us an explanation.'

Mr. Harris smiled. 'I was wondering when we were coming to that,' he said.

'Who was Cabot, truthfully? She said she was taking me to Lucas? Who is Lucas?' asked Sam.

Mr. Harris held up his hand. 'Let me start at the beginning. It's a bit of a long story and an incredible one at that, so bear with me. What have I told you about Pha-yul?' he asked.

'That it is a very ancient community of gifted people. Live in Tibet. You help people like us, who are different,' said Maya.

'That is the basic truth. But there is much more to it.'

'Seriously? You could have fooled me,' said Sam.

'Ouch!' said Mr. Harris. 'I guess I deserved that, but believe me, at no point have I lied to you. I just didn't tell you the whole truth, because I thought you were not ready for it. It takes at least a couple of years of mentoring and training, before children or adults enter our community. I still don't think you are ready for it, but considering the events of the last few weeks, I think you've earned the right to know.'

'Adults?' asked Sebastian.

'Yes, for some people, the powers manifest after they're much older,' explained Mr. Harris. 'What I'm about to tell you is not something you can share with anyone.' He looked around at them, pausing at Cassie a few seconds longer than the rest. She blushed, sheepishly. 'I have not reached this decision lightly. I have conferred with Iola, and she also thinks you deserve an explanation.' The children looked at him eagerly. Finally, an explanation!

'When I said Pha-yul is an ancient community, I didn't mean a hundred years or even a thousand. It is much more ancient. Our ancestors, if we could call them that, came from a planet called Padim. Padim was in another galaxy.'

'Aliens! We're aliens,' said Sebastian, sounding delighted.

'Shut up, Seb,' said the other four in unison.

'Not us, Sebastian, I don't think we can call ourselves aliens, but yes, the original settlers were alien. They were a much more advanced civilization. Their sun was imploding and so they looked for a planet closest in structure to theirs, and they found Earth. Unfortunately, everyone on Padim was not willing to leave. They were not convinced Padim was in danger. Those who believed that catastrophe was imminent, chose to leave. They came to Earth.

They seem to have come at a time when humankind was just getting civilized. Padimites, as they called themselves, have written detailed accounts of life on Earth when they first arrived. Most of the books are preserved at Pha-yul. They were a peaceful society for the most part, but that could be because they were a much older society. They came here and found humans, violent and savage. So, they found a remote area and built a home for themselves. Some scholars at Pha-yul believe that theirs was the lost city of Atlantis, but we have not found proof of that.'

Mr. Harris paused and looked around at the children who were listening, fascinated. He smiled, 'It may all be a bit too much to take in. I understand.'

'No, no, go on, this is… too… too…,' Maya paused, lost for words.

Mr. Harris folded his arms and leaned against the window. 'Well, as I said, the Padimites stayed away from humans. They lived in seclusion, letting our planet develop at its own pace. But after a few centuries, they came to the conclusion that if they did not integrate with humans, they would soon become extinct. Many Padimities took human partners. They were particular about who they chose, to make sure their culture had a better chance of survival. They found that children of the union were born with special abilities, and were more like Padimites than humans. This meant a lot to the Padimites. It meant that they would endure.

But over the years, the balance changed and the children born were showing more human characteristics than those of Padimites. Many children were born without powers. People started leaving the community and living with humans, because they found they had more in common with them, than with the Padimites. But even then, for a long time, if children of those who had moved away from the community, manifested powers, they would be sent to the community to learn to control their powers and get tutored there. They were given the choice of staying or leaving the community, once they were able to control their abilities. No one was forced to stay.

The downside of people choosing to live among humans was that sometimes, children of Padamite ancestry, manifested powers many generations later and they were often ostracized, abused or even killed, because they were not normal in human terms. People were scared of them because of their special abilities. Ever hear of the Salem Witch Hunt? That's just one example. So, the Padimites invented technology which identified children born with the Padamite gene. By then, due to certain events, the Padimites had chosen to move away from civilization to a place where they could continue helping gifted people, without disturbance. They settled in a remote area of Tibet, and there they founded Pha-yul, which means "Homeland".'

Mr. Harris sighed, 'You can understand how difficult it must have been for them. Leaving their planet, trying to live without being discovered, in a new place...'

Sam interrupted, 'But they must have been on Earth for centuries, by then. They should have gotten used to living here.'

Mr. Harris shook his head. 'Sam, being different isn't easy. You kids should know that by now. People of Padimite ancestry will always be different. And that is why the Elders of the community took such pains to find people who manifested powers. To protect them and help them understand what was happening to them. Of course, it wasn't easy to identify children born with the Padamite gene in the days of midwives and home births. But now, as soon as a child is born, a blood sample is taken and this lets us know when a child with a Padamite gene is born. We keep an eye on the children as they grow. Some manifest powers and some don't. And when we do find someone who does, we try to help them.' Mr. Harris paused and looked around. 'Any questions?' he asked.

They had hundreds of questions, but Sebastian asked the first one,

'So we're aliens… at least part aliens?'

Mr. Harris couldn't help smiling. 'Yes, Sebastian, if it makes you happy, yes, you are a tiny bit alien.'

'Who's Lucas?' asked Sam.

'Ah!' Mr. Harris looked pained. 'Lucas! Every basket has some rotten eggs. We're no different. Lucas was part of our community… but…,' he sighed, looking sad, '… he didn't agree with our philosophy and decided to follow a different path.'

'What does he want with me?' asked Sam

'We aren't the only community of gifted people, though we are the ones who follow the principles and rules set by the original settlers. Over the years, several communities have sprung up in different parts of the world. Each one follows a different ideal, they have different agendas. Lucas heads one of the other communities.'

'But why does Lucas want me? And Cabot mentioned a book? What book?' asked Sam. The others had discussed some of this with Sam and with each other. They were also curious to know what it meant.

Mr. Harris hesitated and looked thoughtful for a moment, before he spoke. 'You know how Maya has visions? But she sees the present and only if it involves Sam, apparently, but, of course, it may change as her powers grow. But over the centuries, there have been a few, just a handful of gifted men and women who could see the future. They have been called many names, like prophets, soothsayers, psychics, etc. We called them oracles.'

'That sounds pretty cool. Imagine what you could do with a gift like that,' said Sebastian. 'You could see who wins the big game. You could win the lottery.'

'You would also see how you die, Sebastian. You will see how your friends die, you will see how your family dies and each time you see it, you feel the pain of loss. And there is nothing you can do about it. That's the oracle's curse. That they can see the future, but they cannot change it. Oracles consider themselves cursed, not blessed, and most of them live their entire lives in seclusion, keeping themselves unattached to things. But I'm digressing. One oracle spent his life, writing. A lot of what he wrote is philosophy. But he prophesied that a child would be born on November 16th, and he will become the most powerful and gifted Padamite on Earth.

You were born on November 16th, Sam. Lucas shares your birthday, and for a long time, the community thought Lucas was the one. But there is a sacred Book we have at Pha-yul, which is written in a dialect which we don't understand. We believe it is written in the original Padimite language. There is no one living now, even in Pha-yul, who understands the dialect. It is one of our most sacred possessions. The oracle said that a child, born on that day, will be able to read the Book after he or she turns sixteen. It is the ultimate test. Over centuries, children born on that day have been given the Book to read, when they reached the age of sixteen. Lucas was given the Book to read when he turned sixteen, as well. He couldn't. He wants to find the child who can.'

The children were quiet, as they digested all this.

'I doubt I'd be able to read it. I don't even have any actual powers to…' Sam left the sentence unfinished, looking glum.

Mr. Harris gave him a strange look. 'Even after all that has happened, Sam, you still don't believe in yourself?'

Sam looked puzzled. 'All what happened? I got kidnapped and they rescued me.' He waved his hand at the other four. 'That's what happened. I was useless. I couldn't even help myself,' he said, with barely concealed frustration.

'Sam, that's not true. It's because of you that we're all alive.' It was

Maya who spoke. 'How did you do that, Sammy? We're all curious to know. How did you send the energy? Do you remember what you did?'

'I do remember, but I don't know how I did it. I'm sure if you ask me to do it now, I won't be able to. When I opened my eyes and saw Cassie battling with Cabot, and Maya lying battered on the floor, I just felt such rage and power surging up. But I felt too weak to reach it. I don't know why I asked Maya to reach for it. I didn't even know whether it would work. I just took a chance. I don't think I was even thinking straight.'

'I'm glad you took a chance, because it paid off,' said Cassie soberly.

A nurse bustled in to check on Sam. She looked shocked to see so many people in the room with him.

'Out! Out! All of you! Only one person stays,' she said, shooing them out.

They said their byes and left. Cassie walked with them to the car park to see them off. When she got back, Sam was staring distantly out of the window.

He looked around, when Cassie came in. 'Cas! You know what Cabot told me? She said Lucas would be able to help me discover my powers. What if she's right? What if Lucas can help me? I mean, what do we know about Pha-yul other than what Mr. Harris tells us. It's not like we can go ask somebody, or Google it. No one knows about them. We just blindly believe what he tells us. How do we know any of it is true?'

'Sam, we may be in the frying pan… let's not jump into the fire,' Cassie replied. 'We have no idea what's going on. We'll have to wait and see.'

'But what if he can help me? Mr. Harris doesn't seem to be able to,' persisted Sam.

'It's pretty obvious Mr. Harris thinks that Lucas is bad news,' said

Cassie.

'But that's because Mr. Harris doesn't agree with Lucas's ideas or ideals. We don't even know what Lucas's ideals are. How can we make up our minds about someone, without giving them a chance?' Sam asked.

'Sam, what he did to you.' Cassie shuddered, as she thought about it.

'Cas, he didn't even know about it. Cabot did this,' said Sam.

'Well, then all I can say is that he's a very poor judge of people,' said Cassie.

'Look who's talking,' snapped Sam.

Cassie looked annoyed for a minute, and then she said, 'I admit I was fooled too. But if I had known what kind of a person Cabot was, I wouldn't have her around. Lucas did. What does that say about him? Sammy, all I'm saying is we don't know enough to make decisions yet.' They were silent for a bit, each immersed in their own thoughts. Cassie suddenly burst out laughing.

Sam looked at her. 'What?'

'No, I just remembered how Cabot looked in that crazy outfit, and her cropped hair and the heavy makeup. I don't know what horrified me more. Seeing you half dead or seeing her in that get up.'

Sam laughed too. 'Oof! Enough of Pha-yul and Cabot and Lucas... let's watch T.V. and forget about them.'

'Yes, please, let's just be normal kids for a bit,' said Cassie, picking up the remote. 'What do you want to watch?' she asked.

'Criminal Minds,' said Sam promptly.

CHAPTER 36

It took Sam almost a month, before he could get back to training. The other four had got back to training almost immediately. Mr. Harris didn't seem to think traumatic events deserved a few days off. He had now started them on practicing archery. Sebastian found it archaic and wanted to know, why archery and why not guns. To his delight, Mr. Harris had said they would progress to guns. He had said they had to learn archery, as you never know when you may need to use a bow and arrow. Surprisingly, Cassie was turning out to be the best archer on the team.

Mr. Harris had thought of starting Sam slowly, on simpler routines than the others when he returned, but found Sam fighting fit when he got back. He got back into a routine pretty fast. It was the weekend before Easter, and the kids had spent the morning duelling one another with sticks. Mr. Harris told them to take five and disappeared into his office. The kids sprawled on the football field, exhausted. The summer was promising to be a scorcher.

'I've had enough,' groaned Sam. 'I haven't practiced for a month. I'm hurting all over.'

'Look at it this way. You've been relaxing for a month, while we've been working our butts off,' growled Sebastian, as he sipped water.

Sam smiled. 'That's true. But I don't want to practice anymore. I wish it would snow. Maybe, he'd let us off,' he said.

Sebastian turned over and lay on his stomach, saying, 'Fat chance! He'd make us run in the snow.' As he said that, he felt something splash on his head and cold water trickled down his neck. 'Ew!' he said, wiping it and smelling his hand. 'Is that bird shit?'

'Hey!' said Cassie, as she felt something wet splash on her face. She sat up, wiping her face.

'Guys! Look!' Maya was sitting up, pointing at the sky. They all looked up.

Snow was falling, softly and gently, around them.

'You made it snow! Sammy! You made it snow!' said Maya, grinning and thumping Sam on his back.

Hearing all the noise, Mr. Harris walked out of his office and looked up in surprise as a large snowflake fell on him.

'Sam did it,' called out Ryan, beaming.

Mr. Harris's face broke into a big smile. 'I knew he could do it. I knew it,' he muttered to himself, as he walked over to his circle of five.

Sebastian threw an arm around Sam. 'Dude! You are the coolest kid I know.'

Sam smiled happily, as the five of them sat there, looking up, the snow falling lightly on their faces.

To be continued

###

About Jan Raymond

Jan Raymond grew up in the pages of her favourite books and amongst imaginary friends. With her debut novel, 'Circle of Five', she has fulfilled a lifelong dream to become an author and create a world of her own. When she's not writing, she enjoys watching movies with her daughters, and cuddling with Tristan, her basset hound.

She has just finished the second part of the Pha-yul trilogy, Gransdur: The Games.

She lives in Chennai, where it's always too warm, and is currently working on the third book in the Pha-yul trilogy.

LOS ALAMOS COUNTY LIBRARY
MESA PUBLIC LIBRARY
2400 CENTRAL AVENUE
LOS ALAMOS, NM 87544

28888385R00186

Made in the USA
San Bernardino, CA
09 January 2016